# THE
# ROAD TO
# MALHEUR

## C.J. ADRIEN

First Edition

Originally published in the United States in 2023 by Runestone Books

ISBN: 9798871182024

For more information, visit www.cjadrien.com

*For Bob Boyd, my 7th and 8th grade history teacher who inspired me to make history my career, and whose fur trade project inspired the idea for this book almost three decades ago.*

*For my wife, Crystal, my rock, who has and continues to support my author career.*

*For my son Léo.*

# More books by C.J. Adrien

## THE SAGA OF HASTING THE AVENGER

*The Lords of the Wind*
*In the Shadow of the Beast*
*The Kings of the Sea*

## THE KINDRED OF THE SEA

*The Line of His People*
*The Oath of the Father*
*The Lady of the North*

# TABLE OF CONTENTS

# CHAPTER 1
## TROUBLE IN ST. LOUIS

There I was, knee-deep in the mud, with a gun barrel shoved halfway down my throat. I was a dead man. Oregon Country had not been kind to me, not kind at all. They'd said the Indians would cause trouble. They were trouble enough, but it was one of my own who had turned his rifle on me; it was one of my own with his finger on the trigger. We were supposed to trailblaze and push out the Hudson's Bay Company so Americans could enter the fur trade. To that point, we had mainly turned on ourselves. In my final moments on this earth, I thought about how it had all gone wrong.

With the taste of metallic bitterness in my mouth and cold steel pressed against my skin, memories flooded back, pulling me to the beginning of this ill-fated journey. I'd begun with the hopeful glimmer of a new start before the backbiting treacheries of Oregon Country unraveled our mission. It was 1821, a time when my most pressing concern was the state of my polished boots. I disembarked at the bustling Port of St. Louis, carrying the weight of my East Coast education and aspirations for a better life. The wild world awaited me, as did a man named Boyd.

The port was a swirling dance of activity, teetering on the edge of two worlds: the civilized East and the untamed West. Everywhere I looked, its French roots were evident. Buildings with French colonial facades adorned with ornate balconies and wrought iron railings bordered the waterfront. The melodic tones of French mixed with English as men hollered orders and women negotiated over goods. Young children chased each other through the narrow alleys, their laughter echoing in a blend of both.

The streets of St. Louis, cobblestoned and bustling with cart traffic, whispered of its storied past. Quaint inns and taverns, reminiscent of those I had read about in Paris, beckoned newcomers and old hands alike. The city held on to its European elegance while embracing the rugged spirit of the frontier.

As I adjusted my bag and tried to shake off the journey, a shadow emerged from a nearby building. He was an older man with the sunbaked look of someone who had wrestled with nature and won more times than he'd lost. He reached out a hand to shake mine.

"Are you Christian D... D'Her..." he tried to pronounce.

"D'Herbauges," I corrected him in my native French accent.

"I'm Boyd. Boy, you look like you've strolled right out of a Parisian academy, and you sound like it, too." His voice dripped with amused skepticism.

He was right. I was wearing a tailored suit with fine leather bags over my shoulder. This was my first day on the job, and I had been taught to dress for the occasion. Holding my head high, I responded, "I've traveled here from New York to seek opportunity."

Boyd chuckled, then spat into the dirt. "Opportunity? I've seen many young men like you, all dreams and no real understanding. Do you believe your education will shield you out there?"

Not wanting to seem daunted, I replied, "I've done my research, sir. I know the territories."

His eyes narrowed as he stepped closer. "That knowledge won't warm you in the mountains or deflect a Blackfoot arrow. I've been navigating these parts longer than you've been alive. And it's no place for a city gentleman."

"Thank you for your insight," I said. "But I plan to prove my mettle."

The man smirked. "Well, I've been sent to collect you and get you settled. Let's get this over with."

"Are you and I going to be traveling together?" I asked.

He laughed and clapped me on the back. "I hope not."

As he strode away, I took a deep breath, readying myself for the path ahead. I needed to orient myself and perhaps build some understanding with the hardened trapper, so I hurried to catch up. "Wait," I called out, "I have questions."

Boyd turned, his eyes scrutinizing. "Figured as much."

Swallowing my pride, I gestured to the city around us. "Tell me about St. Louis. It's... different from what I envisioned."

"St. Louis?" Boyd grinned. "It's a gateway, kid. Half the men you see here are dreamers like you, set on heading west. The other half? Well, they've tried and come back or found some other business here." He gestured toward the distant outskirts of town. "The French laid its foundation. That's why you'll hear the lilt of their language in the markets, see their touch in the buildings. I'm not too keen on those Frenchies, can't trust them as far as I can throw, but they're everywhere around here."

I shrugged off his comment about the French. "And the frontier? How different is it from here?"

His face grew serious. "The frontier's a different beast altogether. Out there, it's wild and unpredictable. Nature doesn't care about your education or your fancy clothes. She'll challenge you again and again. And it ain't just nature; the tribes, the rival trappers, are all elements you'll have to reckon with."

Feeling a chill despite the warm day, I asked, "What do I need to know to be successful?"

Boyd pondered my question for a moment. "First, shed any airs you got. Out there, humility and observance will serve you more than arrogance. Learn from those who've been doing it for years. Listen more than you speak. Second, respect the land and its people. You're more likely to receive respect in kind if you show respect. And last," he added with a pointed look, "trust is a rare commodity. Be careful who you give it to."

Our conversation continued as we meandered through St. Louis, with Boyd pointing out places of interest and me soaking in as much knowledge as possible. There was a wellspring of wisdom beneath his rough exterior, and if I wanted to thrive out here, I'd do well to heed his words.

Boyd led me onward, navigating the maze of streets until we arrived at a modest brick building. The sign above read: *American Fur Company*. Though the structure was unassuming, I could feel the pulse of ambition emanating from within. I stepped forward to show myself through the door, but Boyd put a hand on my chest to stop me.

"Listen, kid. It's not too late. You can go back to New York and no one will think the lesser of you."

"I beg your pardon, but I think you underestimate me."

Boyd pushed harder against my chest. "I don't think you understand what I'm getting at, kid. Just one look at you and I can tell you'll be food for crows before we even get to the first fort. The men who come out here... they've got nothing to lose, no homes to go back to. You could go back to New York and be a doctor or a lawyer. The frontier isn't for you."

His words gave me pause. He was right—I'd had more opportunities for a lucrative career in New York. Before setting out West, I had been a lawyer, and a good one.

"I think I belong here more than you know," I insisted.

Boyd crossed his arms. "Tell me why."

I reached into the well of my memory, stirring the pain from which I was running, and said, "If you must know, my wife and son died in childbirth, and the grief drove me to drink. I got into some trouble with the law, and Mr.

Astor fished me out of jail and worked out a deal with the judge."

"Oh." Boyd's demeanor toward me shifted. He took off his hat and held it over his chest, a look of pity in his eyes. "I'm sorry for your loss."

We stood in silence for a moment, surrounded by a swirl of chatter and laughter from passersby, the thundering of carts over cobblestones, and the unsettling distant crack of gunfire.

"Astor's a good man," Boyd finally said. "He helped me out of jail, too. But a young man of your education and demeanor... I'm surprised he sent you out here to do the grunt work instead of keeping you at his office in New York."

"Oh, believe me, it was not my first choice," I said through a chuckle. "Mr. Astor insisted I venture out here to learn the trade before bringing me on at the corporate office. Something about 'you need to know what's in the sausage to sell the sausage.' He's given me the task of securing a trade deal with the North West Company so we can ship our furs back east from Oregon Country, and there's a good-paying job waiting for me in New York so long as I don't flub it up."

"Okay, kid. I get it now. Come on, let's get you outfitted."

Boyd led the way inside. The office was spacious, with neat rows of desks, ledgers scattered about, and clerks busily at work. We were approached by a man who seemed out of place. He wore a suit, no doubt a mark of his position, but his hair was disheveled, sticking out at odd angles. It looked as though he'd been thrust into his role rather than being naturally suited for it.

"Boyd," he said with a nod. Then, eyeing me with curiosity and skepticism, he extended a hand. "And you are?"

"Christian." I shook his hand firmly.

"I'm Randall. I handle the company's business here." He guided us to a desk piled with paperwork. "I assume you want the standard trapper contract?"

"Yes," Boyd cut in, "and whatever else the company provides for beginners."

"Wait." I reached into my coat pocket to procure the letter signed by John Astor and handed it to Randall, who lifted a monocle to his eye to read it.

"You'll want to take this to your company leader," he said.

"What does it say?" Boyd asked, his neck craned over my shoulder.

Randall smirked, handing me a sheaf of papers. "It's all quite standard. A contract for your service, and in exchange, you'll receive a trapper's kit, and equipment essential for your journey."

Boyd sighed audibly as I skimmed through the documents, trying to make sense of the legal jargon. "All this paperwork makes a man thirsty," he remarked.

I could feel his impatience, but looking at the list of equipment and provisions the company offered, I was keen to collect them. "Actually, before that, I'd like to gather my kit."

Randall nodded, scribbling something onto a piece of paper and handing it to me. "Take this to the trade post. They'll set you up with everything you need."

As we left the building, with the promise of a new venture palpable in the air, Boyd playfully punched my shoulder. "Is it always business first with you? Let's get you sorted, then we'll find that drink."

It irked me that he kept insisting on drinking after I had confided in him my troubles back home. There was a disconnect with him, an aloofness married to urgency over finding that next drink. I knew it well. And I wanted to forget it.

The streets of St. Louis were teeming with various characters, each with their dreams and aspirations, all searching for that elusive fortune. As Boyd and I made our way toward the depot, the midday sun cast shadows over the cobblestones, and a boisterous laugh cut through the air.

Coming our way was a group of men led by a striking figure dressed head to toe in deerskin, his garments tailored to his muscular frame. Atop his head sat a sizable round hat adorned with a prominent feather that danced in the breeze. His rugged beard did nothing to hide the smirk on his lips, and his eyes sparkled with mischief.

"For crying out loud," Boyd muttered, wiping his face with a handkerchief. "It's Fergus MacBride. Do me a favor and don't pick a fight with him."

A raw, unfiltered disdain surged when I locked eyes with Fergus. There was a type of man I had learned to detest in my life, one of unchecked ego and bluster, and it was apparent that Fergus fit the bill. Conversely, my city attire and unfamiliarity with the frontier world seemed to brand me as everything he despised.

"Look here, lads," Fergus called out in a thick Scottish accent, his voice dripping with feigned surprise. "A wee lost lamb in his Sunday best?" He motioned to me, causing his cronies to chuckle.

One of the men added, "Looks like he's wandered far from the church, eh?"

I felt a flush rise to my cheeks. I was out of my element, and they knew it. To them, I was just a city boy playing at being a trapper. I opened my mouth to retort, but Fergus beat me to it.

"Do they wear fancy clothes like that on the trails where you come from?" he asked, his voice laced with mockery.

Another added, "He'll be a beacon for all the wild creatures! Easy prey! Won't last a week!"

Boyd, walking beside me, remained silent. His lack of defense was a clear message: I would need to stand up for myself in this world.

Gathering my courage, I again met Fergus' gaze. "Every journey has its beginning," I said. "I might start in these clothes, but it doesn't mean I'll finish in them."

Fergus laughed, a hearty sound that was infectious. "You've got spirit; I'll give you that! Maybe there's hope for you yet." He winked and, with a wave, moved on with his group, leaving me to contemplate the road ahead.

Breaking his silence, Boyd said, "You had better be careful with him; he's a killer."

On the outskirts of town, we arrived at a peculiar cabin. It was built with raw, uneven logs that stood out glaringly amidst the more modern brick and plaster structures we had passed. A roughly burnt sign overhead read *Trade Post*. Its blatant primitiveness seemed almost defiant.

"That's an odd-looking building," I remarked.

Boyd cast me a sideways glance. "That's the idea."

Entering the cabin was like stepping into another world, one far removed from the academic halls of New York's law schools. The overpowering scent of hide, dried herbs, and other miscellaneous trade goods would make any newcomer's head spin. Tall shelves lined the walls, stacked meticulously with sorted furs, while thick strands of dried tobacco leaves swayed gently overhead, a testament to the trade that flowed through the outpost.

Out of sheer curiosity, my fingers reached out to touch one of the tobacco bundles. The texture was stiffer than anticipated, and its resilience momentarily captivated me.

"Those are for smoking, not for your city hands," came a raspy voice dripping with condescension. My gaze shifted to the counter, where a scruffy man stood, his bloodshot eyes sizing me up with an almost predatory keenness. The backdrop of ancient muskets and knives, rusted with age and use, only added to his sinister aura.

Boyd, seemingly unfazed by the man's demeanor, leaned in, their conversation barely above a whisper. My name punctuated their hushed tones multiple times, which only heightened my anxiety. But rather than stand idly by, I chose to busy myself by examining the wares on display. If I was to be a fur trapper, acquainting myself with the tools of the trade seemed a logical first step.

The items were an eclectic mix: from beaver traps of varying sizes to specialized knives and tools I could scarcely identify. A rough hand clamped down on mine as I picked up a peculiar-looking instrument, perhaps a skinning tool.

"That ain't for the likes of you," the scruffy clerk growled, his face inches from mine.

Taken aback by his sudden aggression, I retorted, "I was merely examining it. I've every intention to purchase my equipment here."

His eyes flared with a mix of amusement and disdain. "You think throwing coin about will make you fit for the frontier? You're in for a harsh lesson, city boy."

Everything stood still for a heartbeat. Here was my first real test. Would I bow to the bully or stand firm, establishing my place in this new world?

Pushing back against the weight of his grip, I drew myself up, meeting his gaze evenly. "I suggest you release me. I am here to trade, not to be manhandled."

For a split second, I thought he would lunge at me. But Boyd intervened, his voice slicing through the mounting tension.

"Enough, Jeb. The kid's here with me. He's got coin and intent. So unless you've got an issue with either, I suggest we move on to business."

Jeb released my hand, his eyes never leaving mine. It was clear he did not think much of me. Still, in a show of diplomacy, he pulled out a bottle filled with a tantalizing amber liquid. After taking a prolonged swig, he offered it to me with a challenging glint.

I hesitated for a moment before grabbing the bottle and taking a swig. The liquid burned its way down, and I coughed a little, much to Jeb's delight. But I held on to the bottle a moment longer, locking eyes with him before passing it back.

The rest of the transaction went relatively smoothly. Boyd conversed with Jeb about the necessary supplies, pointing to various items, while I took mental notes. When all was said and done, Boyd threw the paper signed by Randall onto the counter. Jeb read the note and groaned.

"They're giving this kid a fifty-cal Pennsylvania? What a waste."

Still eyeing me, Jeb gathered my supplies on the counter and checked them against the list. As he did, his demeanor shifted from confrontational to something more calculating, a change that didn't escape my notice.

"Your company doesn't cover all of this," he said. "You still owe fifteen dollars."

"Don't pull this crap, Jeb; you and I both know the company covers the whole kit," Boyd said.

"It's fine." I pulled Astor's letter from my pocket. "I have this."

Jeb scanned the letter, running his fingers over the wax seal. He let out a low snicker as he read. As he handed back the letter, he pushed my supplies across the counter.

"Good luck, kid."

When we finally left the trading post, I was laden with the tools of my new trade, a rifle I scarcely knew how to use over my shoulder, and also with the weighty realization that my journey into the wild frontier would be fraught with challenges.

Boyd, sensing my introspection, clapped a hand on my shoulder. "The frontier is a different beast, kid. It won't be like anything you've faced before. But remember this: it's not the wilderness or the animals you need to be wary of most—it's the men."

The sun was beginning to dip below the horizon, casting long shadows on the uneven cobblestone streets of St. Louis. The city's stone and wood structures turned golden in the dying light, their facades hinting at stories of a community carved out from the hinterlands.

Boyd seemed restless as we wove through the streets, his gaze continually drifting to the taverns we passed, each filled with the lively hum of conversation, laughter, and the occasional drunken song.

"Christian," Boyd began, his voice noticeably softer, "I don't suppose we could… you know, make a quick stop? Just a small detour. I could use something to wet my throat."

I frowned, adjusting the strap of my satchel. "Boyd, I'd like to get to our lodgings first. Get settled in, and perhaps have a proper meal. We can drink afterwards."

Boyd looked at me with an expression that was hard to read—a mixture of frustration, desperation, and something deeper, something I couldn't quite put my finger on.

"It's been a long day," he finally said, his voice almost a whisper. "I need it. Just one drink to take the edge off, and then we can move on."

Despite my reservations, the rawness in Boyd's voice struck a chord. I realized that while I was out of my depth in this new world, so was he in his own way. Perhaps, for him, the tavern was more than just a place for a drink; it was a haven, a brief respite from his burdens.

"Fine," I sighed, my resistance waning, "but just one drink. Then you take me to my lodgings."

A brief, relieved smile broke through Boyd's grim facade. "All right," he murmured, guiding us toward the nearest tavern, its dim lights offering a warm invitation against the encroaching night.

The dimly lit tavern was a cacophony of laughter, loud voices, and the occasional clinking of mugs. At first glance, it seemed like any other drinking establishment, but a closer look revealed the rough edges unique to the frontier. The patrons, burly trappers and traders, their rugged features illuminated by flickering candlelight, seemed to blend seamlessly with the wooden interior.

As Boyd and I made our way to an empty table, I couldn't help but notice the subtle changes in his demeanor. Gone was the assertive man who had met me at the docks. In his place stood someone who seemed a tad out of sorts, restlessly glancing toward the counter where a line of bottles sat. It was clear Boyd found solace at the bottom of a glass—an escape, albeit temporary, from whatever demons haunted him.

"Drink? I'm buying," he said, a hint of vulnerability peeking through his gruff exterior.

Before I could answer, a familiar voice rang out. "If it isn't the city boy and his chaperone!"

MacBride. Accompanied by his gang of rowdy trappers, he swaggered into the tavern, every step dripping with arrogance. By his side, a shorter man slithered, his blond hair contrasting sharply with the dim surroundings, his beady eyes focused intently on our table.

"Who's the man next to him?" I asked Boyd, concerned by the look he gave me.

"That's MacBride's lapdog, Lucas MacLane. Not someone you want to cross."

Their approach was deliberate, like wolves circling their prey. And, once again, I found myself the center of their mockery. With startling speed, MacLane lunged, snatching the satchels from my side.

"Let's see what the gentleman has brought with him from the big city," MacLane jeered, flinging one satchel to a crony while rifling through the other. Laughter echoed as they played their cruel game of keep-away, my belongings tossed about like playthings.

Boyd's face grew tense, but he seemed rooted to the spot, his internal struggle evident. My patience, however, had evaporated.

Lunging at MacLane, I tried to reclaim what was mine. Surprise gave me the upper hand for a brief moment, and I managed to wrestle one satchel away. But the numbers were against me. MacBride came at me with a wicked smirk on his face.

"Enough games," he bellowed just before his fist connected squarely with my jaw.

The force of the blow sent me sprawling, my vision blurring, the raucous laughter and jeers growing distant. As darkness threatened to consume me, the last thing I saw was Boyd's anguished face, a torrent of emotions crossing his features.

Then, nothing but blackness.

My eyes fluttered open to the sight of aged wooden beams above me, forming a tight A-frame. A dull pain throbbed at the back of my skull, every pulse reminding me of the brute force of MacBride's blow. I groaned, trying to push myself up, but the room swayed, forcing me back onto a straw-filled mattress.

I took a moment to absorb my surroundings. This wasn't the clean, cozy inn I had pictured. Instead, the shack was cluttered, filled with an array of items like those at the trading post: fur pelts stacked in a corner, tools scattered about, and what looked like dried herbs hanging from the ceiling. The air was thick, laden with the scents of tobacco, hide, and something less identifiable that tickled my senses, a combination of earth and decay.

Boyd stood beside a rickety wooden table, watching me with a mixture of amusement and irritation. His silhouette was backlit by the thin rays of sunlight peeking through gaps in the wooden slats of the shack.

"Finally awake?" he remarked dryly, sipping from a mug. "You sure have a talent for trouble, city boy."

I winced and managed to find my voice. "Where am I?"

"Trapper house." Boyd set down his mug and gestured around the shack. "Had to drag you out of that tavern before things got even uglier. MacBride and his lot had a field day with you. Lucky a couple of them felt bad and helped me gather your gear."

I swallowed hard, memories flooding back—the mocking laughter, the feel of my satchel being yanked from my grip, and the cold, brutal violence in MacBride's eyes.

"Thank you," I murmured, although some of me still bristled at the idea of being saved.

Boyd snorted. "Don't thank me yet. You've made things complicated." He produced a piece of paper from the pocket of his worn coat, unfolded it, then held it out for me to see. I recognized it instantly as an official order from the company.

"You see this?" His voice was laced with frustration. "We leave tomorrow. And you got your wish, I'm going with you. There is no time for any real preparation, no training, nothing. You think you're ready to face the frontier with just that high-and-mighty attitude of yours?"

I tried to sit up again, fighting back the dizziness. "I'll manage," I replied defiantly.

Boyd shook his head, chuckling bitterly. "Manage? The wilderness doesn't care about your education or your pride. It'll chew you up and spit you out if you're not careful." He paused, looking me square in the eye. "MacBride was just a taste of what's out there. There are things far worse than him waiting in the shadows of the forests and mountains."

I met his gaze, refusing to let my fear show. "I can handle it."

Boyd sighed, leaning back against the table. "You've got spirit, I'll give you that. But spirit alone won't keep you alive out there." He paused, running a hand through his unkempt hair. "I've seen too many greenhorns like you end up as food for the wolves or lost to the elements. Listen to me, Christian. It's not too late. You can head back to New York now, and no one will be the wiser."

"Thank you, but I'm committed to seeing this journey through," I said.

Boyd's words hung in the air, and I felt the weight of the journey ahead for the first time since my arrival in St. Louis. Though I had responded to him with courage and pride, inside, I questioned myself. What had I gotten myself into? The employment office in New York had promised riches beyond my wildest dreams, but where were all the men who had made such a fortune?

The rosy fingers of dawn reached out across the Missouri horizon, turning the sleepy town of St. Louis into a realm of shadows and silhouettes. With the crunch of gravel underfoot, Boyd and I made our way to the rendezvous point, our belongings slung over our shoulders, our steps heavy with the uncertainty that lay ahead.

Boyd broke the silence. "You sure you're ready for this, Christian? It's not too late to catch the next coach back east."

"I haven't changed my mind." I squared my shoulders, trying to sound more confident than I felt. "I've come this far. There's no turning back now."

A familiar sneer met us as we approached the gathering point, curdling the morning air. Standing there, surrounded by his gang of roughnecks, was Fergus MacBride. His face lit up in amusement as he saw me.

"God help us," Boyd muttered under his breath. "MacBride is our expedition leader."

Boyd and I approached the assembled men, each busily preparing for a lengthy expedition. Their shadows stretched long over the dusty ground in the rising sun. MacBride's posture was dominant, his authority undeniable. Our first encounter had been less than friendly, and the last thing I'd expected was to find him in charge of the company I was to join.

Boyd seemed to sense my hesitance. "Steady there, kid," he whispered as he nudged me forward.

Before we could formally announce our arrival, MacBride's voice rang out, thick with a Scotsman's pride. "If it isn't the city boy!" His eyes scanned me with disdain before landing on Boyd. "And you brought him, Boyd?"

Boyd, unruffled as ever, nodded. "Got our orders, didn't we? Christian here's not just a pretty face from the city. There's more to him than you might think."

MacBride smirked, taking the bait. "Oh? And what would that be?"

Before I could interject, Boyd chimed in, "He's Mr. Astor's personal pick—that's got to count for something."

I stepped forward and handed MacBride the letter in my pocket. There was a pregnant pause, during which his calculating eyes met mine.

"Christ almighty." MacBride's voice took on a tone of irritation. I could see the cogs turning in his head, the realization sinking in that, as much as he might loathe to admit it, I just might turn out to be indispensable.

"What is it?" MacLane asked, craning his neck over MacBride's shoulder to catch a glimpse of the letter.

"Christian here is our second-in-command," MacBride said.

"Stop playing," MacLane blurted out, swiping the letter out of MacBride's hands. He glanced over the words. "Shit."

MacLane crumpled up the letter and threw it at me, shouting insults so loudly and quickly I could not understand them. MacBride dove in to keep him from lunging at me, and MacLane, his face beet red, did not have the strength to push past him.

"Take a walk, Lucas," MacBride growled. MacLane stormed off down the road on his own. MacBride pulled an intricately decorated silver pocket watch from his pocket, glanced at the time, and adjusted his tunic before continuing, "Well, let's get the introductions over with, then."

He motioned to a burly man, a towering figure with a beard that seemed to have a life of its own. "This here's Sam 'Bear' Barrens, our cartographer. Another Scotsman like me and MacLane."

Bear extended a massive hand, engulfing mine in a firm shake. "Good to meet you."

Next to Bear stood a slender man with pensive eyes. "David Asher," he introduced himself with a nod. "Boston. Handle the accounts."

"New York," I replied, trying to find common ground.

MacBride then pointed to a tall, stern-looking man with bright blue eyes. "Jim Schmidt. Prussian sharpshooter. The best shot we've got."

Jim gave a curt nod, but his eyes were assessing, weighing me.

MacBride swept his arm toward another man, one with sun-kissed skin and a friendly grin. "Michael Roarke. He's come from South Carolina."

"Pleasure," Roarke said, tipping his hat slightly.

Lucas MacLane was next. He had walked back from his tantrum and taken a place among the others. He didn't need to re-introduce himself. The sneering Scotsman's nod was perfunctory, almost dismissive.

Finally, MacBride indicated two rugged-looking men, their appearance a blend of European and Indigenous features. "Georges Saint-Pierre and Jean-Baptiste

Delhommeau. Our Métis guides up the Missouri. Don't speak a lick of English, which is why you're here."

The two men gave a respectful nod. I returned the gesture, eager to establish rapport with those who knew the lay of the land.

MacBride grunted, the introductions done. "There you have it. We're together now. Whether we like it or not." He locked eyes with me. "I hope you know what you're doing."

"I've read all the books and studied up on the trade," I explained. "I promise I will prove my worth to this expedition."

Boyd, sensing the palpable tension, clapped me on the back. "Bet that coach back east is sounding real good right about now."

Despite the animosity, I felt a strange brew of excitement and determination bubble up within me. "No," I replied. "It doesn't."

# CHAPTER 2
# THE FIRST FRONTIER

The dawn light painted the horizon as I stood on the bank of the vast Missouri River. It looked almost benign in its gentle shimmer, a stark contrast to the treacherous tales I'd heard. Even though the morning was just breaking, the heat had begun to press down, foretelling a blistering day ahead.

Nature's morning melodies filled the air. Birds sang spiritedly from the canopy of trees by the river, their songs intermingling with the distant sounds of St. Louis, slowly coming to life. Our path led us along a patchwork of farmland beside the river, far as the eye could see, with an occasional farmhouse and barn fenced off from the dangers of the wilderness beyond.

I took a deep breath, trying to steady my nerves. The air was a medley of scents—the freshwater tang of the river, the earthiness of the nearby wetlands, and now and then, a whiff of tobacco from one of the men's pipes.

But amidst this robust group, I felt like an anomaly. My attire, suited more for a city meeting than an expedition, was already causing discomfort. My dark coat and waistcoat felt like they were sticking to my skin, the rising sun making the fabric unbearable. To make matters worse, my hat, chosen more for style than practicality, did little to shield me from the sun's relentless glare.

Boyd remarked with a smirk, "You should've dressed down."

Wiping the sweat from my forehead with a handkerchief that was quickly becoming saturated, I retorted, "I didn't think it'd be this hot. It's only April."

"It's not that hot." Boyd laughed. "You're just overdressed."

Around us, the other men seemed to effortlessly lead their horses and mules, heavy with supplies. Their conversations flowed easily, filled with laughter and tales of past journeys. Each of them exuded an air of familiarity with the terrain and the task ahead. Meanwhile, every step I took felt clumsy, every tug at the bridle a testament to my inexperience. As we set off on this journey, I couldn't help but feel a daunting sense of unpreparedness.

The sun rose higher, each ray searing down with unyielding intensity. My head throbbed with every step, and the world seemed to blur in the waves of heat emanating from the ground. My coat felt like a furnace, and my feet were begging for relief from the tight leather shoes.

Seeing my labored steps, Boyd slowed down and drew up beside me. "Christian," he said with a chuckle, "you look like a roasted turkey in that getup. Why not shed a layer or two? No one's judging here."

I shot him a defiant look. "I'm perfectly fine," I lied through gritted teeth, my pride stinging from his earlier remark. "Besides, it's not like we're at a summer picnic. There's a sense of decorum to maintain."

Boyd laughed heartily, wiping the sweat from his own brow with his rolled-up sleeves. "Decorum? Out here? The trees and mules don't care what you look like."

I stubbornly pressed on, but with each passing minute, the weight of my choice bore down on me. My vision danced with spots, and my throat felt like parched earth. Boyd, sensing my distress, offered, "Want a sip of water?"

"No, thank you," I said, perhaps too curtly, regretting my tone almost instantly. But the heat, the weariness, and my wounded pride had frayed my patience.

Boyd shook his head with a mix of amusement and concern. "Stubborn kid," he mumbled, pulling ahead slightly but throwing occasional glances back in my direction.

My knees began to buckle after what felt like hours but was probably mere minutes. The world around me swam in a haze. I could feel my coat's weight, my cravat's constriction, and the heat pressing down on me from all sides. As much as I didn't want to give Boyd the satisfaction of being right, my body was screaming at me that I was so very wrong.

With a deep sigh, I finally stopped, reluctantly beginning to shed my coat. I could feel Boyd's eyes on me, his lips curving into a triumphant smirk.

"Feel better?" he asked, genuine concern seeping into his voice.

I met his gaze with both gratitude and embarrassment. "Yes," I admitted, my voice soft. "Thanks."

He nodded, clapping me on the back. "It's a lesson, Christian. Out here, pride won't keep you alive. Adapting will."

I nodded, humbled, realizing just how unprepared I truly was for this journey. But with Boyd by my side, my only ally, I hoped I stood a chance.

As dusk slowly swallowed the river, the farmland, and the far-off forests, the sun's fiery orange gave way to deep purples and inky blacks. Above, the vast expanse of the night sky unveiled itself, an endless canopy of shimmering lights. In all its splendor, the Milky Way stretched like a luminous ribbon across the heavens, weaving a tale of ancient myths and endless mysteries. The celestial bodies twinkled, some with a gentle glow and others with a fervent shimmer, all singing the ageless songs of the cosmos.

The noises of the day faded. Now, the night serenaded us with its symphony. The soft chirping of crickets, the distant hooting of an owl, and the gentle rustle of leaves created a mesmerizing lullaby. Every so often, the mournful howl of a coyote echoed in the distance, a reminder that we were but small players in this vast wilderness.

In stark contrast to the vast, cold expanse above, our campfire provided a beacon of warmth and camaraderie. The flames danced and flickered, casting moving shadows upon the ground and painting our faces in a warm glow. The wood crackled and popped, the embers occasionally taking flight, only to disappear into the night.

The men, scattered around the fire, lounged in varying states of relaxation. Some leaned against their packs, while others reclined, using saddles as makeshift pillows. Each face told a story, illuminated by the fire's glow. Lines of weariness, etches of laughter, scars of past battles—the light momentarily softened all. The Métis set their bedding aside from the rest, and they kept to themselves, carrying on private conversations and paying no heed to the main group.

In his typical boisterous manner, MacBride held court, recounting tales from past expeditions, each more outlandish than the last. His deep voice, enriched with that Scottish lilt, filled the air, soliciting bursts of laughter and inquisitive looks from the expedition's newer members.

Beside him, MacLane nodded along, occasionally interjecting with his own side of the story or emphasizing a particularly exciting point with animated gestures. Compared to the towering MacBride, his shorter stature was compensated by his lively demeanor and sharp, beady eyes that were always evaluating and assessing.

"You think today was hard, lads? Let me recount a little escapade Lucas and I found ourselves in not more than three summers past." He shot a knowing glance at MacLane, who simply nodded, prompting MacBride to continue.

"We'd been trading up in the Rockies, near what you'd call the northern parts. Thick pine forests and cliffs that seemed to touch the sky. Beautiful country, but perilous." He paused, stoking the fire for effect. The flames jumped, casting his face in an eerie dance of light and shadow.

"We'd just brokered a deal with a band of Crow. Good folk, fair traders. But as we left their territory, heading south, we unknowingly crossed into Blackfoot land. Now, the Blackfoot, they're mighty protective of their borders."

MacLane chuckled. "Aye, that's one way to put it."

MacBride grinned. "We were riding through a densely forested patch, the kind where the sun barely touches the ground because of the thick canopy. The air was cold, the scent of pine everywhere. We thought we were alone, but we were sorely mistaken."

"We started hearing whispers," MacLane chimed in, his voice low, "like the wind was carrying secrets. We didn't think much of it until we realized the whispers were growing louder."

"And then the arrows came," MacBride said, his voice dropping an octave. "They flew from all directions, like hornets protecting their nest. We were outnumbered and outflanked."

Jim Schmidt snorted. "Surely you jest. A few arrows and you were scared?"

MacBride shot him a glare, but there was a twinkle in his eye. "Not scared, Prussian. Calculating. The Blackfoot are among the finest horsemen in these lands. Escaping them on the open plains would've been near impossible. But in the dense forest, with the advantage of stealth, we stood a chance."

MacLane took over. "We decided to split up, try to confuse them. While Fergus rode straight, drawing their attention, I took a risky path that led right through a bear's den. But it was a gamble I was willing to take."

"You went through a bear's den? On purpose?" David Asher asked, incredulous.

MacLane smirked. "Aye. With the Blackfoot on our heels, a bear seemed the lesser threat. And true to form, as I sprinted through, the mighty beast emerged, roaring, giving chase. But it also deterred a few of the Blackfoot warriors who had been close behind me."

MacBride picked up the thread again. "I could hear the bear's roars, even as I tried to lead the majority away from Lucas. Just as I thought I'd lost them, my horse tripped on a concealed rock, throwing me off."

Jim leaned forward skeptically. "And let me guess, you fought them all off single-handedly?"

MacBride grinned. "Not quite. But they suddenly halted as I scrambled to my feet, weapon in hand, ready to face them. All of them. There was a moment of sheer silence."

MacLane nodded. "That's when I rejoined Fergus, bear still in tow. The sight of that massive creature, enraged, chasing after me, gave the Blackfoot pause. It was a standoff neither of us had anticipated."

Jim raised an eyebrow. "You used a bear as backup?"

MacBride laughed. "Desperate times, my friend. The Blackfoot eventually retreated, deciding we might not be worth the trouble. And the bear? After a while, it lost interest and ambled back to its den. I don't think it liked the smell of me."

I stared at the two Scots, mesmerized by the tale. The campfire's glow, the distant stars, and the vivid story made the evening surreal.

Jim, ever the skeptic, clapped slowly. "A bear, you say? And yet, here you both sit, unscathed. Remarkable."

"The Rockies are full of wonders, Prussian." MacLane winked. "And dangers. Sometimes, they're one and the same."

The men around the campfire chuckled, the tension from the tale dissipating into the night, replaced by a renewed sense of camaraderie and mutual respect.

The laughter subsided, the men getting comfortable in their spots again, still awed by the story. In the quiet lull, Boyd leaned over to me, the shadows from the fire playing on his face. "You know," he whispered, the hint of a smirk on his lips, "I reckon Fergus MacBride is full of shit."

I tried to suppress a chuckle as we exchanged a look, an unspoken bond forming over shared skepticism amidst the vastness of the night and the tales it concealed.

The next morning, a soft, forgiving light bathed everything in a warm golden glow. Men bustled about camp, gearing up for the day's journey, attending to their mounts and adjusting burdensome loads. The inviting aroma of freshly brewed coffee wafted through the air, drawing a small crowd. Another pot, filled with thick grits, was passed around, and I took my share, thankful for a warm meal.

The coffee, as dark as a midnight sky and robust in flavor, felt invigorating, a warm balm for my tired insides. But soon, an unsettling discomfort made itself known. The realization hit me with all the subtlety of a charging bull: the coffee had stirred more than just my senses.

Trying to maintain a nonchalant demeanor, I shifted in my place. "Anyone know where the nearest... er, place for me to do my business might be?" I ventured, my voice a notch higher than I intended.

MacLane chuckled. "What's the matter, New York? Need a porcelain throne?"

Asher grinned. "Or some plush red curtains for some privacy?"

"I've heard tell of the grand bathrooms of the East." Sam Barrens, our Scotsman cartographer, teased, not looking up from his coffee. "Rooms dedicated solely to the art of... relief."

Desperation mounting and cheeks reddening, I attempted to deflect. "Just seeking a moment of solitude, is all," I responded, trying for levity.

"Careful, lads, that's your superior you're jesting at," MacBride said. His defense took me quite by surprise.

Boyd, ever the observant one, shot me a knowing look. "Head toward that barn yonder," he whispered, nodding discreetly towards the distant structure.

Gratefully, I pocketed a few handkerchiefs and made a beeline for the barn, every step a mounting urgency. The vast openness of the landscape seemed to mock me, but salvation lay just ahead.

I took refuge behind the wooden structure and sighed in relief. Birds sang from a nearby elm tree, the morning sun casting dappled patterns on the barn's old walls.

While my relief was profound, it was also short-lived. Just as I was cherishing the momentary privacy, a harsh voice pierced the calm.

"Hey! Who the hell are you? What are you doing on my property?" A burly man, face red with anger and a rifle cradled in his arms, emerged from the barn's shadowy entrance.

Panicking, I tried to pull my trousers up, fumbling with the fabric in my haste. "I'm sorry, sir! I didn't know —"

"You city slickers think you can just traipse onto any man's land and soil it?" Without warning, the disgruntled farmer raised his rifle and fired a shot into the sky. The deafening boom rang in my ears.

I yelped, a pathetic sound of surprise and fear, and began to bolt towards the camp, pants still perilously low. "Apologies, sir! I meant no disrespect," I shouted over my shoulder, praying he wasn't taking aim.

The farmer's loud, booming laugh chased after me. "Run, city boy, run! And tell your fancy pals not to cross onto my land again!"

As I neared our campsite, I could feel multiple pairs of eyes on me. MacLane doubled over with laughter, Asher unsuccessfully tried to stifle his giggles behind his coffee cup, and even stoic Jim's lips twitched in a suppressed smile.

Boyd hurried over as I pulled up my trousers. "You sure have a knack for finding trouble," he chuckled, handing me my scattered handkerchiefs.

Face burning with a mixture of shame and adrenaline, I managed a feeble retort. "Perhaps a signpost about trigger-happy farmers would've been helpful."

The teasing was relentless for the rest of the morning. Every time someone looked my way, they'd mimic a gunshot before bursting into laughter. My adventures—and misadventures—on this frontier journey were only beginning.

The humiliation clung to me more tightly than the grit and sweat of the day's journey. But as evening approached and the prospect of wearing soiled pants for another day became unbearable, I knew I had to take matters into my own hands. That was when I sought out Boyd's advice, hoping to find a bit of redemption.

"I need to wash these." I motioned to my stained trousers.

Boyd raised an eyebrow but nodded. "All right. First thing: if you're going to wash in the river, always keep an eye out. Currents can be stronger than they seem."

I frowned. "I just want to wash my pants, not go for a swim."

Boyd smirked. "Just trust me on this. And make sure you secure whatever you're washing. I've seen more than a few kids lose their clothes to the Missouri. It's got a peculiar taste for fabric."

I grumbled while gathering a makeshift wash kit. As I was about to leave, Boyd called out, "Oh, and watch out for those slippery stones!"

With a determined huff, I made my way to the riverbank, looking for a spot that offered some semblance of privacy. I found a stretch shielded by tall, thick reeds and sighed in relief. Undressing, I stepped gingerly into the water, holding on to my pants.

The cold of the river was startling but also refreshing. As I scrubbed at the pants, my thoughts drifted away with the river. It was then that I felt a peculiar sensation. A group of curious fish, presumably attracted by my splashing or the soap's lather, were nibbling at my legs.

Startled, I flailed, trying to shoo them away but only managing to lose my balance on one of those slippery stones Boyd had warned me about. I went down with a splash, my trousers floating away with the current.

Coughing and sputtering, I emerged, frantically searching for my pants. It took a moment, but I spotted them caught in a nearby branch. Thank the heavens.

As I made my way back to camp, soaking wet, pants draped over my shoulder, Boyd looked up, struggling to suppress a smile.

"I told you about the currents. Did you at least make some new fish friends?"

Exasperated, I replied, "I think I preferred it when you were just warning me about being overdressed."

He laughed heartily. "Welcome to the frontier, Christian. Every minute's an adventure, whether you want it or not."

We left the quilted plots of farmland behind that day and entered into the vast, unsettled wilderness of the West. A week of similar mishaps whizzed by like a poorly aimed arrow, each day more challenging than the last. From slipping on muddy banks to almost losing my boot in quicksand, it seemed the wilderness had a personal vendetta against me. But as the days went on, the distant horizon began to change. Woodlands and marshes gave way to open, rolling plains. The land was a tempestuous sea of dry grasses, tossing like waves in the wind. Amid that wild expanse, the outline of human-made structures soon appeared in our line of sight.

The fort that lay ahead was an imposing structure. Tall, sharpened logs formed a palisade around several wooden buildings, and tall watchtowers punctuated each corner, with keen-eyed guards monitoring the surroundings. Outside its sturdy walls, numerous encampments spread out, teeming with life. There were canvas tents, some plain and some colored, likely belonging to trappers and settlers. But what caught my attention the most were the cone-shaped dwellings with their intricate designs—teepees, I believed they were called.

"That there's a ronday-view fort," Michael Roarke declared with a confident nod as he sidled up next to me.

"A what now?" I asked, my confusion evident.

"A ronday-view," Roarke repeated with emphasis, puffing out his chest. "It's where trappers and settlers trade and resupply before heading out further into the unknown."

"You mean a rendez-vous," I corrected, pronouncing it with my best French accent.

Roarke raised an eyebrow. "Well holy shit, ain't you fancy with your fancy French words. Hey everybody, did you know this kid speaks French?"

I shushed him, not wanting to draw attention to myself, but the others had all heard, especially MacBride. He sneered, but said nothing.

"Rendez-vous, Ronday-view, potato, potahto. All means the same," Roarke went on, his tone dripping with derision.

I forced a smile but decided not to argue further. "What's with the encampments up front? They don't look like trapper tents."

Roarke squinted, shading his eyes with a hand. "Ah, them's the Otoe. A native tribe that's friendly with the fort. They trade hides, fur, and sometimes guides in exchange for goods."

The Otoe's teepees were truly mesmerizing. Made from animal hides and beautifully decorated with intricate patterns, they told tales of hunts, wars, and legends. Families could be seen around them—children playing, women tending to daily chores, and men discussing, perhaps, trade deals or the day's hunt.

Roarke continued, "You see, these forts—or rendez-vous," he added with a mock French accent and a wink, "are more than just trading posts. They're gathering spots where stories are exchanged and cultures meet. The trappers, settlers, and natives, we all come here with our backgrounds, with our tales. And in this melting pot, everyone benefits."

"I never realized how... diverse it was," I admitted.

"Oh, it is. And while sometimes there's friction, it's mostly peaceful. Everyone here knows the value of trade and partnership."

We slowly made our way toward the fort's main entrance, passing by a group of Otoe warriors. Their faces were painted, and their regalia was both intimidating and beautiful. They watched us closely but didn't stop us, then focused once again on an elder who was conversing with a fort official.

Roarke leaned in, his voice dropping to a whisper. "Always be respectful to them. They're proud folks. They've been here long before us and likely will be long after we've gone."

I nodded, taking in the bustling scene—the chatter of negotiations, the laughter of children, the distant singing from around a campfire. All of this was new to me, a fresh experience in this wild land.

The fort's large wooden gates creaked open to reveal a well-organized interior, with systematically placed buildings for storage, living quarters, and trade centers. Men moved about carrying goods, and in one corner, a blacksmith worked his forge, the clanging of metal echoing through the air.

I took a deep breath to prepare for yet another chapter of this adventure, hoping the fort might offer some respite from my seemingly endless misfortunes.

With his commanding presence, Fergus MacBride quickly drew the attention of a fort official, a tall, wiry man with silver streaking through his dark hair and a face lined with years of frontier life.

"MacBride." He nodded in greeting.

"Bradley," MacBride acknowledged, not one for long pleasantries. "I need canoes. We're trading horses."

Bradley smirked. "Straight to business, as always." He beckoned for us to follow. Amidst stacked supplies and tethered animals, a collection of sturdy canoes lay in wait.

Before negotiations could proceed further, an Otoe procession approached with three women leading the group. Their grace was evident in their gait, their outfits adorned with intricate beadwork that caught the sunlight. Each had a unique aura, but the woman at the front, with piercing eyes and an air of authority, held my gaze.

Seizing the moment, Bradley said, "MacBride, I've got an offer for you. These natives know the Missouri's intricacies better than any map. Interested in a guide?"

MacBride, glancing at his pocket watch, his face a mask of skepticism, retorted, "We've got our Métis. Why would I need them? Especially women."

Bradley bristled. "Oh, well, in that case—"

Boyd chimed in, against all expectation. "Say, MacBride, this isn't a bad idea."

"What do you mean?" MacBride asked him.

"I mean, Mr. Astor put this expedition together, and you and I both know he's never been trapping. He assigned us the Métis thinking any old Indian would do, but they're from Quebec. I've been concerned about having them as guides since we left."

I could sense the tension in the air thickening. The women, however, seemed undeterred. The one at the forefront stepped forward, her eyes never leaving MacBride's.

"I am Blue Fox." Her voice was confident, and it almost seemed to echo off the fort walls. "The Missouri and its secrets are known to me, every twist and turn. Your Métis might know the land, but I know the water."

Her mastery of the English language took me aback. Never assume, as they say.

For a moment, no one spoke. The challenge hung in the air. I felt a stir within, recalling my own recent struggles with the wilderness.

"MacBride," I cut in, "having an extra hand, especially one as knowledgeable as her, might not be a bad idea. Lewis and Clark had native guides. I am sure Jean-Baptiste and Georges are good, but as Boyd said, they're not from here."

MacBride's gaze darted to me, his eyes narrowing. "You suggesting I can't make a judgment on what's best for this journey?"

I swallowed, feeling the weight of his ire. "Not at all. Just that..."

The staredown between us seemed eternal. The men around us, Roarke, MacLane, and even Boyd, waited with bated breath.

Bear finally spoke up. "Boyd and Christian are right. A guide would be useful," he said. "She could help with my maps."

MacBride exhaled. "Fine. One guide. Blue Fox, you're with us. But—" He pointed a stern finger at her. "—prove your worth. Every single day."

Blue Fox nodded, her expression unreadable. "You will see the wisdom of your choice," she said.

Bradley's eyes gleamed with mischief as he leaned in closer, lowering his voice for dramatic effect. "Blue Fox isn't just any guide. She's the best. The rivers are her home, the currents her kin. She knows when to push forward, when to wait out a storm, and where the best hunting grounds lie."

Ever the seasoned negotiator, MacBride raised an eyebrow. "Sounds expensive."

Bradley chuckled. "Expensive? She's priceless. But for you? Fifty dollars for the introduction."

A collective gasp went around our group. The price was steep.

MacBride scoffed. "You're out of your mind."

Before Bradley could retort, Blue Fox stepped between them, her voice laced with pride. "It's not Bradley you should be negotiating with. It's me."

The silence that followed was palpable. All eyes turned to her.

She continued, "My knowledge and skills come at my own price. The waters of the Missouri have their own song. And only a few can truly hear it. I require an equal share of the company profits."

MacBride, trying to regain his footing in this exchange, said, "We don't give shares to Indian guides."

Blue Fox was unfazed. "I know things others don't. Secrets of the river that can save us days, even weeks. You need me more than I need this expedition."

Boyd chimed in with a raspy, unsteady voice. "Look, MacBride, our Métis guides are good, but they're not locals. I reckon this girl will come in useful in a pinch. And I'm willing to give up a small share if it means increasing our chances of staying alive."

MacBride was cornered, and we all knew it. But his pride was still at stake. "I'll commit twenty-five dollars to Bradley for the introduction, as he says. That's my final offer. And since my *employees* seem so certain she's worth the expense, I'll cut her a share of *their* profits."

Blue Fox and Bradley exchanged nods. "Agreed," she replied, her tone suggesting she still held the upper hand.

"Fine," MacBride grumbled, "but the down payment cost falls on you." He jabbed a finger toward me and Boyd. "You're the ones who insisted on her."

"Not a problem," I managed to utter, the weight of my rash decision settling in.

Blue Fox's eyes twinkled with triumph. She had successfully haggled with one of the toughest men in the West, and I couldn't help but admire her for it. The journey ahead promised to be anything but ordinary.

As the group dispersed to see to the new arrangement and the goods, I found myself face-to-face with Blue Fox. Her dark eyes were piercing, sizing me up in a manner that left me feeling exposed.

"Is this your first time out West?" Her voice lilted with a note of mockery.

I hesitated, taken aback by her directness. "Well, yes, but I've studied and read about—"

She chuckled, interrupting me. "Reading about the West and living in it are worlds apart. Just as reading about confidence and actually having it differ greatly."

I shifted uncomfortably, recalling my earlier predicament. "Look, I... I'm adjusting."

She crossed her arms, her gaze unrelenting. "You Easterners, so ill-prepared for the realities of the West. Always thinking your bookish knowledge will save you."

I straightened up, trying to find a firm footing in the conversation. "Books have their value. Just as I believe everyone does, in their own way."

Her eyes narrowed, considering me for a moment. "You're different from the others. Less boisterous, more... thoughtful. But that doesn't mean you're ready for what lies ahead."

"I'll manage," I snapped, surprised at my sharp tone.

She smirked, tilting her head slightly. "We'll see about that."

Stung, I replied, "I bring other skills to the group. Not just physical prowess."

Again she tilted her head. "Perhaps."

I swallowed my rising defensiveness and said, "I might not have your experience, but I'm here to learn. And, in time, to contribute."

She looked me up and down—from my still-clean boots to my tailored shirt. "Time will tell. Time always does."

"And how about you?" I asked. "You speak elegantly for a native woman."

She scowled and, with a nod, moved past me. In Blue Fox, I had found both a critic and a challenge.

The cacophony from the fort's grounds began to diminish as our company and the workers efficiently shifted their attention from horse trading to readying the canoes. The wide and meandering Missouri River beckoned us from the edges of the fort, its currents gentle but insistent.

The canoes lined the banks, their wood polished and gleaming with the overhead sun. Each had been crafted with meticulous care, long and narrow with pointed fronts, ideal for navigating the winding river.

"Ever paddled before, Christian?" Boyd asked as he clapped me on the back with his ever-so-boisterous nature.

"Only in the ponds of Central Park," I admitted.

He chuckled heartily. "Well, this ain't Central Park." He patted the side of one of the canoes. "But don't fret. The river's forgiving at this stretch. You'll get the hang of it."

Just then, my eyes landed on Blue Fox. She was speaking to one of the fort workers, her back to us. The wind tugged lightly at her raven-black hair, which cascaded down her back in a silky flow. Her posture was poised and confident, and despite our earlier confrontation, there was an undeniable allure about her.

Boyd's gaze had followed mine. "She's something, isn't she?" he murmured.

I looked at Boyd, a little surprised at the hint of reverence in his voice. "You seem taken with her."

He grinned, the corners of his eyes crinkling. "Oh, come now, Christian. Can you blame me? She's like no one I've ever met. Such spirit. It's captivating."

I raised an eyebrow. "You fancy her?"

Boyd took a deep breath, his eyes still on her. "Perhaps, though I'd wager she's not the kind to be 'fancied' by the likes of me."

Before I could respond, MacBride boomed, "Men! Gather 'round! Time to assign canoes."

We obediently shuffled over, forming a semicircle around him. MacBride was already flanked by MacLane and the fort's manager. With practiced efficiency, MacBride began doling out assignments, pointing to each canoe and naming the men who would occupy it. I noticed something odd had happened with the Métis. When Blue Fox stood beside them, they made it a point to step away from her and put Bear and Jim between them.

To my surprise and simultaneous anxiety, MacBride announced, "Boyd, Christian... and Blue Fox, with her supplies, you're together in the last canoe."

Boyd shot me a knowing smirk as Blue Fox nodded and gathered her belongings, including a rolled-up teepee and several satchels.

She approached our canoe, her steps measured. "Let's hope you're better with a paddle than you are with your words," she said to me.

Boyd chuckled as he loaded the last of our gear into the canoe. "Looks like we'll get to know each other better on the river."

I took a look around, asking aloud so all could hear, "Why are we leaving at dusk? Shouldn't we have stayed in the safety of the fort for the night?

"Forts cost money I don't want to spend," MacBride chided back. "Now, shut up, get into your canoe, and follow me."

Boyd leaned over as I climbed into the canoe. "MacBride's got a favorite camping spot just up the river from here—we'll be there before dark."

The setting sun cast a golden hue upon the water, turning it into a shimmering tapestry of light and shadow. The scene was breathtakingly tranquil, but the underlying tension within our group lingered.

As the first paddle broke the surface of the water and our journey began, I couldn't help but wonder about the enigma that was Blue Fox. The coming days promised to be full of challenges, lessons, and unforeseen interactions. And somewhere in the mix was the magnetic pull between a desperate city man and a woman who embodied the frontier's beauty, majesty, and callousness.

# CHAPTER 3
# THE MANDANS

The woodland was a realm of whispers, rustling leaves, and ancient boughs that stretched endlessly toward the sky. The sun barely penetrated the thick foliage, casting dappled patterns of amber on the ground. Apprehension buzzed in the air; this was not a leisurely exploration of the forest but a hunt, and at its forefront was Blue Fox, her posture alert, every movement precise and silent. Beside her, MacBride moved with surprising agility for a man of his stature, eyes scanning for signs of game.

The rest of us trailed behind them in a line, our footsteps soft against the forest floor and hands clasped on our rifles. I tried to mimic their stealth, but every broken twig underfoot felt like a gunshot, every rustle of my clothing like the roar of a waterfall. MacBride had insisted I tag along despite my protests, to help them corner game if we found it; what a mistake that was. Sole Bear and Jim had remained at camp to watch over our effects. The closer we delved into the heart of the forest, the more alien it felt. Gone was the reassuring width of the Missouri River. In its place was a labyrinth of trees and shadows, where every rustle could be predator or prey.

MacLane, always MacBride's right-hand man, signaled for us to halt with a finger to his lips.

Immediately in front of me, Boyd whispered a quick "stay low" and dropped to a crouch, his eyes darting around.

I followed suit, my heart beating so loudly I feared it might scare away any potential game.

We waited for several tense minutes. In our stillness, the forest came alive. Birds twittered, water bubbled over rocks somewhere in the distance, and I became acutely aware of the smell—damp earth, the tang of pine, and the musky odor of animals.

Blue Fox gestured toward a clearing up ahead, where the faint silhouette of a deer could be seen grazing, oblivious to our presence. MacBride nodded ever so slightly, unslinging his rifle with practiced ease.

"Christian," Boyd whispered from beside me.

I turned to him, my eyes wide.

"Stay behind. You're noisy enough to wake the dead."

His words stung, but I knew he was right. I was the city boy, out of place and out of my depth in this vast wilderness. I gave a curt nod, signaling my understanding, though embarrassment burned in my cheeks.

The group inched forward, with MacBride and Blue Fox leading the way. Each step they took was deliberate, a dance of shadow and light as they approached their prey. From my vantage point, I could see the grace with which Blue Fox moved—she was one with the forest, a silent specter in this crowded expanse.

The deer, a beautiful doe with large brown eyes, continued to graze, unaware of the danger lurking nearby. Every muscle in my body was tensed, waiting for that pivotal moment.

Suddenly, a twig snapped—not from our group, but from the other side of the clearing. The doe's head shot up, ears pricked, and in a heartbeat she bounded away, disappearing into dense forest. MacBride swore under his breath.

Another group of hunters emerged from the trees, Native Americans, their faces painted and bows in hand. Their leader stepped forward, a man of imposing stature and piercing eyes. He spoke to Blue Fox in a calm, flat tone.

Blue Fox replied in her native tongue, the fluidity of her words musical.

"He is apologizing for scaring off our hunt," she told us.

MacBride stepped forward, extending his hand. "There's more game in the forest. No harm done."

The leader of the natives nodded, clasping MacBride's forearm in a firm grip.

"May your hunt be successful," Blue Fox translated.

As the two groups parted ways, Boyd turned to me, a smirk playing on his lips. "See? It wasn't your noise that scared the game away this time."

Despite the jest, the weight of my inexperience pressed on me. I was an outsider, not only to the wilderness but also to this eclectic group. They had accepted me, albeit with a fair share of teasing, but I yearned to prove my worth.

MacBride, ever the strategist, surveyed the group. "Let's split up. Cover more ground. We'll meet back at the river by sundown." He pointed towards MacLane and the Métis. "You lot with me." Then he gestured to Blue Fox, Boyd, and me. "The other group, head west."

As the parties diverged, I took a hesitant step, inadvertently finding myself beside Blue Fox.

"Who were they?" I asked.

"Mandans," she replied, her voice even and soft. "We're on good terms. They mostly keep to themselves, and when paths cross, it's usually peaceful."

I nodded, processing this. "You handled that well," I began, searching for words. "I mean, you're good at this... hunting and navigating through the wilderness. Would you... erm, perhaps teach me? A thing or two?"

Blue Fox eyed me with a tilt of her head, her gaze inscrutable. "Are you trying to court me?"

"What? No!" I managed to choke on my own spit. When I finished coughing, I added, "I mean, not that you're not—I just meant the hunting! Just the hunting part."

A hint of a smile played at the corners of her lips. "Relax," she teased, clearly amused. "I knew what you meant. I enjoy watching you stumble."

I let out a sigh of relief mixed with embarrassment. "Honestly, I just don't want to be the laughingstock of this expedition any longer."

In that moment, I regretted heading West at all. I would have fared better in a New York jail cell than the wilderness. At least in jail they give you three square meals a day and a safe place to sleep. Oh, how I longed to return to New York just then. I wondered if I could have negotiated better with John Astor to earn my way back to good graces without having to risk my neck in this wild country. But I was where I was. And I had to make the best of it.

Blue Fox regarded me for a moment, her expression softening. "All right, Christian. I'll teach you. You must listen, watch, and most importantly, respect."

Gratitude welled up inside me. "Thank you, Blue Fox. Truly."

She nodded while gesturing for me to follow. "Let's start with tracking. You won't have anything to hunt if you can't find your prey."

As we ventured deeper into the woodland, I couldn't help but think that, in this vast wilderness, I might find more than hunting lessons. With every step, I was learning more about myself and those around me.

The soft crunch of dried leaves underfoot brought a whisper of rebuke from Blue Fox. "Your footsteps are too heavy." She fell back to walk gracefully beside me. "You're announcing your presence to the entire forest."

I frowned, adjusting my stride to mimic hers. "Like this?"

Her lips curled into a smirk. "Better. Feel the ground, don't attack it."

Further along, she stopped me again, but this time to motion me into a crouch beside her. "See it?" Her eyes were alive with the thrill of the hunt.

I squinted. "The broken twig?"

She brushed the ground with a tenderness that imparted deep reverence. "No, the hoofprint. Right here. A deer."

"How can you tell?"

Her gaze locked with mine, a playful gleam dancing within. "Everything leaves a mark."

My heart raced as the distance between us seemed to shrink, the forest sounds fading into insignificance. But just as swiftly, she was on her feet, tugging me along, her voice a hushed command.

"Listen."

Closing my eyes, I strained to catch the subtle notes of the wild. "The water?" I ventured.

Her head tilted, listening intently. "No, the rustle in the bushes. That's our prey."

Triumph surged as I finally discerned the soft, erratic noise. "I hear it."

Her smile was genuine, her pride in my progress clear. "Good. Now, approach silently."

We moved in tandem, every shared step drawing us closer in a dance of hunter and prey. But the moment was shattered by a rustling behind us. We whirled around to find Boyd's grinning face.

"You might want to see this," he panted, gesturing towards a distant hill.

Blue Fox and I trailed behind him until the woodland near the river fell away to the Great Plains, an endless sea of dry grasses roiling like waves in the arid wind. A sprawling village nestled on a slope overlooking the river. The sight was mesmerizing: countless tepees scattered amidst barren land, smoke wafting skyward industriously.

Boyd pointed to the settlement on the distant hill. "What is that?"

Blue Fox followed his gaze, her eyes narrowing. There was a slight pause, a momentary lapse in her confident demeanor. "That's a Mandan village. We're closer than I thought."

"You're familiar with it?" I asked.

She looked thoughtful for a moment. "Yes, I know it. This is one of their larger villages. We weren't supposed to reach it until tomorrow or the day after."

Boyd's eyebrows knitted together. "Is it bad that we're early?"

She exhaled softly. "There is a process to revealing one's presence to the Mandans. Encountering them in the forest is one thing, but they can grow defensive if we approach their village without invitation."

I tried to piece it all together. "Did we veer off course? Are we at risk of offending them?"

There was a hint of regret in her eyes. "Perhaps we didn't choose the best path, but we're here now. We need to proceed with caution."

Boyd glanced between us, trying to gauge the situation. "So what's our next move?"

"We should set up camp and wait for the morning," she replied with authority. "Now that we're this close, they will come to us."

I nodded, my thoughts still racing from the day's close interactions with Blue Fox and the unexpected challenges that lay ahead.

We made our way back to the canoes, our earlier camaraderie replaced by a weighted tension. The landscape around us shifted from a shaded woodland to a heavy, humid swamp nearer the river. The other group had already returned to the river, and from their disappointed expressions, it was evident they'd had no better luck than we did.

Scanning the horizon, MacBride turned his discerning gaze to us, obviously expecting a report. "What have you found?"

"A Mandan village," Blue Fox said, "much closer than I anticipated."

He frowned and exchanged a wary glance with MacLane, vigilant as always at his side. "And you didn't expect it to be there?"

"I didn't realize how close we had come," she admitted. Her usual confidence had waned just a bit, replaced with cautious reservation.

Boyd chimed in, trying to ease the tension. "She says they're good people. Peaceful."

MacBride shot him a look. "Every village has its warriors, every tribe its protectors. How do you suggest we proceed?"

"We should make camp here," Blue Fox said firmly. "If they've seen us—and they have—they'll send someone. It's their land. We can't ignore them or turn back now."

MacBride's lips thinned. "And if they're not friendly?"

Blue Fox looked him squarely in the eye. "We wait for an invitation. If they extend one, we must accept. It's the only way to ensure peace and safe passage."

There was a collective nod among the group. We all understood the importance of diplomacy in unfamiliar territory.

Boyd, ever the voice of levity, piped up. "Well, if they have any of that corn beer they're known for, it won't be a total loss."

MacLane chuckled while shaking his head. "Always about alcohol with you, isn't it?"

The group began to unpack, the day's events weighing heavily on our minds. Our proximity to the village meant that every action had to be considered, every move calculated. But as the evening settled in and the campfire began to glow, there was an underlying angst that the Mandans had us at their mercy.

As we continued setting up camp, the two Métis, Georges and Jean-Baptiste, approached Blue Fox with swift purpose. They exchanged rapid-fire words in a language unfamiliar to my ears, but the escalating tone was unmistakable.

The intensity of their conversation caught the entire group's attention, and all eyes shifted to the unfolding scene. Without warning, Jean-Baptiste lunged at Blue Fox, who swiftly sidestepped and pushed him back, showing an impressive command over her movements.

Boyd and I exchanged glances of alarm. "What the hell's going on?" he muttered.

"Damned if I know," I replied, equally clueless. "But we can't let this go on."

MacLane, Roarke, and Asher moved closer, their faces etched with concern, but none intervened, perhaps out of uncertainty or respect for the Métis duo's seniority.

As the conflict escalated, my protective instincts kicked in. I lunged between Blue Fox and the two angry Métis. "Enough!" I shouted.

Blue Fox's face was a mix of anger and surprise, her chest heaving. Her eyes momentarily softened in gratitude —at least, until she was again glaring at her two rivals.

Georges, his face flushed with rage, yelled something in their language, pointing a finger at her. The accusation, whatever it was, seemed grave. My heart raced; it was clear that this was not a mere disagreement.

MacBride stepped forward, his voice full of authority. "What is this about?"

Georges looked at him, then back to Blue Fox, hesitating for a moment before replying in French, "We are in danger. She's not to be trusted."

I felt a pang of confusion and concern. "Danger? What are you talking about?"

Jean-Baptiste spat as he stared down Blue Fox with undisguised contempt. "Some of my things are missing. I'm sure it was she who stole them."

I translated for MacBride, whose eyes narrowed. "Is this true, Blue Fox?"

She straightened her posture, eyes blazing. "I am many things, but a thief is not one of them."

The air was practically electric with distrust and anger. "Let's all calm down," I said. "We're on the same side, aren't we?"

After what felt like hours, Georges finally relented, his shoulders sagging in defeat. "She's not to be trusted," he warned, eyes still locked on Blue Fox.

Since we had brought her on at the fort, Georges and Jean-Baptiste had kept their distance from her. Something about her bothered them. It was hard for me to gauge what because they kept to themselves, seldom talking with the rest of us. This outburst was a complete surprise.

Later, as the camp came alive with the evening's activities, the two Métis approached me, their faces marked with evident concern.

"Monsieur Christian," began Jean-Baptiste in a heavily accented French, "we must speak with you."

I nodded. "Of course, what is it?"

Georges' brow furrowed as he said, "It's about Blue Fox. We think she is lying about knowing the river."

Jean-Baptiste chimed in. "A good guide wouldn't have been caught by surprise by the Mandans like we were today."

The weight of their words hit me. Could what they were saying be true? Was our newest guide deceiving us? The thought sent my heart aflutter.

Georges continued, "From now on, we should be the ones to guide the expedition, not her. We are not from here, but this is not our first journey up the Missouri. We can manage the Mandans and the rest, and if we need her help, we will ask for it."

I sighed, understanding their frustration. "I will speak to MacBride about this."

Jean-Baptiste shook his head. "No, we want you to tell her."

"What makes you say that?" I asked.

They looked at each other and shrugged. "You are better with words," Jean-Baptiste said.

It made sense to me. They probably hoped that by speaking to me, they could avoid any more public confrontations. I had sensed that both men seemed to regard MacBride with an air of deep suspicion. They hadn't said a word to him the entire expedition.

"I don't want to go behind MacBride's back on this. I should really consult him first," I said.

"Please, Monsieur Christian, we would like to handle this quietly, for the sake of the expedition. We think you can do it," Georges insisted.

"Fine. I'll speak to her and then MacBride."

The two men nodded, seemingly relieved.

"Thank you, Monsieur Christian," said Georges. "We just want to ensure the safety and success of this expedition."

On their suggestion, I moved towards where Blue Fox was unpacking her supplies. I had hoped for a calm conversation, one in which we could talk about the way forward. She didn't meet my gaze as I approached, and I could sense the tension radiating from her.

"Blue Fox," I began, my voice gentle, "I've spoken with the Métis. They ask that, for now, you hang to the side a little. Lie low. They want to handle the Mandans."

She finally looked up, her brown eyes unwavering. "You haven't asked me my side of things." Her voice was soft yet edged with anger. "Those men resent me because I know the way better than they ever will, and they feel threatened."

"Do you have proof of that?"

"Proof?" she snapped. "They attacked me, not the other way around. I have nothing to prove, Christian, and the fact that you think I do shows how little you trust me."

I sighed, running a hand through my hair. "Look, there's a lot I don't know. I trust you—I do—but I also have to trust them."

Her expression remained steely. "I will remember this, Christian."

"I didn't mean to offend you," I tried to explain, but she turned away, clearly hurt and angered by my words.

Her back was to me; her shoulders stiffened as she took a deep breath. "If that's what you think is best," she said quietly, her voice barely above a whisper. It wasn't just her words but the very tone that left me feeling uneasy.

I reached out, attempting to bridge the widening gap between us. "Blue Fox—"

But she cut me off with a swift, dismissive wave of her hand, her message clear. Now wasn't the time to talk. I retreated, my heart heavy, unsure how to mend the bridge it seemed I had unintentionally burned.

I then approached MacBride's tent, determination fueling my steps. Pushing past the canvas flap, I stepped inside, meeting his piercing gaze.

"MacBride," I began confidently, "the Métis asked that I handle the Blue Fox situation, so I did. I think we should put her under watch for the time being and let them handle the Mandans until we can figure out if their accusations hold water."

He stared at me for a moment, his silence adding weight to the room. Then, finally, he repeated, "They asked you?" His tone was dripping with sarcasm. "Why you and not me?"

I paused. "I... I'm not sure, perhaps because I—"

He cut me off sharply. "Just because that letter gave you second place in our chain of command does not give you permission to go around making critical decisions about the expedition without my consent."

Trying to maintain some semblance of dignity, I added, "I only want what's best for the expedition, sir."

MacBride's eyes were cold, his posture tense. "This is my expedition. My command. And while I might have come to the same conclusion about the Métis and Blue Fox, that was *my* call to make. Not yours."

I shrank under his glare. "I apologize. I overstepped."

He took a moment to let the silence punctuate his displeasure. "See that it doesn't happen again. Remember your place, Christian."

As I stepped out of the tent, my cheeks still warm with embarrassment, Maclane was waiting outside, leaning casually against a tree. He raised an eyebrow, an amused smirk playing on his lips.

"He'll kill you if you do that again, you know," he remarked, a hint of seriousness beneath his light tone.

I sighed. "I gathered as much."

MacLane took a step closer, his smirk fading. "I hope he does."

I swallowed hard. He was serious. Rather than push back, I retreated to my tent. I went to sleep that night with my rifle in my arms.

The first thing I was aware of when consciousness seeped back was the soft trill of birds and the distant sound of water lapping against the canoes. The sun's warmth on my face was a little too intense. I blinked my eyes open, expecting the usual scene of my compatriots preparing for the day, but instead, I was met with an extraordinary sight.

A group of Mandan warriors stood just a few feet from where I lay, their powerful frames outlined by the early morning sunlight. There must have been at least fifteen of them. Their faces were marked with striking ocher and white clay streaks, making their dark eyes appear even more intense. They had long hair pulled back behind their heads and held in place by long feathers. This hairstyle, a marker of their warriors, added to the fierce aura they projected.

Their bodies, bronzed from the sun, rippled with muscle. They wore minimal clothing—strips of hide hung loosely around their waists, while intricately beaded bands wrapped around their biceps and forearms. Some bore necklaces made of animal teeth or carved bone. Each warrior carried well-used and well-maintained weapons: bows strung taut, arrows with razor-sharp points, and clubs adorned with menacing spikes.

But what struck me most was the confidence with which they held themselves. They stood with a regal air, as if they owned the very ground they stood upon. This was their land, after all.

Two particularly imposing figures conversed with MacBride and MacLane a few feet away from the main group. One was taller than the rest, with intricate tattoos that ran from his wrists to his shoulders and across his chest. The tattoos depicted scenes of hunts, battles, and what I guessed might be stories of their people's history. Beside him was a slightly shorter but broader warrior, his presence almost as commanding, his face marked with a blue crescent moon under his right eye.

The rest of our group formed a semicircle around this discussion, their expressions a mix of curiosity, respect, and, in some cases, thinly veiled apprehension. Blue Fox was also there, her posture rigid. I could tell she was on high alert, perhaps even more than the rest of us. We were on their land, uninvited. Any wrong move or misunderstanding could easily escalate tensions.

MacBride was speaking in slow, deliberate English, using expansive hand gestures to aid his communication until Blue Fox could interject with a few words in their native tongue, clarifying or elaborating on what MacBride was trying to convey.

I pulled myself to a sitting position and quickly ran my fingers through my disheveled hair to make myself look somewhat presentable. As I did so, the taller of the two Mandan leaders glanced my way, his dark eyes briefly locking with mine before returning to MacBride.

Trying to shake off my grogginess and the discomfort of my stiff muscles, I slowly got to my feet and joined the rest of the group. I felt foolish for having overslept and potentially missed crucial parts of the discussion.

Boyd, noticing my arrival, leaned in and whispered, "Quite the awakening, huh?"

"You could say that," I murmured back.

Just then, the meeting came to some conclusion. MacBride and the two Mandan leaders shared a respectful nod before the war band began to disperse. As they did, they studied our group, a silent reminder of their power and our precarious position in their territory.

MacBride, his broad shoulders tight but his face glinting with satisfaction, turned to address us. MacLane stood just behind him, a subtle frown marking his otherwise stoic features.

"Good morning, everyone," MacBride began confidently. "The Mandan have extended an invitation to their village. They're offering us a feast."

A murmur went through the group, a mix of relief and curiosity.

MacLane added, "And it's not just hospitality they're offering. They're keen on trade as well."

MacBride continued, "It seems our reputation precedes us. They're well aware of our journey and its purpose. They've expressed an interest in some of the goods we carry, especially the glass beads."

Roarke, ever the optimist, piped up. "When do we go and visit them?"

"I'm not keen on going into their village." Boyd shook his head.

Blue Fox spoke up, clear and calm. "It is the Mandan way. Hospitality is highly regarded, especially to those who come in peace. Refusing their invitation would've been a sign of disrespect. We are on their lands, and it's in our best interest to build a good relationship with them."

I couldn't help but notice the slight tension in her posture. She was trying hard to mask her anxiety, but I could sense the weight of responsibility she bore.

Asher chimed in with evident curiosity. "So what exactly will this feast entail?"

MacBride, who was glancing at his pocket watch, smirked. "I suppose we'll find out soon enough, lad. But if their reputation holds true, it'll be a spread of local delicacies: roasted game, fresh vegetables, and perhaps even some fermented beverages."

Boyd, always looking for a light moment, grinned. "Forget what I said. All you had to say was fermented beverages! What are we waiting for?"

MacLane's voice cut through the jovial atmosphere. "Remember, this isn't just a social gathering. It's a chance for us to further our goals and establish strong trade relationships. We must be respectful and show gratitude."

MacBride nodded in agreement. "Lucas is right. We are guests in their territory. Let's not forget that. We'll prepare ourselves and head to their village shortly."

With that, the group set about their tasks, a din of excitement and uncertainty. As for me, I couldn't help but wonder what the night would hold. I had barely managed to get my bearings when MacBride approached me, his face hardened, eyes sharp and piercing.

"Christian," he began, his voice dripping with the authority he wielded so effortlessly, "I've given it some thought. You'll stay here and guard the camp with Blue Fox. Everyone else will join the feast."

I was taken aback, my mouth open in surprise. "You can't be serious! I can't miss this opportunity."

MacBride's steely gaze held mine. "Consider it a lesson. You overstepped yesterday, and this is the consequence."

My frustration boiled over. "It's just a simple meal! I've come all this way, suffered so much—"

His hand whipped out, fingers curling into the fabric of my shirt, pulling me close. His face was inches from mine. "I'm the leader of this expedition, not you. You'd do well to remember that and keep your educated mouth shut."

I braced myself, expecting a blow, but it never came. Instead, a voice broke the tension, clear and firm.

"Enough!" It was Sam Barens. He stood between us, his eyes locked on MacBride. "He's made mistakes, but this is not the way. We got our orders—let's stick to them. If the chain of command breaks down out here, we're all dead men."

MacBride, taken aback, loosened his grip on my shirt, his eyes narrowing. "You're right."

For a moment, there was an uneasy silence. The weight of their gazes and the air's electricity was almost palpable. The entire camp had turned their attention to the unfolding drama, waiting with bated breath.

MacBride finally broke the silence, his voice cold. "Christian and Blue Fox, you're on watch here. The rest of you, follow me."

He turned on his heel and walked away, leaving the two of us in the middle of the clearing. I tried to find words, but she held up a hand.

"Not now," she said softly, then turned away to attend to her tasks.

The sounds of the departing group had barely faded when I found myself seated opposite Blue Fox, the campfire crackling between us. The flames danced, casting fluctuating shadows on her face and momentarily illuminating her eyes. They were distant and reflective, and I couldn't help but think she was lost in some memory all her own. The ambience was thick with apprehension, and though the flames provided warmth, a noticeable chill hung in the air.

"Look..." I began, "I'm sorry for yesterday—for making that decision without consulting you. I was wrong."

She remained silent, only the soft sigh of the wind in the trees filling the void.

"I just... I wanted to do what I thought was right. I wanted to prove myself. You were right. You were honest. I should have known that. I hope you can forgive me."

Her face was unreadable. "You have a lot to learn."

I sighed, shifting uncomfortably. "Tell me about yourself, about where you come from."

For a moment, she hesitated, her gaze once more distant. "I am from a Mandan village further north," she began quietly, "or at least my mother was. My father... he was a trapper, a wanderer from another world."

I leaned forward, intrigued. "Two worlds... Must've been hard."

She chuckled softly, a sad smile playing on her lips. "Yes. Growing up, I always felt like I had a foot in both worlds. Never fully belonging to one or the other. Always caught in between."

I thought of my own past, my own divided heritage. "I know what that's like," I confessed. "My father was French, and my mother American. I, too, grew up between two worlds."

Blue Fox's surprise was evident in her eyes. "I wouldn't have guessed," she said.

I chuckled. "There's a lot you don't know about me."

For a moment, she just studied me, her gaze intense. Then, slowly, she rose and moved to sit beside me, close enough that I could feel the warmth of her body. The fire seemed brighter, the night less chilly, and I was strangely at home amidst the vast wilderness.

The warmth of Blue Fox beside me was comforting. Her closeness made the vast wilderness around us feel a little smaller and more intimate.

"So," she said, "you've mentioned your parents briefly. But tell me about New York. And how did you end up with the American Fur Company?"

I cleared my throat, memories from a long-ago life flooding back. "My family moved to New York when I was three to escape the war in the Vendée. I grew up amidst the hustle and bustle of New York City. My father was a wealthy businessman from France, always traveling, always looking for the next big opportunity. I didn't see much of him."

"And the company?"

I glowered, remembering the chance encounter. "After my wife and son passed away in childbirth, I crawled inside a bottle to drown my sorrow."

"How awful, Christian. I am—"

I cut her off. "It cost me my law career. After a bad night on the town, I was jailed for starting a brawl at a tavern. My mother runs with the who's who of New England, and she pulled a few strings with some friends of hers. Mr. Astor paid my bail in exchange for a contract to work for him as one of his corporate lawyers. He was desperate for someone of my education and skills who could also speak French and understand the laws in Quebec."

"Odd that he would send a lawyer into the wilderness," Blue Fox said.

"You're right. Part of the deal was that I have to spend at least two years out West, away from the temptations and vices of the city. To 'sober up,' as he put it."

Her eyes gleamed with a mix of curiosity and surprise. "Ah, I understand. You're here for redemption."

I shrugged. "You could call it that, yes."

I poked at the fire with a long stick, stoking the flames. We sat in silence for a moment. I wanted to share with her everything I was feeling, all my secrets. Perhaps it was the loneliness of the expedition that drew me to her, or the wounds in my heart from what I had lost. But I refrained.

Blue Fox gazed at me, her eyes studious. "I've heard the others complain about your rank. They say you don't deserve it."

"It's because of my degree," I explained. "In Astor's companies, men with degrees start up higher than men without them. I've also been tasked with brokering a deal with the North West Company. No one better than a lawyer for that."

"What kind of deal?" she asked.

I hesitated, and she noticed. "I can't say yet."

She nodded thoughtfully. I could tell she wanted to press her question, but she showed restraint and moved on. "So is this journey meeting your expectations so far?"

I sighed. "In many ways, yes. The beauty, the vastness, the challenges... it's all there. But it's also lonely, trying to find my place among men who've done this for years."

She smiled, her gaze warm and understanding. "Everyone finds their place eventually."

Blue Fox had listened intently, her eyes reflecting the flames' dance. After I'd finished, she took a moment, collected her thoughts, then began gathering herself as if to stand up and leave.

"What about you? How did you end up a guide? And one who speaks such impeccable English?" I asked. My question brought her gaze back across the flames to me.

"There's not much to tell. My father was a French trapper. My mother was from a village north of here, and her tribe cast her out for what my father had done to her."

She paused, her gaze distant. "I grew up around the English-speaking rendezvous forts closest to St. Louis. They became my playgrounds, my classrooms. Mother and I would often stay near them, waiting for my father's return, trading with the other travelers, and hearing tales of lands beyond."

Her fingers played with the edges of her satchel. "You could say the forts raised me. I learned the languages of the tribes, the ways of the traders, and the tricks of the rivers and forests. As I grew, I began guiding traders and explorers, using the knowledge I'd gathered."

"Do you hope to see your father again?"

Blue Fox scowled. "He had better hope I never do."

I raised my hands as if her glare was an arrow pointed at my heart. "I'm sorry, I didn't mean to..."

She softened as she faced me again, her eyes deep pools in the firelight. "Like you, Christian, I was born between two worlds, never fully belonging to either. But that has made me who I am."

"I can understand that sentiment."

A smirk tugged at her lips. "Then it will not surprise you to know that the meeting I had with the Mandans was them reminding me that I am not welcome in their village."

"This was the village your mother was banished from?"

"No, but one of the hunters we met in the woods recognized me, and they went out of their way to remind me of my place as an outcast to their people. It's a small community."

Despite our vast differences, that single common thread of existing between two different worlds, cultures, and languages formed a bridge between us. The walls we'd built seemed to crumble, replaced by a newfound respect and camaraderie.

As her story came to an end and the weight of our confessions settled between us, I felt an unexpected boldness take hold.

"Blue Fox, I could kiss you right now," I declared, looking into her eyes, searching for a hint of reciprocation.

Her gaze hardened, and her response was swift and sharp. "Don't mistake my sharing a story as an invitation. Know your boundaries, Christian."

I felt my face flush. "I apologize," I managed to say, gazing down at the fire.

She took a deep breath, her eyes still fixed on mine, ensuring her words had truly sunk in.

As the intensity of the moment lifted, a hint of a smile played at the corners of her lips, a subtle, almost imperceptible softening. It was a fleeting expression, but it was enough to suggest that while I had been too forward in this moment, all was not lost between us.

"You have much to learn, Christian," she said, her tone gentler now. "And not just about surviving in these lands."

I met her eyes, reading the layers of meaning in them. "I'm a willing student," I replied.

Her smile deepened, and for a moment, there was an understanding between us, a shared anticipation of what was to come. The night's conversation was far from over, and I felt renewed hope for our budding connection.

Later that evening, the rest of our company returned from the Mandan camp gleaming from a successful trade and enjoyable feast. The Mandans were evidently excellent hosts. Passing through their territory was assured.

# CHAPTER 4
## FIRST BLOOD

We spent two or three weeks navigating through Mandan territory without incident, until we reached the confluence of the Missouri and Yellowstone rivers. The sun cast a brilliant golden glow over the shimmering water and the distant calls of birds created an idyllic scene, contrasting sharply with the sudden tension at camp.

Blue Fox had been conversing with a group of Assiniboines, their exchange lively and engaging. She laughed, pointing at a particularly large fish one of the tribesmen had caught. At this moment, MacLane, ever the bold opportunist, saw fit to make his move. Striding up to the group with a twisted smirk, he reached out and gave Blue Fox's backside a firm grab.

The atmosphere turned electric. Blue Fox, her face a mixture of shock and rage, whirled around and slapped MacLane hard across the face. The Assiniboines, clearly not comprehending the exact nature of the interaction but sensing the violation, took a step back, their hands inching toward their weapons. My face reddened as anger and jealousy flared within me.

MacLane, rubbing his now-reddening cheek, let out a low chuckle. "Touchy, aren't you?"

Her voice was ice-cold. "Keep your hands to yourself."

I charged toward them with thunderous steps. Even Blue Fox seemed surprised. MacLane sneered at me, his hand still on his face.

"What in God's name do you think you're doing, MacLane?" I seethed.

He replied with a chuckle, "Oh, calm down. It was just a bit of fun."

Blue Fox's voice rang out, cold and firm. "If you ever touch me like that again, I'll cut you where the sun and moon don't shine."

From the corners of my eyes, I could see the gathering camp members, drawn by the commotion. The Assiniboines, with whom Blue Fox had been laughing moments before, fled on their horses, our crucial trading with them ended by MacLane's foolishness.

Before I could process the situation further, a firm hand gripped my shoulder and spun me around. MacBride's face, inches from mine, was a mask of fury. "You think you can run this camp, boy? Yelling at MacLane like you own the place?"

MacBride's sudden anger, directed solely at me, took me aback. My eyes darted to MacLane, who was enjoying the scene, smug satisfaction on his face.

I tried to explain. "Sir, I was only—"

MacBride cut me off, pushing me back slightly, his voice dripping with menace. "Know your place, Christian. Keep your temper in check, or you'll find yourself out of this company. Understood?"

I nodded, swallowing my pride. "Understood."

MacBride gave me one last glare before storming off, leaving me to simmer in my own fury and humiliation. I couldn't help but wonder if this journey was more treacherous than I'd imagined. Not because of the wilderness but because of the men I was traveling with.

My pulse quickened, and I jabbed a finger toward MacLane. "What about MacLane and what he did to Blue Fox? Huh?"

MacBride paused, his face contorted in contempt. "What about it?"

"You don't see anything wrong with that?!" I could hardly contain my rage.

MacBride stopped in his tracks and growled. "I see that the commotion scared off our trade partners, and MacLane will pay for that. But that's my business, now, not yours."

MacLane, nearby, shot MacBride a smug smile but said nothing.

My hands clenched, knuckles white. I wanted nothing more than to wipe that smug look off MacLane's face. But I also knew the risks involved. He was the leader's pet, and his place was practically above mine in this wilderness.

Blue Fox, however, took a step forward. Her eyes, normally calm and collected, burned. "I am not your toy, nor his," she spat, her gaze flicking to MacLane. "You will regret it if you ever again lay a hand on me."

MacBride looked between us, amusement dancing on his face. "Well, well. Looks like we've got a love story blooming here." He chuckled, his laughter grating to my ears. "Stay out of things that don't concern you, Christian. And as for you—" He looked at Blue Fox. "—know your place. You are our property; act as such."

She shot back a withering look, but both of us knew that, for now, we'd have to pick our battles.

Staring down at MacBride, I felt the weight of the situation pressing on me. In a desperate attempt to protect Blue Fox, I found myself blurting out, "Look, I paid for her to join this expedition, so she's my responsibility."

The camp fell silent, every eye turning in my direction. I felt heat rise to my face, realizing the implications of what I had just declared. How could I stand by as MacBride declared another human being property? The very idea was repugnant to me.

Blue Fox's eyes widened, shock and hurt evident in them. I mentally cursed myself, thinking I'd just lost any trust or connection I'd managed to build with her.

But then her expression shifted ever so slightly. There was understanding in her eyes, a recognition that I wasn't claiming ownership but trying to shield her from the malicious intentions around us. It was a reprieve I hadn't expected.

"I am not a possession to be passed around or bartered over," she said slowly, her voice low but commanding respect from all who heard.

My heart raced. I had no intention of treating Blue Fox as an object, and her acknowledgment of my protection was both humbling and heartbreaking. I looked down, battling my emotions, the guilt of the declaration, and the relief of her understanding.

MacBride, sensing that he'd lost the upper hand in the conversation, grumbled, "Fine, keep your little trinket safe then." With that, he strode away, leaving a tense atmosphere in his wake.

"What made you intervene, Christian?" she whispered so softly that only I could hear amidst the murmurs of the crew.

"I can't bear the thought of anyone harming you," I admitted, eyes locked onto hers, a silent plea for her to understand the depth of my concern.

I took a deep breath, my thoughts a whirlwind. But how else could I keep her safe in this lawless land, where men's desires seem to override their sense of decency? How had we gotten to this point, where a person's worth could be equated to beads or trinkets? It was unfathomable.

We made our way back to the canoes to continue upriver. On our way, we passed the Métis who stood leaning against a tree, arms crossed, and a smirk across their faces. They saw that Blue Fox had started to drive a wedge through the company, and I imagined that made them happy considering they had distrusted her from the start.

As we steadily advanced up the river, the rhythm of the paddles in the water became our metronome, punctuating the passage of time. The world around us was changing, metamorphosing from the vast openness of the plains to the inviting embrace of dense forests.

The Missouri had been our guide, a fluid pathway through a land of varied wonders. It seemed as if every bend in the river introduced a new vista, a fresh spectacle for our ever-curious eyes. The horizon, which had once been a distant line on the vast prairies, now began to close in, hemmed by the towering pine trees that seemed to touch the very heavens.

Whereas the plains had an expansive grandeur, with undulating grasslands and the play of light and shadow as clouds drifted lazily overhead, the forests had a different charm. It was an intimate beauty, an ecosystem that invited you to delve deeper, to become one with the intricacies of its design.

I found myself constantly looking up, neck craned, as the pine trees, with their straight trunks and evergreen foliage, vied for the sun's attention. They stood like ancient sentinels, guarding secrets of the land known only to them. Here and there, a break in the canopy would allow a shaft of sunlight to pierce through, spotlighting a patch of the forest floor and illuminating the myriad ferns and other undergrowth in a golden hue.

The air was different here, too. The arid breath of the plains had been replaced by a moist, earthy scent that filled our nostrils with every breath. The aroma of pine needles mingling with the dampness of the soil was refreshing and invigorating. Every inhale seemed to cleanse the soul, connecting us to the very essence of nature.

As we paddled, the gentle murmur of the river was accompanied by a symphony from the forest. Birds serenaded us with their melodious songs, each species contributing its unique note to the harmonious chorus. Squirrels darted between branches, their rapid movements accompanied by the rustling of leaves. And every so often, the haunting call of a distant loon would echo down the river, a reminder of this place's wild, untouched beauty.

In these parts, the river was a clear, sparkling stream, its bed a mosaic of pebbles and rocks of every conceivable hue. We often saw fish, their silver bodies flashing beneath the surface, darting between the shadows of the trees that dappled the water.

As the days passed and we journeyed further into the heart of this pine-clad realm, our bond with the land grew. It was as if the river and the forest were whispering their ancient tales to us, stories of epochs gone by, of creatures that had once roamed these lands, and of the timeless dance between nature and those who revered it.

Blue Fox seemed to come alive even more amidst this verdant landscape. Her keen eyes would often spot details that most of us would overlook—a rare bird perched on a high branch, a patch of edible berries, or the tracks of an animal on the forest floor. She was clearly attuned to the pulse of the wilderness, her senses heightened, her spirit in harmony with the world around us.

As for me, I found solace in this untouched realm. Each day on the river, amidst the embrace of the pines, was a balm to the soul. The stresses and strains of the expedition, the constant danger, and the friction with MacBride and the others seemed to melt away, replaced by a profound peace.

During these moments, surrounded by nature's raw beauty, I felt a deep kinship with Blue Fox. Our conversations, which had started as mere exchanges of information and curiosities, had evolved into profound discussions about life and our place in the world. The forest and the river became our shared sanctuaries, places where our spirits could commune freely, unburdened by the prejudices and constraints of the world beyond.

But as much as we reveled in the pristine beauty of the landscape, we were also always vigilant. The dense woods, while enchanting, could also hide dangers. Bears, wolves, and other predators roamed these parts, and we had to be constantly on guard. Still, the sheer majesty of the untrammeled wilderness around us was a constant reminder of the wonders of the natural world—a world that, despite its challenges, held endless possibilities for discovery, understanding, and connection.

But then the serenity of dense pine forest and the gentle rhythm of the river were shattered in an instant. Ahead, nestled in a clearing on the riverbank, a camp came into view. White linen tents gleamed in the dappled sunlight, unmistakable against the rich green backdrop, but it was the flag that caught our attention—a proud Union Jack fluttering in the gentle breeze.

Before I could register the implications of this detail, MacBride's voice, edged with urgency, reached my ears.

"Hudson's Bay trappers," he hissed, eyes narrowed. The color drained from his face. It became clear at that moment that our journey had suddenly taken a perilous turn.

I was unfamiliar with the intricacies of the fur trade, but MacBride's reaction told me all I needed to know. We were intruding on the territory of a formidable rival, one that had dominated these lands long before the American Fur Company came along.

Before any of us could react or discuss our next move, a chilling sound pierced the air—the unmistakable crack of a musket. Another shot rang out, followed by another. Bullets whizzed past us, some embedding into the wooden frames of our canoes, others sending splashes into the water.

Panic erupted within our ranks. Paddles slapped the water haphazardly as everyone tried to maneuver out of the line of fire. MacBride barked orders, attempting to bring some semblance of strategy to the chaos.

"Paddle! Get to cover! Move!" he shouted.

I glanced back to the Hudson's Bay camp. Eight men, muskets in hand, were emerging from the tree line, their expressions a mix of rage and determination. They weren't in a welcoming mood.

Blue Fox, ever composed even in the face of imminent danger, steered our canoe with swift, deft strokes towards a clump of bushes along the riverbank. We ducked low, hoping to avoid being easy targets. The air was thick with the acrid smell of gunpowder.

Once we were relatively shielded by the foliage, I turned to MacBride, looking for answers. "Why the hell are they shooting at us?!"

He gritted his teeth, frustration evident in his eyes. "This is their territory, lad. They see us as interlopers. The fur trade isn't just business—it's war."

My mind raced, trying to find a way out of this dangerous predicament, trying not to feel helpless. Blue Fox's voice broke through my thoughts.

"They have us outnumbered."

MacBride looked at her, then at me, determination set in his features. "We need a plan and fast. Before they decide to finish what they started."

The weight of the situation pressed down on us. Here, on the banks of the Yellowstone River, deep in the heart of the wilderness, we found ourselves in a standoff that could determine our fate.

Blue Fox's eyes scanned the surrounding trees and brush, her mind working rapidly. "The smoke." She pointed towards the camp.

Their freshly lit campfire was sending up a thick plume of white smoke, partially obscuring the trappers' line of sight.

MacBride's eyebrows furrowed. "Go on."

She continued, "They think they've pinned us down, but we can use the smoke to get away. They don't know this river like I do. Just a short distance downstream, there's a tributary—shallow but wide enough. If we can navigate silently into that waterway, it'll circle back around and bring us behind their camp."

I smiled at her plan. "You want to flank them."

Blue Fox nodded. "Exactly. While they're focused on the river and where they last saw us, we can approach them from the rear, catching them off guard."

MacBride's face showed a mix of admiration and concern. "It's risky. One wrong move and we're sitting ducks."

"But it's a chance," I said. "They'll never expect it."

MacBride weighed the options for a tense moment before nodding in agreement. "All right, Blue Fox, lead the way."

She gave a sharp nod, and we set off, paddling with a purpose. The sound of the Hudson's Bay trappers grew distant, their shouts and gunshots a stark contrast to our stealthy retreat.

With Blue Fox guiding us up the mazelike tributary, we felt a glimmer of hope. Her intricate knowledge of the land and its waterways was our secret weapon, our surprise.

As we neared the end of our detour, the noise of the rival trapper camp issued through the trees. The scent of woodsmoke grew stronger. We hunkered down, grounding our canoes on the muddy riverbank, then readied ourselves, weapons at hand, preparing to face our adversaries with the element of surprise.

The dense forest canopy shielded us, the gentle sway of the pines and their fragrant aroma surrounding us. The birdsong was almost deafening, a surreal contrast to the situation we found ourselves in. Blue Fox led our approach, her footsteps silent and her movements swift, blending seamlessly with the shadows of the underbrush.

Then she motioned for silence, signaling us to remain low and in the shadows.

From our concealed vantage point, we observed the Hudson's Bay trappers. They seemed at ease, their guard down as they shared laughter around a campfire. Their weapons, which had brought such terror moments ago, had been casually set aside.

MacBride's face was a mask of intense concentration. He whispered, so soft I could barely hear, "We have the advantage. Let's not squander it."

While most of our party prepared their weapons, I fumbled with my rifle. It was a beautiful piece, expertly crafted, but my inexperience showed. I struggled to load it, my hands shaking from the apprehension.

MacLane, smirking, whispered harshly, "Haven't fired one of those before, have you, city boy?" His jeer drew quiet snickers from a couple of the men, making my face burn with embarrassment.

Ignoring MacLane's taunts, I finally managed to get my rifle ready. By this time, Blue Fox had already nocked an arrow to her bowstring, her eyes never leaving the unsuspecting trappers. She gestured to a few of our marksmen, who took aim, ready to strike.

The world seemed to slow as we waited for the opportune moment. Blue Fox's fingers flexed slightly, her gaze fixed. I took a deep breath, trying to steady my racing heart and shaking hands.

With a sharp nod from MacBride, our motley crew unleashed a volley of musket fire. The woods echoed with the sound of our gunfire, interrupted only by the screams of agony and surprise from the Hudson's Bay trappers. Our initial advantage was clear. Yet, with their notorious inaccuracy, muskets would not be our winning ticket in this skirmish. It was a fact made even more clear by the smoke and debris that soon filled the air, making visibility poor.

Before the smoke could clear, MacBride bellowed, "Charge!"

With adrenaline pumping, our party rushed into the enemy camp. The transition from long-range fire to up-close combat was jarring. Every sense was heightened, every movement critical.

I sprinted towards one trapper, clumsily attempting to use my rifle as a makeshift club. But before I could raise my weapon, he smashed the butt of his rifle into my knee. Pain shot through me, white-hot and debilitating. The world tilted, and I collapsed, the ground rushing up to meet me. From my fallen position, I caught a glimpse of Roarke clutching his shoulder, blood seeping between his fingers, his face contorted in pain.

Perched high among the tree branches, Jim acted as our guardian angel. His rifle fired in rhythmic bursts, each shot purposeful and targeted. His experience in such combat was evident, and his strategy was clear: give us the advantage from up above.

MacBride engaged in a fierce brawl with one of the Hudson's Bay trappers as the chaos continued. He managed to subdue the man with incredible skill, putting him in a choke hold and rendering him unconscious. He secured us a prisoner by dragging the limp body away from the heat of battle.

Seeing their comrade captured and overwhelmed by our onslaught, the remaining trappers began to retreat, disappearing into the thick woods. Our company, panting and bloodied, began to regroup.

"Get the wounded to safety!" MacBride ordered, his voice hoarse from the battle cries.

I tried to lift myself, my hands pressing into the earth, but my knee refused to support me. The pain was agonizing, a reminder of the high cost of this altercation.

The dust settled, and MacBride motioned for us to gather around the captured trapper as we assessed the damages. He was tightly bound to a tree, sweat and dirt streaking his face. MacBride approached him, knife in hand, but hesitated upon realizing there was a language barrier.

"He speaks French," I noted, hearing the man's muttering.

MacBride shot me a look. "Translate. I need to know everything."

I nodded, took a deep breath, and addressed the man. "Qui êtes-vous? Pourquoi êtes-vous ici?" *Who are you? Why are you here?*

The prisoner responded cautiously, "Nous sommes de la Compagnie de la Baie d'Hudson. Je m'appelle Etienne." *We are from the Hudson's Bay Company. My name is Etienne.*

I relayed the message to MacBride. His eyes narrowed. "Ask him about the numbers. How many men? Where are the other camps?"

"Combien êtes-vous? Où sont les autres camps?"

"Des douzaines... peut-être plus. Plus au nord et à l'est," the man replied, his voice shaking slightly.

"Dozens, he says. Maybe more. Further north and east."

MacBride grunted in acknowledgment, then asked, "What's their purpose here?"

"Quel est votre but ici?"

The man hesitated, then sighed, "Ce n'est pas seulement pour les fourrures. C'est pour vous."

I looked at MacBride, a sinking feeling in my gut. "He says they're here for us."

He nodded. "I suspected as much. Someone tipped them off about our mission."

MacBride's words struck me as odd. "What mission?" I asked. "Surely they don't want us dead just for trapping?"

A smile tugged at MacBride's lips. He drew his hunting knife from his belt and played with the blade with his fingertips before thrusting it into the prisoner's heart. The man's shocked eyes met mine briefly before life left him. MacBride let out a guttural moan.

"Mon Dieu!" I exclaimed, stepping back. "Why? Why did you do that?"

MacBride cleaned his knife, his voice steely. "Know your place, Christian."

I stared at the dead man, realizing the gravity of my plight. I was standing in a war zone. And I was no soldier. MacBride sheathed his knife, took out his pocket watch, glanced at the time, and said, "Let's move out."

We continued upriver, more silent and cautious than before. My mind swirled with what had happened and what MacBride had said. As we paddled onward, the terrain shifted gradually, the dense forests of pine giving way to the rugged outline of the Rocky Mountains on the horizon.

Every day began with the same ritualistic break of camp: packing our gear, loading the canoes, and making sure everything was secure before setting off. The monotony of these tasks was offset by the ever-changing beauty of the landscapes we were traveling through. Birds soared overhead, singing unfamiliar tunes. Fish leaped out of the river, their silver bodies gleaming in the sunlight.

I tried to ground myself in the natural beauty, but an undercurrent of dread ran through the group. The encounter with the Hudson's Bay Company trappers was a stark reminder of the stakes we were playing for. We all felt the weight of our mission now more than ever.

One evening, as we set up camp beneath the twilight sky, Roarke, nursing his shoulder wound, pointed out a trail of smoke rising in the distance.

"Could be another group of trappers," he murmured.

MacBride, always alert, scanned the horizon. "We need to be cautious. From now on, no fires in daylight where they could see our smoke, and slow burns at night."

Always resourceful, Blue Fox taught us techniques to minimize our visibility and scent. We learned to cook with lower heat, which produced less light and smoke, and to set up camp in more concealed locations.

I found myself working closely with her during these lessons. Her knowledge was vast, her skills honed by years of living in this unforgiving wilderness. And in those shared moments, our bond deepened. The memory of MacLane's affront and MacBride's disdain still fresh, it was clear she felt safer near me. And I was glad for her presence.

As the next few days unfolded, we continued our journey, always wary of potential threats. MacBride's leadership became more authoritarian, his decisions unquestionable. The rift between him and the rest of us deepened, but we knew better than to challenge him. We had a mission to accomplish, and every man, regardless of personal feelings, was integral to its success.

The looming mountains grew closer each day, their majestic peaks casting long shadows over the land below. As we paddled on, I often found my thoughts drifting to the days ahead. What would we find at our destination? And at what cost? MacBride was in no mood to slow down, and Roarke was looking worse day by day, losing strength and color. Despite Georges and Jean-Baptiste's best efforts to heal him, the grueling pace of our advance gave him too little time to rest and heal.

The most concerning part of the entire ordeal was how useless I'd been in the battle. I knew now I was woefully ill-prepared for combat, amongst company or on my own, if they decided to turn on me. MacBride would take no issue discarding me as he had our prisoner, and so, in my mind, I was now at war with him as much as the other trappers.

A few nights after our skirmish, as the campfire cast a flickering orange glow over the encampment, the soft murmurs of men discussing the day's events hanging in the air, punctuated by occasional laughter, I decided to seek out Jim's help with my rifle. He was cleaning his gun meticulously beside the fire, the light catching the polished barrel as he worked. I approached him with my own rifle held awkwardly at my side.

"Jim," I began hesitantly, "I need help."

He raised an eyebrow. "You waited until now, after all these weeks, to admit you don't know how to use that?" A smirk played on his lips.

I swallowed hard. "I thought I could manage, but after our fight…" My failure weighed heavily on me. "I can't pretend any longer."

Jim took the rifle from me and examined it closely. "Well, well," he said. "A fifty-cal Pennsylvania. This is some good stuff. You have better equipment than you realize, Christian."

I shifted uncomfortably. "I just want to know how to use it properly."

Jim gestured for me to sit next to him. "All right, let's begin. Given our situation, we'll have to forgo firing for now."

Under the canopy of stars, with only the light of the campfire and Jim's patient instruction, I learned the intricacies of my rifle. He taught me the basics of loading and priming, how to aim accurately, and the importance of maintaining the weapon.

"Always keep your powder dry," he said as he showed me how to ensure the flint was sharp. "And remember, Christian, this rifle, it's a part of you now. You treat it right, and it'll never let you down."

Hours seemed to fly by, and before I knew it, the fire had reduced to embers and the camp had fallen quiet. I felt a renewed sense of confidence, grateful for Jim's guidance.

"Thank you, Jim," I whispered, clutching my rifle close.

He nodded, his eyes reflecting the dying firelight. "You're welcome. Just remember, it's the man behind the rifle that matters." He gave me a pointed look. "In the right hands, it can change everything."

# Chapter 5
# The Crow

**A**s we paddled on, my thoughts dwelled heavily on MacBride. Boyd had said he was a killer. The memory of how he'd executed that prisoner played itself out over and over in my mind. The steely glint in his eyes and the pleasure he'd derived from it was unsettling. What dark past drove him? I couldn't help but wonder if he had once been a convicted felon, wearing the chains of punishment before finding his way to the fur trade.

And Lucas MacLane—he was another enigma. With his ready smirk and fiery temper, it wouldn't be too far-fetched to imagine him having a sinister past as well. How little I truly knew about the men I was traveling with. Our true colors were coming to light in this wilderness, where laws seemed nonexistent.

There was an old French saying my father used to recite: "Dit moi qui tu fréquentes, et je te dirais qui tu es." *Tell me who you associate with, and I will tell you who you are.* Pretense fell away out here, surrounded by the wild and the unknown. If I did not stand up for my principles, I might soon become as bad as them. Some of my companions might have had no issue abandoning their humanity for the sake of survival, but I refused.

Hence, a few days after our encounter with the HBC, the memory of the execution swirling in my mind, I snapped. I felt I had to act. Someone in the group needed to confront MacBride for what he'd done.

As the sun dipped below the horizon, painting the sky with hues of orange and purple, the company settled for the night on the riverbank. Campfires were lit, and the hum of conversations filled the air. Blue Fox, as always, set up her teepee at a distance from the main group. I could see her silhouette against the light of her fire, and something about it felt grounding amidst the chaos of the day.

With every step towards MacBride's tent, my heart pounded louder. The weight of what I was about to do pressed on me. Taking a deep breath, I lifted the flap and entered. Sitting on a makeshift stool, MacBride looked up from cleaning his gun. His expression remained neutral, but his eyes held a glint of challenge.

"I had a feeling you'd come," he murmured.

"I wasn't told there would be murder on this expedition," I began, struggling to keep my voice steady. "John said this was just a fur trapping venture. Simple, straightforward, and profitable."

He set his gun aside, standing to face me. "You're right. John did sell it that way. But can trappers carve out a place in an already saturated market? Especially one dominated by giants like the Hudson's Bay Company and the North West Company?"

I blinked, taken aback. "I thought we were just... competing."

MacBride took out his pocket watch, glanced at the time, and smirked. "This isn't a friendly competition, lad. This is war. A war for control, for market share, for territory. The Oregon Country isn't just a pristine wilderness; it's a battleground. The Hudson's Bay Company and the North West Company have held their grip on this land for long enough. And we're here to challenge that."

"You didn't have to kill that man," I pressed.

He leaned in, and I could smell the tobacco on his breath. "If I had let him go, he'd be back on our tails to kill us. It's kill or be killed. I've seen too many a man killed by his mercy."

"There must be a better way, such as diplomacy. Surely they are willing to talk," I suggested.

"Christian, you don't challenge empires by asking politely. You challenge them with force."

"I wish someone had told me about this," I muttered through gritted teeth.

"I do apologize for the secrecy. Not everyone in our party would have signed up knowing what we expected out here, including you."

"And you and MacLane?" I asked. "You're not just trappers, are you?"

A slow smile spread across MacBride's face. "No, we're not. Lucas, Bear, and I served in the 42nd Regiment—the Black Watch. We fought at Waterloo. We're not here because we know how to trap a beaver. We're here because we know how to fight."

My stomach churned. "So you're mercenaries."

MacBride shrugged. "Aye, if that's the word you want to use. John Astor wanted the best. He wanted men who wouldn't flinch at bloodshed. He got us. And he got you to do the business part. Consider yourself lucky that you have us. You'd be dead otherwise."

I took a step back, trying to process everything. The idealism I had harbored about this expedition was shattered. And with that disillusionment, anger surged. "You should've told us the truth."

MacBride's eyes darkened. "And risk mutiny? Panic? No. It's better you know now when there's no turning back. I need every man here. John needs every man here. It was hard enough to cobble this expedition together. Men aren't jumping at the opportunity to come out here and die."

For a moment, we stood there, locked in tense silence. I felt the weight of MacBride's experience, his battle-hardened resolve. And in that moment, I knew I was out of my depth.

"Go get some rest," he said finally. "Tomorrow, we move on."

As I exited his tent, the cool night air fell heavy on my skin, filled with the revelations and burning questions of loyalty, purpose, and the price of ambition.

The night's stillness resonated with the gentle hum of insects and the distant murmur of the river. I was deep in thought, trudging back towards my tent, when a deep voice with a distinctly German inflection called out to me.

"Christian!" Jim was sitting by a campfire with a pipe between his teeth, his slender frame outlined by the orange glow. His sharp blue eyes fixed on mine as I approached.

I hesitated for a moment but then walked over.

He gestured to a log beside him. "Sit down."

Reluctantly, I did. The warmth of the fire was comforting, but the heaviness in the air was palpable.

Jim took a long drag from his pipe, exhaling slowly. "You look as if you've seen a ghost. MacBride, he told you everything, yeah?"

I nodded, pressing my lips together. "More than I wanted to know."

Jim chuckled dryly. "That's MacBride for you. But you know, having soldiers on this journey, it is not so bad."

"And you're one of them, I suppose." I should have known—MacBride had introduced him as a sharpshooter.

The corner of Jim's mouth quirked. "John Astor knew what he was getting into. He needed protectors and fighters."

"So you're—"

"A Hessian," he finished for me, a hint of pride in his eyes. "Soldier for hire. Look, Christian, this land is vast, unpredictable, and filled with challenges from nature and man. John Astor wanted to make sure that those of you who are real trappers—like Roarke, Asher, Boyd, and yourself—are protected."

"But why not tell us?"

Jim sighed. "Sometimes it's better to keep the soldiers in the shadows until they're needed. Keeps the group focused on the task at hand rather than anticipating battles."

I leaned back and stared into the fire. "It still feels deceitful."

He shrugged. "War and trade are two sides of the same coin. There is always some level of deception involved. But remember this: our presence here is for your safety. You focus on the trapping, and let us worry about any threats."

Jim's tone conveyed a certain sincerity, a stark contrast to MacBride's cold pragmatism. And for the first time that night, I felt a small measure of comfort. Not all the protectors in this company were devoid of heart.

"Thank you, Jim," I said quietly.

He nodded, taking another puff from his pipe. The fire crackled, casting flickering shadows on the ground, and for a while, we sat in silent camaraderie, each lost in our own thoughts.

As the night deepened and the fire continued its gentle dance, I glanced over at Jim. "Why did you join this expedition? Truly."

He exhaled, the white plume of his breath mingling with the smoke from the fire. "For the money, like you," he began, his accent giving his words a deliberate weight, "but there's more."

I leaned forward. "Go on."

His fingers tightened around the stock of his rifle. "Hudson's Bay Company... they have an officer named Jean-Louis. That man killed my brother when he was out west, trying to earn a living in Oregon Country."

"I'm sorry."

Jim's eyes, reflecting the firelight, took on a hard glint. "My brother, he was just an innocent trapper. He considered Jean-Louis his competition but not his enemy. But then he just... ended him." His voice cracked. "I couldn't be there for him. But on this expedition, I thought I might have a chance at revenge."

It all made sense now—the intensity with which Jim approached this journey, his expertise, his determination. It wasn't just business for him; it was deeply personal.

He stoked the fire, sending embers floating into the night sky. Around us were the soft murmurs of our men, punctuated by occasional laughter. I sat there, weighed down by the rifle in my lap, by everything I had learned. My eyelids grew heavy, and so I took my leave. As I limped towards my tent, the flickering firelight cast an ever-shifting shadow on the ground.

As I passed Blue Fox's teepee, she called out to me. "Christian?"

I turned to find her peering out from the entrance, her features bathed in soft light.

"Yes?"

"How is your knee?" she asked, genuine concern evident in her eyes.

I grimaced slightly. "It's seen better days, but I'll live."

"Let me have a look," she insisted, beckoning me inside.

The interior was warm and filled with the familiar scent of herbs and hides. She gestured for me to sit on a blanket, and I obliged, carefully stretching out my leg.

She examined it with gentle hands, her touch sending a tingle up my spine. "It's swollen," she noted, her brow furrowing. "You need to rest it. Here, let me apply a poultice."

She fetched some herbs from a small bag and began to mix them with water. As she applied the cold and soothing mixture, the pain lessened.

"Thank you," I said.

She locked eyes with me. "I've noticed you've been distracted."

I hesitated for a moment, trying to find the right words. "Things have changed since we left Mandan territory. It's just all overwhelming."

She nodded, understanding. "We're far from the world we once knew. But remember, you're not alone. We're in this together."

Those words brought a small comfort, and I felt a spark of hope for the first time in days.

"Thank you, Blue Fox," I whispered.

She smiled, her fingers lightly brushing against my knee. "Rest now. We'll need our strength for the journey ahead."

She traced a gentle circle around the poultice on my knee, her touch calming and grounding. The intimate silence between us was powerful, a world of unspoken thoughts and emotions swirling underneath.

Breaking it, I cleared my throat, my thoughts shifting to another member of our company. "How is Roarke? His shoulder looked bad when he came into camp."

Blue Fox sighed, her eyes taking on a distant look. "The bullet went clean through. It missed any major arteries but will be sore for a while. I cleaned it, applied a poultice similar to yours, and bandaged him up."

I winced in empathy. "Is he going to be okay?"

She nodded. "In time, yes. He's strong and stubborn. But he'll need to be careful. The shoulder is tricky; if he strains it too much, it could hurt him."

A sense of relief washed over me. "I'm glad you are here, Blue Fox. I shudder to think what would've happened to Roarke—or any of us—without you."

She looked down, a faint blush painting her cheeks. "It's what I do. Healing, guiding—it's my way of being part of this world."

We shared another moment of silence. I was in awe of her strength and wisdom. She was a beacon of hope in this unforgiving wilderness, amidst all the uncertainty and danger.

"Thank you," I whispered. "For everything."

"It's time to sleep," she said.

She helped me to my feet, ushered me out of her teepee, and closed the entrance behind me. I felt the pang of unrequited love as I hobbled to my tent.

The early morning was thick with fog, the river's mist intertwining with the gray sky to create an ethereal curtain. The company was bustling about, prepping for another day on the river. The soft lapping of water and muffled conversations echoed faintly through the morning haze.

Suddenly, Blue Fox stiffened, her eyes locked onto something in the distance. I followed her gaze, trying to see past the thick veil of mist. A lone figure on horseback stood atop a ridge overlooking our camp. The rider was motionless, almost a statue. From this distance, and with the fog as a cloak, it was hard to discern much detail.

"Who is it?" Unease had crept into my voice.

"It's a Crow warrior," Blue Fox whispered.

MacBride's eyes sharpened as he observed the distant figure. "Hold your positions. Don't make any sudden moves."

MacLane glanced nervously between MacBride and the warrior. "What's he doing here?"

Jim, shading his eyes to get a better look, replied, "Observing, perhaps. Or maybe sending a message."

Roarke, clutching his injured shoulder, squinted up at the ridge. "That's no ordinary scout. He's making a statement. A reminder that we're in their territory."

I felt a chill down my spine. The silent figure gave off an unsettling aura, amplified by the fog.

Blue Fox continued, her voice a near-whisper, "The Crow respect strength and courage. His presence is both a warning and a challenge."

The horse beneath the Crow warrior shifted slightly, and for a brief moment, he locked eyes with Blue Fox. Then, as silently and mysteriously as he had appeared, he turned his horse and disappeared beyond the ridge, leaving us in the midst of the fog with an atmosphere thick with uncertainty.

MacBride broke the silence. "We move out. Now."

Paddling with soft, deliberate strokes, we made our way up the river, the only sound the gentle slap of water against the sides of our boats. The fog, now lifting, revealed the thick tree line that hugged the riverbanks. Its shadows, combined with the dense underbrush, created impenetrable pockets of darkness.

As we continued, a rustling caught my ear. At first, I dismissed it as the work of woodland creatures. But then the sound became more pronounced, and I wasn't the only one who noticed.

MacBride signaled for the group to slow. He squinted, scanning the thick woods intently. MacLane, holding his paddle, looked uneasy. The hairs on the back of my neck stood on end.

Whispers of movement darted between the trees like phantoms just beyond our reach. Every now and then, the slight glint of something reflective or the hint of a silhouette would betray the presence of someone—or something—in the underbrush.

Blue Fox softly murmured what sounded like prayers, her voice barely above a whisper.

"Be alert. We are not alone," she said to us.

Roarke, still pale from his injury, hissed from another canoe, "Do you think it's the Crow?"

Jim shook his head. "Too stealthy. Crows would be more direct. This feels different."

Suddenly, a sharp bird call echoed from the woods, and the rustling noises stopped. An eerie quiet took over.

We held our breath, waiting for the next sound or movement.

Blue Fox tensed. "It's a signal. They're communicating."

MacBride motioned for the group to gather closer. "Get in a tight formation. Be ready for anything."

And as we paddled onwards, every one of us remained on high alert. The eerie stillness continued, but the feeling of being watched never left. The shadows seemed to close in on us, and the once-gentle river now felt like a winding path leading us deeper into danger.

We continued our journey, each paddle stroke methodical and precise. With every inch we progressed, the tension grew, our senses straining to pick out any signs of movement or danger. The woods seemed to press in all around us, a silent and watchful guardian.

Just as the stifling atmosphere became unbearable, the dense forest thinned out, revealing a large, craggy hill that broke the continuous line of green. It rose majestically from the water's edge, its rocky surface a stark contrast to the tree-covered landscape we had grown accustomed to.

As we approached, the river widened and the swift current lessened, allowing us a moment's respite. The bend offered a panoramic view of what lay ahead: a sprawling clearing bathed in the glow of the midday sun, its edges defined by the continuation of the forest beyond.

Silhouetted against the sky atop the hill was the figure on horseback. Again I had the impression of a statue. Then, as if sensing our gaze, the figure turned the horse and disappeared behind the hill.

Blue Fox pointed. "There. Did you see?"

I nodded. "Who was it?"

"Sentinel, most likely," MacBride said. His eyes were fixed on the spot where the figure had vanished. "Scouting, watching. But for whom?"

"Oh, no," MacLane cut in. "It wouldn't be Blackfoot Indians, would it?"

"God help us if it is," Asher said.

"What's wrong with the Blackfoot?" I asked.

Blue Fox shot me a look she rarely gave, one of fear. "They despise white men. If it's Blackfoot, more than likely, you will all be dead by nightfall."

The clearing beckoned, a seemingly safe haven after the tension of the forested journey. Yet the sight of the lone figure had added a new layer of unease.

"We need to be cautious," Blue Fox said. "Open spaces can be more dangerous than the thickest woods."

Roarke, gripping his rifle, said, "We've come this far. Whatever's waiting for us, we'll face it together."

With a collective nod of agreement, we adjusted our course, paddling slowly towards the beckoning expanse of the clearing, prepared for whatever challenges lay ahead.

The paddling grew laborious as we approached a peculiar sight. It was a logjam—a blockade of logs floating on the river's surface, interconnected in a web that prevented our passage. The water flowed freely beneath, but there was no way for us to continue upstream in our canoes.

"We've got to portage," MacLane shouted to the group.

As we pulled our canoes ashore, a resonant drumming filled the air—the distinct sound of hooves against the ground. A formidable group of warriors emerged from the tree line, their faces painted and determined, riding on robust horses with intricate patterns adorning their coats.

The company froze, our hands instinctively reaching for our weapons, but it was clear we were outnumbered. The warriors swiftly surrounded us in a semicircle.

Blue Fox took a cautious step forward as the leader, bedecked with a headdress of raven feathers, dismounted and approached us with a deliberation that commanded respect. In his hand, he held a red bonnet, a symbol that held a world of meaning. Hudson's Bay Company wore those bonnets.

He addressed Blue Fox, his words foreign and melodic, and she listened intently before translating for the rest of us. "This man is the Crow chief. He wishes to know if we are with the Hudson's Bay Company."

MacBride hesitated at the sight of the red bonnet. The implication was clear: these warriors had had altercations with the HBC, likely violent ones.

"We are not with the Hudson's Bay Company," she replied in the chief's language, gesturing to our group to reinforce her statement.

"He says their men kidnapped his daughter. He's searching for her," Blue Fox translated.

"Tell him we wish to avoid the HBC as much as possible. They, too, are our enemy," MacBride said.

The chief's gaze flitted between us, evaluating, weighing the truth of our words. His eyes lingered on me for a moment, long enough to give me pause. Every rustle of the trees and chirp of the birds amplified the quiet standoff.

After what felt like an eternity, the Crow chief gave a subtle nod, seemingly satisfied with Blue Fox's words. The message was clear: we were not their enemy, but that didn't necessarily mean we were their friends either. We were strangers in a complex and volatile landscape, navigating the intricacies of alliances and hostilities, with each encounter holding the potential to tilt the balance.

The Crow warriors stepped back with wary grace, providing us enough space to drag our canoes around the logjam. Their gazes followed our every move, eyes sharp and evaluative as if gauging the very nature of our souls. I felt an unspoken acknowledgment, a nod to the balance of power and understanding that had been briefly established.

MacLane led the way onward, his motions quick and methodical. Roarke, despite his wounded shoulder, helped with the other canoes, a grimace on his face indicating pain but also determination. MacBride shot frequent glances at the Crow, ensuring we weren't overstaying our welcome.

The minute we cleared the logjam, we rushed back into our canoes and paddled with a newfound urgency. Having no more business with us, the Crow retreated into the trees from whence they'd come. But even as the distance between us grew, I couldn't shake the feeling of being observed, the sensation of eyes boring into our backs.

The forest on either side of the river thickened, a dense green curtain that concealed any number of threats, real or imagined. It wasn't just the wildlife; every rustling leaf or snapped twig could be a scout or another war party, friendly or otherwise. The world around us was alive with mystery and danger.

Hours seemed to stretch as we paddled, the sun beginning its descent behind the tree-covered peaks, casting long shadows on the water's surface. Our arms ached, and the tension was almost unbearable. We needed to find a suitable place to set up camp and soon.

Finally, as the sun neared the horizon, painting the sky with hues of red and orange, we found it—a relatively flat stretch of land by the riverbank. A small clearing surrounded by tall trees provided some level of concealment and strategic advantage.

We quickly went about setting up camp. With practiced efficiency, Blue Fox erected her teepee while the rest of us set about pitching tents, starting a fire, and ensuring our perimeter was secure. The night brought its own set of challenges, but at least for now, we had a momentary respite from the perils of our journey.

Wrapped in the cloak of night, with the fire's glow reflecting off the faces of our small company, I felt a blend of gratitude and trepidation. We had navigated one challenge but knew that countless others lay ahead in our pursuit of territory in this untamed land.

The campfire's soft glow cast eerie shadows as night draped itself over us. Around it, the men talked in low murmurs, occasionally punctuated by the crackling of wood. Their voices were mostly hushed, a subconscious acknowledgment of the danger that loomed on the peripheries of our expedition.

As I took a moment to stoke the flames, a soft, melodic voice beckoned me.

"Christian," Blue Fox called from the entrance of her teepee. Her silhouette, graceful against the warm light that filtered through the tent's fabric, had my full attention.

I approached, still limping. "Yes?"

"Your knee." Her voice was tinged with concern. "Let me take another look. The journey today was long."

I followed her inside, the intimate space of the teepee immediately wrapping around us, cocooning us in its warmth. She motioned for me to sit, her hands moving deftly as she inspected my leg.

"You're healing well," she observed after a few moments. Her touch was gentle, fingers lightly grazing my skin.

"Thanks to you," I murmured.

She looked up at me. There was a vulnerability in her gaze, a fleeting moment of raw emotion that she soon hid. "It will be cold tonight," she said after a slight hesitation, "and the nights are only getting colder as we move forward. It's good for warmth if you stay. Just for the night."

A blush crept up my cheeks, a rush of emotion flooding me. The dynamics between us had always been complex, a dance of attraction and respect, of cultural boundaries and growing intimacy. To share a night beside her was to cross a threshold, even just for warmth.

"Are you sure?"

She nodded, a small smile playing on her lips. "Yes, Christian. Tonight, let the world outside stay outside. In here, we will rest in warmth."

We settled side by side, the rhythmic pattern of our breathing soon synchronizing. As the hours slipped away and the chill of the night intensified, our bodies gravitated towards each other, seeking comfort in the embrace. Outside, the world carried on with its mysteries and dangers, but inside the teepee, we had a momentary respite from the relentless struggle to survive in the wild.

The first hint of dawn had barely pierced the horizon when the sound of MacBride's roaring voice shattered the serene atmosphere of the early morning.

"Christian! Where the bloody hell are you?" MacBride's tone was livid.

Startled, I scrambled up, the previous night's warmth rapidly giving way to the cold realization of my oversight. My watch. I'd drawn the first watch last night and had completely forgotten.

I quickly exited Blue Fox's teepee, coming face-to-face with a fuming MacBride, his face crimson with anger. Behind him, a few members of the company were stirring, drawn by the commotion, their expressions a range of annoyance and concern.

"You had the first watch, boy!" MacBride growled, towering over me. "We could've been ambushed, attacked! Your negligence could've cost us everything!"

A sinking feeling filled my chest. "MacBride, I... I forgot. I'm sorry."

"Forgot? You think forgetting your duty is an excuse?" He shot back, his voice dripping with disdain. "Your dalliances with Blue Fox have left this camp exposed!"

His words struck deep. I felt the accusing stares of the men, the silent judgment. But it was Blue Fox's look that hurt the most: a mix of concern, surprise, and a touch of guilt. I had put the group at risk, and our budding relationship was now under scrutiny.

Jim interjected, trying to ease the tension. "Easy there, MacBride. We all make mistakes. He will not forget again."

MacBride glared at both of us, his temper flaring. "This isn't about forgetting. It's about priorities, and clearly, Christian's are misplaced."

Feeling the weight of my negligence, I said, "I'll take double shifts tonight, MacBride. It won't happen again."

"It better not," he spat as he walked away.

The others dispersed, returning to their tasks. I approached Blue Fox, trying to gauge her reaction. She met my gaze, her face unreadable.

"I'm sorry," I began.

She shook her head. "I am to blame, too. If I had known, I would have made sure to wake you."

Just as I thought the confrontation was over, MacBride spun around to face me once more, his eyes cold and calculating. "You're fired," he declared with a steely tone.

I stared at him in shock, his decision sinking in. "What?" I stammered.

"You heard me."

Jim stepped forward, incredulity evident in his voice. "MacBride, you cannot be serious. We are in the middle of nowhere. He can't just walk back to St. Louis!"

MacBride shot Jim a venomous look. "That's his problem, not mine."

Roarke chimed in as well, "MacBride, he made a mistake, but abandoning him here is a death sentence!"

MacLane smirked, evidently enjoying my predicament, but didn't add his voice to the conversation.

Before anyone else could protest further, MacBride's face contorted into a terrifying rage. "Enough! My decision is final. I won't have anyone jeopardizing this expedition," he roared, his voice echoing through the clearing.

His outburst had the intended effect. The others, momentarily silenced by his display of raw fury, exchanged anxious glances. The air grew tense, and for a moment, I felt a genuine terror of the man standing before me.

Boyd muttered under his breath, "He's lost it. Damn Scot's gone mad."

Blue Fox looked equally distraught but held her tongue, knowing that to push MacBride now would be futile. Her eyes met mine, filled with worry.

"Get your things and be gone," MacBride growled, his voice dripping with venom. "Or I'll make sure you're gone."

I nodded slowly, my heart sinking. Cast out in the wilderness, with little knowledge of the terrain and with predators lurking, both animal and human, my chances of survival were slim. But I had no choice. MacBride had made up his mind, and there was no changing it.

As I began to pack my meager belongings, still reeling from the shock of my sudden dismissal, Blue Fox came up behind me. Her eyes were soft and determined. "I will go with you," she said firmly, her voice barely above a whisper.

Before I could respond, MacBride, coming up right behind her, snapped, "You're staying."

Blue Fox stood her ground. "I decide where I go," she said with quiet strength.

MacBride, his patience clearly wearing thin, grabbed her arm and yanked her toward him. "You're my guide. You stay with the expedition!"

Enraged by his audacity, I lunged at him, fists clenched, ready to defend her. But MacBride, with his soldier's reflexes, was prepared. He sidestepped my charge and shoved me to the ground. As he stood over me, I wondered if this was how the HBC man had felt before MacBride ended his life.

A sharp whistle broke the tension and drew all our gazes to Georges and Jean-Baptiste, who had their rifles trained on a target across the river. MacBride whipped around to face the threat, and my jaw dropped. Three dozen native warriors atop mounts, donning black-and-ocher war paint and raven feathers, lined the bank opposite us. Their leader, a large man with a crow-feather headdress and a buffalo robe over his shoulder, his face painted red, raised his hand in a kind of salute.

"Crow?" I asked.

Blue Fox helped me to my feet, terror in her eyes. "Blackfoot."

# CHAPTER 6
## THE BLACKFEET

MacBride didn't move a muscle as he said out of the corner of his mouth, "Everyone, gather the supplies into the canoes."

"Do you still want me to pack my things and head home?" I asked, also frozen as we faced off against the Blackfoot.

"Christian, now is not a good time to make jokes," he voiced.

"He's got a point," Boyd chimed in. "You did fire him."

"I think, given the circumstances, it's fair to say I take it back. We'll deal with your disciplinary action when we're not about to be slaughtered."

The warriors stared us down as we packed, climbed into our canoes, and paddled away upriver. Unsettlingly, they made no sound at all. It was as if they wanted to play with us, as a cat plays with a mouse before eating it.

"So that's it?" I said as we paddled together. "They're just going to let us go?"

"They're giving us a head start," Blue Fox said.

"A head start for what?" I asked.

"Dammit, Christian, didn't any of your books talk about the Blackfoot?" Roarke blurted out. The others shushed him.

I lowered my voice to an audible whisper. "No, they didn't."

"They've sworn whites as their mortal enemy, vowing to kill us wherever they might find us," Boyd said. "Like in MacBride and MacLane's story."

"They gave us a head start because they intend to hunt us for sport," MacBride muttered. "Let's hope we can shake them before too long."

No sooner had he said it than the thundering of galloping hooves filled the air, just as the river narrowed. The warriors stormed ahead, as if to cut us off—and they did. Several bounded into the shallows, knowing precisely where to stand to not submerge their steeds, and fired arrows that hit our canoes. One grazed my arm.

"Paddle back! Paddle back!" MacBride cried out as the river ahead filled with Blackfoot at the narrowest part.

They had set a trap for us, and we had fallen right into it. Our company paddled with all the fury we could muster to turn tail and run, aided by the flow of the river. But the Blackfoot had anticipated our move. More of their warriors rushed the riverbank, with nocked arrows and spears aimed at us.

In that moment, it occurred to me: *we are all going to die.* Where before I might have melted away in cowardice, for the first time in my life, I thought of my companions first. I had missed my watch, I had left us undefended, and I had put us into this predicament. I had to make it right. If the Blackfoot wanted a hunt, then a hunt I would give them.

"Move us closer to the riverbank," I said to Blue Fox and Boyd. They both looked at me, puzzled. "Trust me."

They paddled with me, helping me to drift the canoe away from the group and closer to land. Behind us, the cracking of gunfire echoed across the water as Jim, Roarke, and MacLane managed to load and fire off a round.

"What are you doing over there?" MacBride called out, spotting us breaking formation.

I took Blue Fox's hand in mine and looked deep into her eyes. "Forgive me for what I am about to do."

She didn't have time to reply before I hurled myself overboard and waded with my rifle over my head like mad to dry land. Blue Fox screamed for me, but I could not make out what she said with water in my ears. I pulled myself up through the reeds, and as soon as I felt steady on my feet, I cried out, "Hey, you Blackfoot bastards! You want a chase? Chase me!"

I took aim at them, fired off a round, and darted into the trees behind me, yelling and screaming to draw their attention. It was a gamble, and I hoped beyond hope they wouldn't ignore me. The veil of pines near the river gave way to an open, arid landscape at the base of the mountains, towering granite monoliths that jutted out of steep hills and ravines. It took no time at all for my attackers to give chase. At least part of their war band split off after me, and I hoped it was enough to allow my company to sneak through and escape.

And here again, I was about to die. The ground shook from the rumbling of the enemy's hooves. They would soon strike me down with an arrow. At least I would die for a cause greater than myself—to save my companions from certain death. Except I didn't.

The Blackfoot warriors galloped past me, made a wide, sweeping turn, and galloped back. They encircled me, but without launching a single projectile. Trapped, I stopped running. The chief and two of his warriors dismounted and approached me. He spoke in their language, which I of course did not understand, but I gathered his meaning from the movements of his hands. His men started to cut the clothes from my body with their hunting knives, stripping me down to nothing. They even took my shoes. Laughter filled the air as the chief motioned for me to start running.

Not one to argue with a Blackfoot chief, I started running downriver. The sandy soil underfoot made the running less painful, except for the occasional rock nestled within it. I did not have much speed to give them, but they seemed content to watch me fumbling away, laughing at clumsiness. In the open, I did not stand a chance of escaping them, so I made for the river, but in the opposite direction of my company.

As I reached the peaceful riverbank, I wondered if they would be satisfied with my disgrace. Hoping it was so, I slipped into the water and swam for a log ensnared by the reeds. I pulled the log into the river's flow with me, and together we glided effortlessly with the current. But soon, the galloping of hooves filled the air once more. The Blackfoot communicated through hoots, haws, and bird calls that blended in with the sounds of nature. Had I not known they were after me, I might have missed their presence entirely. Eventually the sounds melted away into the wilderness. They were out there, but I could no more see them than I imagined they could see me.

Minutes turned to hours, and I need to get my shivering body out of the water. Praying I had finally lost them, I kicked back toward what I thought was the safer of the two riverbanks. I emerged with an uncontrollable shiver. As I stepped away from the edge of the river, a warrior bounded from seemingly out of nowhere and swung his club at my head. I leaned back, and it missed my nose by a hair. My attacker had thrown all his momentum into the swing and failed to stop himself from falling into me. I parried and shoved him into the water. That was when the real chase began.

I hugged the river, knowing that moving away from it meant certain death. My every step was a gamble between the relative safety of the water and the naked exposure of the land. My breaths came in ragged gasps, each one a victory against the clutches of the icy Yellowstone.

The landscape around me was a blur of green and brown, blending into the relentless sound of the river churning beside me. My mind was empty of all but one thought: survive. There was no room for strategy or cunning, only the instinctual drive of a hunted animal seeking refuge.

Despite my desperate efforts, the Blackfoot were expert hunters, and they seemed to predict my every move. A whistle cut through the air, sharp and commanding, and I knew they were coordinating, preparing to end this chase. I dared a glance over my shoulder and saw them fanning out in a wide arc, bows at the ready, their horses' nostrils flaring with exertion.

My heart pounded against my rib cage, each beat a thunderous echo to the pounding of hooves on the earth. A cold realization settled over me—I would not outrun them on land. I needed the river, its capricious currents, its offering of cover and camouflage.

With a burst of the last bit of strength I had, I lunged for the water, my skin scraping against rocks and brush. Arrows whistled by, thudding into the earth where I had been just moments before. I plunged into the cold embrace of the Yellowstone, the shock of cold stealing the breath from my lungs.

Submerged and swept along by the current, I kicked with numb legs, forcing myself to stay under as long as my lungs would allow. When I surfaced for air, gasping, I was far from where I had entered. To my relief, the shore before me was devoid of Blackfoot. They had lost sight of me— for now. But I knew the respite was temporary. They would soon pick up my trail again.

I had to make a decision, and swiftly. I could continue downriver, where the terrain was more open and the chances of evading my pursuers were slimmer, or I could attempt to disappear into the dense underbrush that lined the riverbank.

Choosing the latter, I mustered what little strength I had left and swam towards the tangled greenery. The cold had leeched the energy from my limbs, but fear proved a powerful motivator. I dragged myself onto the bank, my body covered in mud, cuts, and bruises.

There, hidden by the brush and with the river as my ally, I waited for darkness to fall. The shadows grew longer, and the sounds of the wilderness began to change. The hoots and calls of the Blackfoot faded into the background, replaced by the evening songs of crickets and the occasional splash of fish.

As night settled over the landscape, I made my move. Creeping from my hiding spot, I traveled in the direction I hoped my company had gone, relying on the stars for guidance. The riverbank was a treacherous ally, offering concealment but revealing traces of my passing.

Hours passed in silence, and the moon climbed high, casting a silver glow over the water. My nakedness was both a curse and a blessing—no rustling clothes to give me away, but every thorn and bramble was a fresh agony against my bare skin, every jagged rock or stone a foe to my feet.

Eventually, the first light of dawn began to breach the horizon. I had put some distance between myself and the Blackfoot warriors, but I was not naive enough to think I was safe. Not yet. My survival depended on reuniting with my company, and for that, I would need the rising sun to guide me back to them. But for now, all I could do was move forward, step by trembling step, clinging to the fragile hope of salvation with the tenacity of a man who has nothing left to lose.

Through the underbrush and the softening darkness, a rustling noise grew louder and closer, setting my heart to hammering against my chest once more. My fingers curled into fists, ready to fight, ready to flee, though I knew not which.

Then, a whisper through the trees, a voice I had come to recognize even in my most fevered dreams. "Christian?"

Blue Fox stepped through the foliage like a vision, her presence a balm to my frayed senses. For a moment, I simply stared, unsure if she was real or another trick of my weary mind. But then she was upon me, her hands clasping my arms, her eyes wide with concern and something more, something I'd dared not hope for.

"You're alive," she breathed, her voice a mix of relief and reproach. "We thought..."

Words failed me, so I simply nodded, allowing the relief to wash over me in waves. She did not seem to care for my nakedness, or if she did, her concern for my well-being overshadowed any embarrassment.

"Come," she said, her voice firm. "Our camp is not far. We moved it farther from the river onto Crow land, for safety. You're lucky I went scouting for the Blackfoot when I did."

With her at my side, I found the strength to move, to follow her lead. She guided me with a gentle but insistent hand, weaving through the wilderness with a confidence that belied the danger we had just escaped. The sky began to brighten, painting the world in shades of gray and pale blue.

As we walked, I realized how much I had longed for her presence during those harrowing hours by the river. Her strength, her resilience, her unspoken understanding of the land and its dangers. In her, I found an anchor, a kindred spirit whose quiet determination mirrored my own.

We arrived just as the campfires were being rekindled. The others were there, their faces etched with lines of worry that eased when they saw us. They rushed to my side with blankets and food, their questions and exclamations a cacophony that filled the space around us.

Boyd clapped a sturdy hand on my back, nearly knocking the wind out of me, his face breaking into a wide, relieved grin. "You crazy son of a gun," he boomed, the laughter in his voice a welcome sound. "We thought you were a goner for sure!"

Asher, stoic and reserved, nodded in agreement, a rare smile tugging at his lips. "That move you pulled, leading the Blackfoot away from us," he said, his voice earnest, "that was something else. You saved our hides, Christian."

Even Bear, the quietest among us, stepped forward. His large hand engulfed mine in a firm shake. "Thought we'd lost another," he muttered, his voice low. "Glad I was wrong."

Their praise, though humbling, struck a chord within me. Up until that point, I'd often felt like an outsider among them, the city boy who'd stumbled into the wilderness, full of book learning but lacking the hardened edges this life demanded. But now, seeing the genuine respect in their eyes, feeling the warmth of their acceptance, it was as though I had crossed an invisible threshold.

"We mourned you, brother," Boyd added, clapping me on the shoulder again. "You've got the spirit of a mountain lion in you, Christian. We all see it clear as day now."

As the laughter and chatter began to subside, MacBride made his way through the group, his usually stern expression softened with relief. "Christian," he started, a smile crinkling the corners of his eyes, "you've done more than prove yourself today."

He reached into his coat, withdrawing the silver pocket watch I'd seen him check a hundred times a day—it was his measure of time, his anchor in the boundless wilderness. He flipped it open, glanced at it, and snapped it shut.

"For a moment there, I thought I'd have to record the exact time of your... dismissal," MacBride said, the jest clear in his tone, and the others chuckled. "But it seems you're not quite done with us yet. Nor we with you."

I met his gaze, understanding the unspoken message.

"You're not fired, lad. In fact, I daresay this company needs you—just as you are, just as you've been today.

Alive and... decidedly undressed for success," MacBride quipped, eliciting a fresh round of laughter from the group.

With those simple words, he had not only shown his appreciation but had also reaffirmed my place among these people. I was more than just an employee; I was part of a collective that valued courage and quick thinking over conventional experience. I was part of a makeshift family, bound by the wild threads of frontier life.

The words were a balm to the loneliness that had haunted me since we'd first set out. In the raw openness of their faces, I found a sense of belonging that I hadn't realized I was seeking. They had seen me at my lowest, chased naked and trembling through the wild, and yet, in that vulnerability, they found strength.

There, in the flickering light of the campfire, with my companions around me and Blue Fox at my side, I felt a shift within me. A revelation that perhaps, amid the danger and the terror, I had found something far more profound than survival.

Within hours, we set out once more. The stillness of the river seemed to hum with a quiet warning as we paddled, and the absence of the Blackfoot's pursuit felt like the calm before a storm. My arms worked the paddle automatically, muscle memory keeping pace, but my senses were on high alert, eyes flicking to the banks, ears straining for the telltale sounds of nature disturbed.

Our canoes cut through the water's embrace, a quiet splashing that seemed unnaturally loud in the expectant hush. Then, as the river graciously yielded, revealing a more expansive vista, the unexpected silhouette of an encampment appeared, an island of tumultuous life amid the serene wild.

"HBC." Boyd's whisper cut through the silence, its undertones a blend of grudging respect and inherent rivalry.

I felt a tightness in my chest, an instinctive reaction to the sight of our competition's stronghold. Our arrival here was as unwelcome as wolves at a feast.

They must have spotted us before we could turn around, four figures lined the perimeter, a silent testament to the HBC's vigilance.

"It's clear why the Blackfoot backed off." Asher's voice was low. "They wouldn't dare come within a stone's throw of this lot."

The camp was alive with the scents and sounds of human industry, stark against the backdrop of the untamed land we'd been threading through.

A man stepped out to the water's edge. He was tall, the green and black tartan of the Hudson's Bay Company wrapped around him, his hat crowned with the feather of a golden eagle—both markers of his standing.

He didn't shout a challenge or a question. Instead, his hand rose, signaling the others. There was a blatant intention in his movement that set my heart racing. It seemed he recognized us—not as mere travelers, but as the very company they had been searching for.

Desperation gripped us as we dug our paddles into the water, seeking to reverse our direction, to escape the looming threat that lay upriver. We sought the fleeting safety of the wilds we had just navigated, the open river behind us.

But our hearts sank as cries pierced the mist—a haunting sign that the Blackfoot had not abandoned their chase after all. They emerged downstream, cutting off our retreat, ghosts turned flesh, as relentless as the river's pull.

Musket balls sang through the air like demonic bees, urging us to a desperate frenzy. With a swift, collective maneuver, our canoes veered toward the HBC's shore—a tactical decision forged in the flames of survival. The Blackfoot, ever our shadows, unleashed their own fury, their arrows slicing through the morning mist with deadly intent.

"Paddle! For God's sake, paddle!" MacBride's command was a guttural roar over the cacophony of gunshots and war cries.

Our muscles burned, our spirits fueled by adrenaline as we made the banks of the enemy's territory. The thud of our canoes hitting the shore synchronized with the thunder of our hearts. We disembarked into chaos, the HBC's lead biting the air around us, their men a blue-coated menace emerging from the tree line.

"East! Head east!" Boyd bellowed as we scrambled from the canoes. The underbrush clawed at us, but we plunged into the woods, an impromptu escape into the dense embrace of the eastern wilds.

In the bedlam, I lost sight of our group—only Blue Fox's presence remained a constant at my side. We dodged, weaved, and ran, the world reduced to the deafening report of muskets and the sharp exhales of our flight.

We pushed on, the forest closing behind us like a curtain, shrouding us in its precarious sanctuary, our path forward as uncertain as the fate of our friends. We hurried away from the river, the echoes of the skirmish receding behind us. The land rose and fell like the waves we had just escaped, and as we ascended a steep incline, my breath came in sharp, painful gasps. It felt as though the very air was being squeezed out of me, each step forward a monumental effort. But there was no time to rest, no moment to catch a fleeting breath.

At the crest of the hill, we dropped to the earth, our bodies pressed against the dirt and scrub, the natural rampart providing us both cover and a vantage point. Cautiously, we peered over. Below us, the open valley stretched out, a theater of despair. The Hudson's Bay Company men were rounding up our friends, tying their hands, prodding them with the cold steel of musket barrels. The Blackfoot watched on horseback from their side of the river, then vanished as swiftly as they had appeared. The scene pierced me sharper than the cold: our friends, taken captive before our eyes.

I clenched my fists until the knuckles whitened, the urge to rush down there and fight overwhelming. But Blue Fox's hand on my shoulder held a word of caution. We were two against many and ill-prepared for a direct confrontation.

"I can't just watch this," I whispered fiercely, anger and desperation threading my voice.

"We have to be smart, Christian," she returned, her whisper fierce as a winter gale. "We need help."

That was when I thought of them—potential allies in this land overrun with our enemies. "The Crow," I said with conviction. "They despise the HBC as much as anyone. If we can reach them…"

Blue Fox followed my gaze, out past the valley and towards the distant hills that the Crow called home. "It's an idea," she agreed.

We slunk back from the ridge, the image of our friends in bondage burning behind my eyelids, igniting a fire that no river could quench. With each step away, I swore an oath to return, to bring back an army if need be. Blue Fox moved like a shadow beside me, her resolve as unshakable as the mountains that watched over us.

The path to the Crow was a gauntlet, each mile fraught with danger, the possibility of running into more HBC patrols or Blackfoot hunting parties. But we moved with a stealth born of necessity, a shared understanding that the fate of our friends now rested on our ability to forge an alliance.

By nightfall, we had put miles between us and the river, the stars above a canopy of silent witnesses to our flight. We made no fire, ate sparingly, and spoke little. The gravity of our situation needed no words; it was conveyed in every hushed step, in every cautious glance.

We would find the Crow. We had to. Hope was a thin thread indeed, but it was all we had left. And I would cling to it with all the strength that remained in me.

The signs were subtle at first: a displaced stone here, a broken twig there. The wilderness spoke in a language of silence and shadows, and I had learned enough of its tongue to read the signs. Blue Fox sensed it too; her strides became more cautious, her eyes darting like a hawk's.

We were being watched.

A sudden rustle from the bushes made us freeze, hands instinctively reaching for our weapons. A familiar warrior emerged atop a horse, his posture as rigid and imposing as the pines around us, a red bonnet hanging from his belt. He regarded us with an unreadable expression, his eyes piercing.

Without a word, he turned his mount and started off at a trot. We exchanged a glance, an unspoken agreement passing between us, and followed. Our footsteps were quiet, our presence as inconspicuous as shadows chasing the fading light.

We had not gone far when the war band materialized around us. They were specters born from the very earth, so fluid and silent was their approach. We were encircled, a ring of horses and warriors, their expressions unreadable behind paint and the stoicism borne of countless battles.

The initial warrior who had revealed himself to us now dismounted, approaching with a confidence that spoke of his authority. His gaze lingered on me, then shifted to Blue Fox, recognition flickering in his eyes.

"We seek the Crow," I began, my voice steady despite the thundering of my heart. "We need your help."

As Blue Fox translated, a murmur rippled through the group, a forest stirred by sudden wind. The warrior before us raised a hand, and the voices fell silent.

"You are in our lands," he said in the language of the Crow. His voice was roughened by the open plains and winters colder than steel. "Why should we aid you?"

I drew a deep breath, my mind racing to gather the shards of our desperate situation into a plea they could not ignore.

"Our friends have been taken by the Hudson's Bay Company," I said, "aided by the Blackfoot. We are enemies to them, as you are."

A spark of interest ignited in the warrior's eyes. I pushed on, embellishing the tale with every truth and half-truth that might sway them—our battles, our escapes, the common enemies that plagued our footsteps. Blue Fox, in conveying my words into the Crow tongue, added her own gestures and emphasis.

The warrior watched us for a long, breathless moment before nodding solemnly. He turned and spoke to his comrades, his voice rising and falling like the undulating plains. I caught no more than the essence, but it was enough.

He turned to us again, his decision etched in the lines of his face. "You will come with us." It was not a question but a command, and one laced with a promise—of either alliance or confrontation.

We followed. Behind us, the war band closed ranks, a phalanx of shadows ushering us into the heart of their territory, towards an uncertain fate that yet shimmered with the possibility of salvation.

He spoke rapidly to Blue Fox, and she listened intently, her eyes narrowing as she absorbed his words. "He remembers us," she murmured to me, "from the river a few days back."

I recalled the brief encounter, the wary eyes that had asked us if we were HBC men, and the red bonnet he had shown us.

"Will he help us?" I asked, my voice low.

Blue Fox turned her attention back to the chief, who was waiting with an expectant tilt of his head. Their conversation was a dance of gestures and sharp nods. Finally, she turned back to me.

"He will help us," she began, "but he wants something from us first."

"What is it?"

Her eyes betrayed angst as she uttered the single word that seemed to hang between us. "Me."

I felt a surge of protective anger, my hands balling into fists at my sides. "No," I said, the word cutting through the tension like a blade. "We cannot agree to that."

The Crow chief watched me, his expression impassive, as if he had anticipated my refusal. Blue Fox stood silent, a stoic statue, her resolve hiding any fear she might have harbored.

I stepped forward, closing the distance between myself and the chief. My next words were firm, heavy with desperation. "We need your help to save our companions, not to give up one of our own."

His eyes, dark and unyielding, held mine. Blue Fox translated, her voice steady despite the uncertainty I knew she felt.

I continued, pitching my voice to carry conviction I barely felt. "Let us fight with you. If we succeed, you get your revenge and you can claim all the spoils of our victory—the horses, the pelts, all of it. But we keep our people intact, Blue Fox included."

There was a long silence, the chief's gaze never leaving mine. He seemed to be weighing the sincerity of my offer, the potential gains against the traditions and codes by which he led.

Blue Fox's hand found mine, a silent plea for trust as we awaited his response.

Finally, the chief spoke, his voice a low rumble of consideration. Blue Fox listened, then turned to me, a faint trace of surprise on her features. "He will consider your proposal," she said. "But he wants to know why you fight so hard for me."

I didn't hesitate. "She is one of us. We do not leave our own behind."

The chief nodded slowly, his decision clear in the set of his jaw. He turned to speak to his men, who had been watching the exchange with the intensity of hawks.

We stood there, caught in the vast expanse of wild country, a land where every alliance was tested, every loyalty measured. In the eyes of the Crow chief, I had seen a reflection of our own struggles—loss, determination, and the fierce bonds of makeshift families forged in adversity.

Whatever his decision, we had offered all we could. Now it was in the hands of the Crow.

The chief returned to where we stood, his steps deliberate, his presence commanding the scene. He spoke, and though the language was not my own, the resonance of his voice held a power that transcended words. Blue Fox relayed his message, her voice a bridge between our worlds.

"He says that the whites often treat his people like animals, and that such treatment has sown deep hatred. But today, you have shown something different."

I waited, the tension between one heartbeat and the next stretching thin.

"He is moved by how you defended me, claiming me as one of your own," Blue Fox continued, her eyes locked with mine. "He believes perhaps you are different. That perhaps not all white men are enemies."

The chief's eyes, which had held so much calculation, now softened with a glimmer of respect. "For this reason, he will help us," she finished.

"And—" She hesitated for a fraction of a moment before continuing. "—he also seeks revenge against the Hudson's Bay Company for kidnapping his daughter. Their presence here is a thorn in his side, a threat to his people's way of life."

I let out a breath I hadn't realized I'd been holding. "Tell him we share a common enemy," I said. "And in this battle, we will stand with him."

Blue Fox translated, and a murmur of approval rippled through the Crow warriors. The chief raised his hand, and his men responded with a unified cry that cut through the air—a fierce, resolute sound that promised a storm on the horizon.

In that moment, we were no longer strangers. We were allies bound by a common cause, united by a shared sense of justice and the impending thrill of a battle against a mutual foe. The road ahead was fraught with danger, but with the Crow at our side, we would face the Hudson's Bay Company with a fighting chance.

# CHAPTER 7
## THE BATTLE

The sun began its descent, casting long shadows across the vast landscape. Every muscle in my body ached from the hike, and my stomach growled like a lion, but I had finally found an optimal vantage point: a jutting hill with a colossal rock that seemed to have been placed just for me, a gift from the land itself. Ensuring Blue Fox and I were still hidden from the HBC camp's view, we approached cautiously, sliding our backs along the smooth, cold surface of the rock.

The buzz of camp life below was a stark contrast to the tranquil environment atop the hill. The clinking of metal, the crackling fires, and the occasional loud voice reached my ears, distorted by the distance. Laying out my musket, I checked it meticulously, making sure the powder was dry and the ball was properly seated. My heart raced at the pivotal role I'd play in the upcoming attack.

From my position, the camp looked like an organized hive of activity. Tents formed straight lines, with pathways meticulously cleared. Smoke rose from several fires, around which men sat, talking and laughing, unaware of the storm that awaited them. At the center of the camp stood a large tent adorned with the Union Jack, undoubtedly the command tent. The sight of that flag stirred a deep resentment within me, a reminder of the ruthlessness of the Hudson's Bay Company.

I reached into my bag and pulled out the small glass I'd acquired in St. Louis as part of my trapper's kit. Focusing on the camp, I identified key targets. Gunmen on the periphery, supply areas, and places where the horses were tethered. There were also larger boats anchored near the riverbank, no doubt the ones they'd use for a quick escape if the need arose.

I felt my breath grow uneven, a cocktail of fear and anticipation bubbling within me. This wasn't a mere rescue mission; it would be a battle. The stakes couldn't be higher, not just for me but for Blue Fox, my companions, and the Crow warriors who had placed their faith in this plan. I inhaled deeply, trying to find my center.

With each passing minute, the sky dimmed. My mind raced back to our companions. Where were they being kept? Would they be in one of those tents? Or had they been moved elsewhere? The thought of them being harmed consumed me, and I had a burning motivation to see this plan through.

After tucking the glass back into my bag, I adjusted the position of my musket, ensuring I had a clear line of sight. The weight of the bullets was a reminder of the deadly intent behind each shot. They were more than just lead; they were the culmination of everything I'd endured so far, each one carrying the burden of my resentments, anger, and hate.

I thought about the sequence of events that had brought me to this point, from my boisterous recruitment in New York to the whispers of treachery and the explosive revelation of our real mission. I was no soldier. But here I was, on the front line of a conflict much bigger than myself. My chest felt heavy at the thought.

With a final glance at the camp below, I mentally prepared myself. The attack would commence soon. The Crow warriors would be positioning themselves, waiting for my signal. I took another deep breath, closed my eyes, and looked at Blue Fox's face, her strength and courage my inspiration. This was it. The moment of reckoning.

I carefully measured out the gunpowder, pouring it down the barrel of my fifty-cal Pennsylvania. The familiar process, which once seemed so foreign to me, now was almost second nature, yet my hands were unsteady. I packed the bullet in, taking a moment to steady my aim.

Looking for a key target, I spotted an HBC officer confidently directing his men. Exhaling slowly, I squeezed the trigger, and the rifle's sharp report echoed through the silent evening.

Panic erupted in the camp. Men shouted and pointed, trying to discern where the shot had come from. I could hear their frantic calls: "Sniper! Sniper on the hill!" My heartbeat pounded in my ears as I began the slow process of reloading. This wasn't like the stories back home, where shots were fired in quick succession. The reality was a painfully slow dance of powder, patch, and ball.

As I took aim for my second shot, bullets began to whizz past me, hissing through the air and making sharp pings as they ricocheted. Every moment spent reloading felt like an eternity. With the rifle ready again, I peeked over the rock and fired into the chaos below.

The return fire intensified. I could feel the impact of each bullet that collided with the rock I was hiding behind. Each hit sent a jolt of fear through me, making the reloading process even more difficult.

"Come on, come on." I urged my trembling hands to work faster.

Doubt began to creep in. What if the Crow had decided it was too risky? What if they had abandoned the plan? As these thoughts plagued me, a searing pain jolted my left arm. A bullet had grazed me, leaving a trail of warm blood running down to my fingertips. I gritted my teeth and tried to shake off the pain, focusing on reloading my rifle.

Two Hudson's Bay men had started climbing the hill, no doubt aiming to take out the sniper causing them so much trouble. Their ascent was swift, their eyes locked onto my position. I forced myself to focus, ignoring the pain in my arm. Aiming carefully, I squeezed the trigger one more time. The rifle roared to life, and one of the men collapsed, rolling back down the hill. Blue Fox took aim with her bow and loosed an arrow that found its mark.

We didn't have time to celebrate. We had drawn their attention and knew we couldn't hold out for much longer. The hope that the Crow would hold up their end of the bargain was the only thing that kept us going.

As the men's lifeless bodies tumbled down the hill, the awfulness of what I'd done hit me. The air around me seemed to thicken; the weight of my actions pressed against my chest. I'd taken a life. A human life. My hands, still clutching the rifle, began to shake uncontrollably, the cool metal now feeling foreign and grotesque.

I tried to rationalize it, to tell myself it was kill or be killed, that I'd done it to save my own life and the lives of my companions. But the piercing, haunting finality of that man's end cut through all my justifications. A kaleidoscope of dark thoughts raced through my mind. Who was he? Did he have a family waiting for him somewhere? Would they ever know what happened to him?

My gaze remained fixed on the spot where he'd fallen. I could see the dark stain spreading on the ground around him and the other HBC man. Two more men climbed toward us, past their bodies, now hesitating, looking torn between avenging their fallen comrades or fleeing from the unseen shooters.

The noises of the camp, the shouting, and the gunfire all seemed to blur and fade, drowned out by the thunderous beating of my heart and the ringing in my ears. I felt detached, as though I was watching this all unfold from somewhere else, unable to believe that I, Christian, had just taken a life.

The adrenaline and shock coiled tightly inside me, making it hard to breathe. The smell of the gunpowder, the metallic taste in my mouth, and the burning sensation in my grazed arm became oppressively overwhelming.

I wanted to shout, to scream, to tell them all I was sorry, that I hadn't meant to, that it was all a mistake. But I couldn't. Words wouldn't form, and I found myself paralyzed, trapped in the horrific realization of the irreversible act I had committed.

Over the clamor of my heavy breathing and the distant cries from the camp came a chorus of high-pitched battle cries. From the opposite side of the camp, the Crow warriors emerged, a sea of riders storming out of the trees. The setting sun cast long shadows behind them, making it seem like an army of giants was descending upon the Hudson's Bay Company men.

The element of surprise was entirely in the Crow's favor. Most of the trappers' attention had been diverted towards me and the direction of my shots. The camp was plunged into chaos. Men scrambled for weapons, but the sheer speed of the Crow's charge caught many off guard.

I watched, wide-eyed, as the battle unfolded before me. The Crow warriors, skilled horsemen, handled their mounts with exceptional dexterity. Arrows zipped from their bows, finding their mark with deadly precision. The trappers tried to form a defensive line, but the initial surprise had scattered their ranks.

Close combat ensued, and the very ground seemed to tremble. The clang of metal, the screams of wounded men, and the desperate shouts of commanders trying to rally their troops filled the air. One Crow warrior engaged a Hudson's Bay Company officer in a fierce duel. Their blades danced in a lethal ballet, each looking for an opening. With a swift maneuver, the Crow fighter disarmed the officer and took him down with a blow to the chest.

But it wasn't all going in favor of the Crow. Some HBC trappers had managed to form small defensive pockets, fighting back with grim determination. Muskets fired, sending deadly lead into the Crow ranks. One warrior, struck in the shoulder, toppled from his horse, only to be trampled in the chaos.

The smell of gunpowder, blood, and sweat was thick in the air. Time seemed to blur, with moments of intense combat stretching into what felt like hours. But the Crow had momentum on their side. Their ferocious war cries began to tip the balance.

Slowly, the Hudson's Bay Company's resistance began to wane. Their defensive pockets were overwhelmed. Working in tandem, the Crow warriors used their mobility to devastating effect. They would isolate a group of HBC men, encircle them, and close in, leaving no room for escape.

As the last survivors fled to the river, a triumphant roar went up from the Crow warriors. They had done it. Against a numerically superior force, they had emerged victorious. The camp, which had been bustling with activity just hours ago, now lay silent, save for the moans of the wounded and the soft whinnies of horses.

Atop his mount, the Crow chief held a small girl in his hands. She was alive and moving. He turned his gaze towards where I was hiding, giving me a nod of acknowledgment. The diversion had worked, and while the price in lives was steep, the Crow had exacted their revenge against the Hudson's Bay Company and rescued the daughter.

The victorious warriors began gathering their wounded and tending to them while others started to loot the camp. The very air seemed to hum with a mix of relief, triumph, and mourning for the fallen. The seriousness of my recent actions and the intense battle I had just witnessed left me drained and numb. But one thing was clear: alliances were invaluable in this vast, unpredictable wilderness. And the Crow had just proven themselves to be powerful allies.

From my vantage point, I tried to find familiar faces among the captured, hoping against hope that my companions were safe. The HBC encampment, now a scene of turmoil and devastation, looked entirely different from the well-ordered layout I'd observed earlier. Tents were torn or flattened, supplies scattered, and the wounded and dying were everywhere. Smoke from fires set during the raid or from abandoned campfires mingled with the fading light, giving the entire scene the look of a passage from Dante's *Inferno*.

With caution, Blue Fox and I made our way down, stepping over bodies and discarded weapons. As I moved, I became aware of the stares I was drawing. Crow warriors, busy looting and securing the area, glanced at me, their expressions a mix of curiosity and suspicion. I kept my head down, focusing on the task at hand: finding our companions.

Our search ended outside a wooden shack. It was set slightly apart from the main cluster of tents, a simple, rough-hewn structure that, at first glance, looked like a storage shed. As I approached, I could hear muffled voices from inside, familiar voices.

I called out, "Jim? Boyd? Is that you?"

A series of surprised exclamations answered me. "Christian?! How in God's name did you get here?"

Blue Fox hurriedly worked on the lock, using the butt of her ax to break it open. The door swung inwards, revealing the familiar faces of Jim, Asher, Boyd, Roarke, and the Métis guides. Their relief was undeniable, and I felt a wave of gratitude wash over me.

Looking worn but unharmed, Boyd stepped forward and pulled me into a rough embrace. "You crazy fools," he muttered, his voice thick with emotion. "That's twice I owe you now." Pulling away, he glanced bashfully at Blue Fox and patted her on the shoulder. "Thank you."

"Where's MacBride?" I asked.

Boyd answered, "Not with us." He rubbed at his wrists where the ropes had dug in. "They took him, MacLane, and Bear to see their leader just before everything kicked off."

My heart sank. "Are they…?"

Boyd shook his head, his face grim. "Don't know. But knowing MacBride, he would have gone down fighting."

"Let's go find them," Blue Fox muttered, pushing her way out of the shack.

The rest of us scurried behind her while I brought everyone up to speed on all that had happened. The camp around us was settling down, with the Crow warriors gathering their spoils and tending to their horses.

As we made our way deeper into the camp, Jim nudged me, gesturing at the chief's tall figure, his face painted with vibrant colors. "That's him, isn't it? The Crow chief?"

I nodded and approached the warrior, my footsteps firm.

He met my gaze. "Your shots were well-timed. Their attention was fixed on you, making our charge even more effective."

I pressed my palms together and said, "Thank you. I'm glad we could do our part, and we could not have saved our friends without you. I am in your debt."

The chief nodded to acknowledge my thanks. "We each have gained much together today."

"Three of our company are still missing. We believe they were taken to meet the camp leader before your attack."

The chief looked thoughtful. "The Hudson's Bay men have a tent near the center of the camp, larger than the others. But be cautious; there might be men ready to fight."

With a nod of gratitude, I motioned for our company to follow me. Without MacBride, I was second in command, and it fell on me to ensure the company's success. At first, leading them felt natural. Not until I gave it a thought while trudging through the camp did I realize what it meant. A heaviness soon weighed on my shoulders. The tent the chief mentioned wasn't hard to locate, given its size. As we approached, the low murmur of voices reached our ears, and the flap was thrown open to reveal a pair of HBC trappers. Their eyes widened at the sight of us, and their hands flew up in surrender. They were beaten and weary; it seemed the fight had left them.

"Where are MacBride, MacLane, and Bear?" I demanded, keeping my voice steady and cold.

The trapper on the left, a man with a rough beard and tired eyes, spoke first. "They were taken just before the Crow attacked."

"Taken where?" Blue Fox snapped, stepping forward.

The other trapper, younger and visibly more frightened, quickly responded, "By canoe. They're heading west. The Hudson's Bay Company governor wants to put MacBride on trial."

"On trial for what?" I growled.

"For attempting to assassinate Jean-Louis Foucher."

A pit of dread settled in my stomach. Here I was, breaking my friends out of captivity, believing we were the good ones. But the young trapper had just confirmed there was more that MacBride had not told me. Just like our first confrontation with the HBC, when I'd discovered our company owner and leader had not brought us on under clear pretenses.

"We need to pursue them," Jim said.

At that moment, I froze. I had no desire to save the Scots. They were soldiers. We had saved the men who mattered. With only the trappers, Asher, and Jim, we could hunt in Oregon Country as planned, and I would still be able to negotiate a deal with the North West Company as I'd been sent to do.

"We need to help them," Asher insisted.

"It's too risky. We have our trappers." All that mattered was that I complete my mission: get back to New York and the high-paying job I had been promised.

"Have a heart, man!" Roarke cried out.

I looked to Blue Fox for support, but she gave me nothing. She stood there, steely and unfeeling. All the others looked at me with pleading eyes, like a litter of puppies begging to be taken home.

"Jesus." I knew if I refused them, they would refuse to follow me. I sank my head into my hands for a moment, exhausted. "All right. We go after them."

Boyd, ever resourceful, pointed to a few nearby canoes. "There's our ticket."

I turned to the captured trappers. "Get your wounded and leave this place. If you know what's good for you, you'll never come back."

Our prisoners fled, and we rummaged around the camp. With the Crow gone, it had the somberness of a ghost town. Thankfully, there were ample supplies still strewn about that the Crow had not touched, and it was clear that we had a golden opportunity to replenish our resources.

While the others set about searching for guns and ammunition, Blue Fox and I were drawn to the scent of freshly cooked meat. My stomach growled—a cruel reminder that it had been days since we'd had a proper meal. Following the aroma, we found a makeshift kitchen area where a pot still hung above a smoldering fire. Inside there was a stew, its broth thick and inviting. Without hesitation, I grabbed a ladle and we started devouring it.

Beside the stew, there was a basket full of eggs that appeared to be freshly laid. I cracked a few, cooking them quickly over the open flame. The taste of the eggs, slightly charred and seasoned by the smoke, was pure bliss. It might have been the hunger speaking, but at that moment, they tasted better than any gourmet meal I had ever eaten.

As we relished our unexpected feast, Boyd approached with a wry grin. "Enjoying the spoils of war, I see."

"Can't remember the last time I ate." I wiped my mouth with the back of my hand. "We should gather as much food as we can."

Boyd nodded. "Jim and Roarke are working on it. David found a cache of dried goods. We'll be well stocked."

"I want to look for supplies for healing," Blue Fox said between bites of stew.

Besides food, we discovered a small armory tent. Inside, rifles were neatly lined against the walls, and boxes of ammunition were piled in corners. With a gleam in his eyes, Jim began loading up on bullets, filling his pockets until they bulged. Asher and Roarke took several rifles, checking their mechanisms and ensuring they were in working order. When we emerged fully reloaded with arms, Blue Fox met us carrying bagfuls of supplies for her own designs.

The moon rose overhead, casting the camp in silver hues as we worked. It was a welcome beacon, considering our recent ordeals. By the time we were ready, our canoes were laden with supplies. It starkly contrasted the meager rations we'd been working with before.

"We have enough to last us weeks," Asher said, clearly satisfied with our haul.

"And the firepower to take on any challenge," Jim added as he patted a newly acquired rifle.

With our supplies secured, we took a moment to rest. I leaned against a canoe, letting the moonlight kiss my face. The intensity of the past days, the exhaustion, and hunger had taken a toll, but for the first time, I felt relief.

Boyd joined me, offering a canteen of water. "You did good today," he said.

"I didn't do it alone," I replied, taking a sip. "We've got a long way to go, but at least we're prepared."

Boyd nodded, patted me on the shoulder, and stood silently with me for a moment while sipping from the canteen.

By the pale moonlight and glowing embers of the burning camp, we set our sights on the winding river ahead, ready to pursue our captured comrades and face whatever challenges the journey presented.

The forest's inky silhouette flanked the meandering river as our canoes glided through the water. The rhythmic sound of our paddles dipping in and out harmonized with the subtle chorus of the wilderness. A soft wind rustled the leaves of the cottonwoods overhead, and the faint chirping of crickets slowly began to rise. We soon found a suitable place to make camp and rest.

The following morning, the sky painted another masterpiece of deep purple and blush pink as the sun rose over the horizon. It was a beauty that one might have found solace in during simpler times, but our circumstances allowed no such luxuries.

We rowed hard all day. Roarke and Jim worked in tandem in the lead canoe, their paddles cutting through the water with trained precision. I could see Roarke was a bit slower but didn't think anything of it at first. Behind them, Boyd and Asher followed suit, occasionally sharing snippets of conversations about past expeditions. As for me, I joined Blue Fox, followed by our two Métis guides. Our strokes quickly found a rhythm, and we made good headway.

However, later that day, the strain of our earlier trials began to manifest. Every stroke felt heavier than the last, and my muscles screamed for respite. I could also see it in the others, especially in Roarke's tightening grip and Jim's increasingly labored breaths.

"We need to find a place to set camp," Boyd called out, concern evident in his voice.

Georges, more familiar with this stretch of the river, nodded. "There's a small clearing upstream," he said in French. "It's sheltered and has good access to fresh water."

Once I'd translated, Jim grunted in acknowledgment, and we continued. The ambience soon shifted. The looming mountains cut our daylight hours short, and soon the land plunged into night. We spent the last leg of our journey in the dark. The occasional hoot of an owl or splash of a leaping fish complemented the chirping of crickets.

Asher suddenly called out, pointing to the riverbank. "Look! That clearing Georges mentioned—I think that's it."

I strained my eyes and made out the faint outline of a flat stretch of land bordered by thickets and tall trees. It looked inviting, the promise of rest too enticing to resist.

As we steered toward the bank, a sense of relief washed over me. The soft ground would provide a comfortable sleeping spot, and the trees would shield us from the wind. The group, running on our last embers of energy, began the process of unloading the canoes and setting up camp.

Boyd and I worked on gathering firewood while Asher and Jim dug a firepit. The Métis guides and Blue Fox, with their uncanny knack for the wilderness, had already begun constructing nests from branches and large leaves.

A moment later, frantic shouts echoed through the clearing.

"Roarke!" Jim's voice was tinged with panic.

There at the water's edge was Roarke, pale and sweating, collapsed next to his canoe. He had returned to it to collect supplies and apparently had lost his strength. I ran with the others to the river. His breathing was shallow, and his eyes were glazed. The events of the past few days, combined with his shoulder injury, had taken a toll.

Boyd shouted, "Get him to the camp! Now!"

As the cold cloak of night draped over us, the fate of our comrade hung in the balance. Everything else—the camp, the journey, the mission—faded into the background. All that mattered now was Roarke.

Jim and Boyd gently laid him down on a blanket in the dim light, carefully avoiding any sharp rocks or uneven ground. With his lips a bluish hue and his face glistening with sweat, he looked more fragile than I had ever seen him.

Boyd, a steady hand in any crisis, began carefully peeling back the bandages around Roarke's shoulder. The pungent smell that greeted us immediately confirmed our worst fears. The wound was clearly infected, a grotesque mix of angry red and purple.

"Oh no," Asher muttered under his breath, his usually calm demeanor replaced by a veil of worry.

Jim clenched his jaw, grimacing as he examined the wound. "It's festered. The infection has taken hold."

Jean-Baptiste moved closer, taking a cursory look at the wound before rummaging in his satchel. "In my travels, I've seen wounds like this. We need to treat it, and fast."

Blue Fox stood over him. "Can I help?"

"I can handle it," Jean-Baptiste said.

He produced a small bundle of dried herbs. "We can make a poultice. It's a remedy from my people. It might help draw out the infection and reduce the fever."

Gratitude flooded me. "Please, do whatever you can."

Boyd nodded in agreement, lighting a small fire nearby. "We'll need hot water."

The next moments were a flurry of activity. While Jean-Baptiste prepared the herbal concoction, Asher and I gathered more wood to ensure the fire burned throughout the night. With her vast experience in wilderness survival, Blue Fox helped to fashion a compress with the available materials. For the first time, she and Jean-Baptiste acknowledged one another and even worked together. The distrust between them had cleared for a moment.

Applying the poultice to the wound, Jean-Baptiste whispered a soft prayer in his native tongue, a gesture both touching and desperate. Roarke's labored breathing became the haunting backdrop to our grim tasks.

The night deepened, and a hush settled over our camp, save for the occasional crackling of the fire and the ever-present song of the river. We took turns watching over Roarke, each of us silently pleading for his recovery.

"How did I not notice sooner?" I whispered, guilt gnawing at me.

Boyd placed a hand on my shoulder. "It's not your fault, kid. None of us knew it would come to this. Now we just do what we can."

The burden of the day's events pressed heavily on us. The hope was that, with the dawn, Roarke's condition would stabilize. But for now, all we could do was wait, hope, and trust in the knowledge of our Métis companion and rest our weary bodies as much as our minds would allow.

A raw, guttural scream tore through the pre-dawn quiet. The sheer intensity of it jolted me awake, my heart racing and my senses on high alert. Blinking against the dim light, I tried to focus on the scene before me. It was Asher. It didn't take me long to realize the source of his anguish.

Roarke lay motionless, his once-ruddy complexion now ashen, his chest no longer rising with breath. The fever had taken him.

Asher, knees buckling, collapsed beside Roarke, his tears falling freely onto the still form of his friend. Jim stood a few feet away, staring at the body with vacant eyes. Grief was etched into his face; the lines around his eyes and mouth seemed deeper now, more pronounced.

He had once lost a brother, and this loss seemed to reopen that old wound.

He murmured softly, "Not again... not another one."

Boyd's usually stoic face was a picture of despair. He approached Roarke and placed a gentle hand on his forehead. "You were always the brave one," he whispered.

The air was thick with an oppressive grief that bore down on us all. Georges and Jean-Baptiste stood at the edge of the camp, their expressions somber. Although they had not interacted with Roarke as much as the others, their saddened eyes spoke of the shock of the loss.

As for me, I regretted not getting to know him better. He had kept his distance from me most of the journey, especially after I corrected his pronunciation of rendez-vous. I had lost him then, and he never warmed to me. It felt like I had amends to make, and I would never again have the chance. Blue Fox stood at my side, her gaze steely. I couldn't tell if she had no tears, or held them back.

"Such is life," she whispered.

Her callousness gave me pause.

"We need to give him a proper burial," Asher choked out between sobs.

Jim nodded in agreement. "Yes, we owe him that."

We set to work, using our limited tools to dig a shallow grave near the riverside. It was backbreaking labor, but it gave us all a chance to process our grief, each shovel of dirt a testament to our deep respect for Roarke.

As the sun rose, casting the first warm rays of light over the river, we lowered Roarke's body into the ground. Asher said a few words, recalling their shared adventures and good times. Boyd recited a short prayer, and Jim, voice thick with emotion, sang a soft German lullaby he remembered from his childhood.

Still grappling with the shocking turn of events, I could only stand silently, paying my respects to a man I had only just begun to know. But the bonds forged in adversity were strong and profound in this wild, unpredictable land.

A solemn promise hung in the air as we finished filling the grave. We would not let Roarke's death be in vain. We would see this mission through, not just for ourselves but for him as well.

The river's gentle flow was eerily quiet as we pushed off from the banks and began to row once more. The rhythmic splash of our paddles was the only sound that broke the stillness of the early morning. Every so often, the distant cry of a bird or the rustling of trees in the breeze would remind us of the world outside our bubble of grief.

In spite of it all, we paddled with renewed determination, propelled by the burning need to rescue our comrades. The Hudson's Bay Company had taken more from us than we had ever imagined possible, and our resolve to confront them was only hardened by the pain of our recent loss.

Georges and Jean-Baptiste, aided by Blue Fox, led our small flotilla, constantly scanning the riverbanks for signs of the HBC's passage. Their keen senses, honed by years of navigating these waters, were our best hope of catching up.

As the morning wore on, Jim, sitting at the front of our canoe, suddenly held up his hand for us to halt. "Look there," he whispered, pointing to a spot on the opposite riverbank. I strained my eyes and saw that he was referring to a recently extinguished campfire, still sending up faint wisps of smoke.

"They couldn't have been gone long," said Boyd, hope flashing in his eyes.

We cautiously approached, finding footprints in the mud and discarded food wrappers. Clearly, the HBC had made camp here. And from the looks of it, they were moving fast.

"We're gaining on them," said Asher, his voice filled with determination.

A torrential rain soon overtook us, slowing down our advance. But we pushed through, taking only short breaks to rest our aching muscles. Our every thought was consumed with catching up to the Hudson's Bay Company and saving our friends.

As dusk began to fall, Jean-Baptiste, navigating the lead canoe, gestured for us to follow him closer to the river's edge.

"There." He pointed to a clearing up ahead. Canoes were pulled up on the shore, and faint voices reached our ears.

It was the HBC camp. We had found them. It was time to take back what was ours.

But the hushed conversations we overheard as we approached the camp were not in the expected British and French accents of the Hudson's Bay Company men. Instead, they were in the distinct drawling of American English.

"Damn," whispered Asher. "American trappers."

Hiding in the shadows, we observed the campsite. The men moved around freely, laughing and sharing stories around a fire. The stars and stripes flew alongside their tents, confirming what their accents had already told us.

Jim sighed in frustration. "We're losing precious time."

I held up my hand, signaling for us to hold our positions. "Let's go say hello. We have no quarrel with these men. And besides, they might have information on the Hudson's Bay group. We will approach them cautiously and diplomatically. Americans value fairness and might help us if we present our case."

With a nod of agreement from the group, I stepped out from our hiding spot, raising my hands to show we meant no harm. The activity in the camp ceased immediately, and a dozen or so guns were trained on me.

"Easy, friends," I called out. "We're not here to fight. We're just looking for some information."

A tall man with a grizzled beard and a weatherworn hat approached me. "Who are you?" he demanded, his voice cautious but also curious.

"My name is Christian. My companions and I have been trailing a group from the HBC. We thought this might be their camp, but clearly we were mistaken."

The man relaxed slightly and extended a hand. "I'm Samuel," he said. "We did see a group of HBC men this morning. They're headed further west."

"Did they have prisoners? We're looking for our friends. Three men: MacBride, MacLane, and Bear."

Samuel shook his head. "We didn't get that close. They fired warning shots at us, and it wasn't a fight worth picking."

"Thank you," I said.

The American trapper seemed to understand our urgency. "If you need supplies or assistance, let us know. The HBC's reach has been growing, and it's pushing many of us out. We've got our own reasons to be wary of them. It never hurts to join forces when the conditions are right."

I looked to my company, their eyes wide with hope, then turned back to Samuel. "We welcome it."

As the night deepened, we formed an unexpected alliance with the other Americans, sharing stories of the Hudson's Bay Company's monopolistic practices and territorial ambitions. Sitting around the campfire, our new allies generously shared their provisions with us. The night deepened, and more trappers joined our circle, drawn by the news of strangers in their midst. By midnight, the circle had widened considerably, and we found ourselves amidst a sea of faces.

The trappers told tales of their adventures, each more unbelievable than the last. Just as Asher was recounting a particularly riveting story of his own, a hush spread through the crowd, and everyone's attention shifted towards the entrance of the camp.

A figure emerged from the darkness, flanked by two guards. He was an older man with piercing dark eyes and a commanding presence that silenced the murmurs around him.

"Manuel Lisa," Samuel whispered to me when he noticed my puzzled expression. "He's a legend among us. Founded the Missouri Fur Company. If you've got a problem in these parts, he's the man you go to."

Lisa sat by the fire, his guards taking up positions behind him. All conversation had ceased. He scanned our group with a discerning eye, then turned to me. "I hear you've got a bone to pick with the HBC."

I nodded, swallowing my nervousness. "They've taken our friends. We intend to get them back."

"What's your name?" he asked.

"Christian. And these are my companions: Blue Fox, Asher, Boyd, Jim, Georges, and Jean-Baptiste."

Lisa looked me up and down, then leaned back, steepling his fingers. "The HBC's been a thorn in my side for too long. Pushing their boundaries, encroaching on territories they have no right to. Tell me—Christian, was it? What's your plan?"

We shared our story, our pursuit, and our intentions. As we spoke, Lisa listened intently, occasionally nodding or interjecting with a question. He leaned forward when I explained my plan to strike a deal with the North West Company.

"You know they've signed a deal with the HBC, don't you?" he interjected. "I even heard talks of a merger."

"I had not," I said. "I must have missed that part. Mr. Astor said they hate the HBC as much as anyone."

"That might be true," Lisa said, scratching at his beard. "But they're both tied to Mother England, and she pulls the strings in the end."

I sat back, feeling embarrassed. My pride in my education crumbled in light of having missed such a critical piece of information as a deal between the North West Company and the HBC.

"You're brave," Lisa said, "I'll give you that. But bravery won't be enough against the HBC. They're intent on stopping any American expedition from accessing their territory. You need allies. As do we."

"I was sent here to make deals," I said with a slight nod and a smile.

Lisa grinned, a sly twinkle in his eye. "Well then, you're in luck."

He held out his hand to shake mine. We would work together for the time being. Over the next few hours, Lisa shared vital information about the HBC's movements, numbers, and intentions. He also introduced us to some of his most trusted men, with whom we shared food and drink.

As the night dwindled, my company and I retired from the campfire to gather our things from our canoes. Blue Fox had already set up a teepee underneath the drooping lower branches of a massive pine tree.

"Where did you get that?" I asked her.

"I found it in the HBC camp," she said.

She kept the flap open, an obvious invitation. I entered the teepee and rested my head beside hers. We kept each other warm for the night, and for the first night in many, I slept well.

As the rising sun cast a golden glow over the camp, I felt renewed purpose and resolve. With Lisa's help and new allies by our side, we stood a real chance of rescuing our friends and challenging the Hudson's Bay Company's dominance in the region.

# Chapter 8
# The Pacific Fur Company

The majestic Rocky Mountains towered ahead, their snow-capped peaks glistening in the sun. The air was crisper here, carrying the promise of unexplored lands and challenges yet to be faced. A deep sense of awe washed over me as we paddled onward, the mountains looming large over our ongoing journey. It would be the most dangerous leg of our trek, or so our fellow trappers insisted.

Lisa, navigating effortlessly up the Yellowstone River, had taken the lead of our expanded group. We had more than twenty canoes banded together. I had been initially wary, reluctant to trust a stranger, but I could make an exception for one with as formidable a reputation as Manuel Lisa.

We had already spent many days on the river, and it only started to narrow after we met our new allies. As the current grew stronger, our journey slowed, until one day we reached impassable rapids. Lisa ordered his men to drag their canoes to land and portage up the hill. We followed suit. Thankfully, the canoes were light, but since we had to take turns carrying them, we had to leave some of our supplies behind. It would have taxed us too much to take them all.

Climbing a mountain was hard enough, but with a canoe over my shoulder? I could hardly bear it. And no one else complained about the weight or the fatigue, which made things worse. I didn't want to be the one to give out first. To my relief, one of Lisa's men collapsed during our trek. When he did, Lisa finally called for a rest.

We kept on like this for several days, carrying our canoes into the mountains. Lisa seemed to know where he was heading. The loose, dusty soil of the mountainside soon turned to mud; and soon after that, we encountered snow. A strong wind blew down at us from the jagged peaks, freezing our noses and our bones. Evidently, winter had held on longer than it should have. The heavier clothes I had loathed at the outset of our journey now brought me some warmth and comfort, though I still felt a shiver that would not let up. Blue Fox had too little clothing as well, and to my relief one of Lisa's men offered up a spare buckskin overcoat that kept her just warm enough. It was a blessing.

We had seen signs of the Hudson's Bay Company— abandoned campfires, trampled underbrush—but had yet to catch up to them. One morning, as we broke camp to continue our arduous march, Blue Fox returned from scouting and foraging, claiming she has seen their camp. I called us all together.

"We're close," I said. "The HBC is right up ahead of us."

"If that's true, we may catch them before we reach the mountain pass," Samuel said.

"That would be ideal," Lisa added.

"How far is the pass?" I asked.

"With the canoes over our shoulders? Another two days or so," Lisa said.

Samuel turned to me with a furrowed brow. "We should be prepared. We've no idea what's waiting for us on the other side."

"Let's not wait around. If we can catch them, let's go," I urged.

Lisa put a hand on my shoulder and sighed. "Listen, kid. I know you're in a rush. But at the pace we've been going, our men are going to tire out. If there's a fight ahead, we should be rested. I'd hate to catch up to them and not have the strength to fight. Let's keep moving, and if we catch them before the pass, great. If not, we'll plan from there."

I gave him a decisive nod. What he did not know was that my urgency to catch up to the HBC was not all my own. It was for the benefit of my company. Lisa had given me permission to slow down without losing face. And so I did. After all, Roarke's death had taught me the perils of pushing past one's limits.

Lisa's estimate proved correct. For the next two days, we climbed further into the mountains on the heels of the HBC group. Evenings were spent around the campfire, sharing tales and speculations. Jim often played his fiddle, and the melancholic tunes added to the air of uncertainty that hung around us.

Jean-Baptiste, with his deep knowledge of the wilderness, had grown close to Lisa. Together, they pored over maps and charts, planning our next move. Boyd and Asher often joined them, contributing with their insights and anecdotes.

On the morning we were to reach the mountain pass, Lisa gathered us around.

"Tomorrow, we'll need to be vigilant," he said. "The pass can be unpredictable. We'll face snow, maybe even avalanches. But if we stick together, we'll make it through."

"Avalanches?" I scoffed. "Isn't it almost summer?" I had lost track of time, but not so much that I had lost my sense of the season.

Lisa chuckled. "Mountain passes can stay snowbound well into summer, kid. I like to prepare for the worst. Let's hope it's dry, but be ready if it isn't."

We set out early under a sky painted pink and orange. As we began our ascent, the terrain changed rapidly. Pine trees gave way to patches of snow, and the incline grew steeper.

Lisa led the way, his experience evident in the way he navigated the challenging terrain. We followed in a single file, each step measured and deliberate. The silence was only broken by the crunch of snow beneath our feet and the occasional cry of a distant bird.

By midday, we reached a narrow gorge, its sides rising steeply. The snow was deeper here, and we used ropes to drag the canoes behind us. It was a relief. As we trudged on, I felt my breath grow shallower, the altitude making each gasp a little less satisfying.

But the promise of what lay beyond spurred us on. The Hudson's Bay Company, MacBride, MacLane, and Bear seemed within reach. With the combined might of our group—perhaps forty in total—and Lisa's guidance, we would face whatever challenges the mountains threw our way, united in our pursuit of justice and wealth.

The wind whispered eerie secrets among the peaks as we trekked through the mountain pass. The jagged walls of the gorge surrounded us, the pathway narrowing and casting long, deceptive shadows on the snow-covered ground. Every sound seemed magnified, from the crunch of our boots to the distant echo of a falling rock.

A bird's sharp cry caught my attention, and I squinted into the blinding reflection of sun on snow, trying to spot its origin. Then it hit me—it wasn't a bird's cry but a signal. My head snapped to Lisa, who had paused and was scanning the ridge above us.

It all happened in an instant. The echo of a gunshot rang out, and a bullet whizzed past, embedding itself in the snow beside Georges. Chaos erupted as men, draped in the colors of the Hudson's Bay Company, descended upon us from all directions. They had been lying in wait.

"Take cover!" Lisa bellowed as he pulled out his firearm. The gunfire was deafening in the narrow passage. Each of us scrambled for shelter, hiding behind boulders and the natural indentations in the walls of the gorge.

Asher and Boyd worked together, firing back and providing cover for each other. Despite his size, Samuel was nimble, darting between spots and taking shots whenever he saw an opportunity. Jim stood his ground, pipe in mouth, firing rounds into the mountainside and, I presumed, finding his mark.

"Jim, get down!" I urged him.

"I'll be fine. They can't aim," he chuckled while reloading his rifle.

Blue Fox tugged at my shirt and led us behind a large outcropping for cover. I was loading my rifle when I felt a hand on my shoulder. It was Georges—he pointed to a vantage point higher up. I nodded eagerly, and we made our way there to get a better angle on our attackers. Before we could sneak off, an HBC man appeared with a saber in hand. Blue Fox nocked an arrow, took aim, and fired. Her arrow struck him square in the chest.

"Nice shot!" I said.

Blue Fox glowered at me.

"Did I say something wrong?"

From our new position, it was clear the Hudson's Bay men outnumbered us. Reinforcements must have joined them from the other side of the pass. They were strategically placed, their experience in such skirmishes evident. But we had the advantage of the high ground. They hadn't expected us to find such a vantage point and to retaliate with such force.

A bullet grazed my arm, and I gritted my teeth against the pain. Georges took aim and shot down the man who had shot me. Blue Fox knelt beside me to examine the wound.

"You're clumsy," she said, tugging at the ripped fabric of my tunic. "It's just a scrape. I can heal it later."

Hours seemed to pass, though in reality it might have been mere minutes. It took so long to reload our rifles, there were ominous gaps between the exchanges of fire, in which my beating heart drowned out all other sounds around me. Lisa's men pressed forward with the support of our cover fire, fighting hand to hand with the HBC men. Jim soon joined us, and with his marksmanship supporting Lisa's men, the Hudson's Bay Company retreated.

Lisa used this moment to regroup. "We need to move." His face was grim. "They'll be back and in greater numbers."

Wasting no time, we began our descent, helping the wounded and ensuring no one was left behind. We'd known the mountain pass would prove arduous, but we'd had no idea it would be a treacherous trap. The skirmish had taken several lives. Lisa ordered us all to leave the bodies. We had no time to bury them. A looming storm, harboring hail and snow, was approaching, a harbinger of death for those still on the mountain at night. We had to hurry to a lower elevation.

The once-breathtaking views of the mountains were now masked by a foggy dread, and every rustling of a tree limb or chirping bird made my heart race. We moved cautiously, trying to maintain a low profile. But the HBC was relentless. Just when I thought we had lost them, a sharp whistle cut through the silence, followed by the crack of a rifle.

A bullet flew past, narrowly missing me. The second ambush was as sudden and fierce as the first. I lost my footing in the panic and tripped over an outcropped root. My arms flailed as the ground gave way beneath me, sending me tumbling down the steep incline of a ravine. Blue Fox tried to catch my arm, but missed.

"Christian!" she screamed.

The world was a blur of green and brown, each jarring bump and scratch intensifying my disorientation. With a splash, I found myself submerged in the icy-cold waters of a narrow, fast-moving rapid. The current was strong, pulling me along with a force I couldn't resist. Heavy with water, my clothes weighed me down, making each stroke a desperate fight against the stream's pull.

Gulping for air, I managed to grasp on to a jutting rock and pull myself up. The roar of the water was deafening, but it could not drown out the sounds of battle—shouts, screams, and musket fire.

Coughing and shivering, I assessed my surroundings. The stream had carved a deep channel through the mountainside, its walls steep and covered in thick foliage. Climbing out was not an option. My only choice was to follow the stream, hoping it would lead to a safer exit point.

Hours seemed to pass as I navigated the rocky rapid, sometimes wading and sometimes swimming while battling the current. The cold bit into my bones, and the weight of my drenched clothes sapped my strength. As night began to fall, I was driven by a single thought: I had to find my companions.

Eventually, the rapid widened, signaling that I was approaching its end. Exhausted, I finally dragged myself onto the riverbank, collapsing onto a bed of wilted grasses. As I lay there, trying to catch my breath and still my racing heart, the stars overhead seemed to spin, reminding me of the dizzying slide down the ravine.

The soft rustling of tree branches made my heart jump. My instincts were screaming at me. I turned toward the disturbance, and that was when I saw it: a large bear, its dark fur glistening in the dappled sunlight, scratching its massive back against a tree.

Our eyes locked, and the world slowed down. I could see its nostrils flare, catching my scent. I hoped that my sodden, river-soaked appearance might dissuade it, but my luck wasn't about to change. The bear moved toward me, each step deliberate and menacing.

I bolted downstream, a new surge of adrenaline fueling my movements. My wet clothes were heavy against my skin, my boots squishing with every step, making it hard to sprint. Soon, I heard the roar of water echoing through the trees. I skidded to a stop, taking in the sight. A massive waterfall cascaded down, a sheer drop of at least thirty feet, ending in a swirling pool below. To my left, the cliffside revealed a potential escape: a jagged path that led downward.

My heart pounded in my ears as I began my treacherous descent, clinging to the slippery rocks, trying not to look down. Halfway there, I noticed an overhang behind the waterfall, hinting at a possible cave.

Without a second thought, I clambered over to the cave entrance, the spray making the rocks slick and challenging to grip. Inside, the sound of the waterfall was a deafening roar, with mist surrounding me like a veil. The cave was deep, offering some solace—or so I hoped.

Moments later, a shadow cast over the entrance. The bear, curious and persistent, had followed. It sniffed the entrance, its massive body partially blocking the light. Panic surged through me, leaving me with little choice. Taking a deep breath, I ran full tilt towards the edge of the cave, pushing past the bear, and jumped.

The drop felt eternal. The wind rushed past my ears until I plunged into the icy depths below. The current once again gripped me, pulling me downstream. Gasping for breath, I surfaced, only to see the bear at the top of the waterfall, its eyes locked onto me. It roared, a sound that sent shivers down my spine, before leaping off the edge and into the water after me.

The chase was on. The bear, although large, was a strong swimmer, and it was gaining. I swam with all my might, hoping against hope to escape. Ahead, the river widened, revealing a steep riverbank dense with trees.

Mustering my last bit of strength, I headed towards it, my limbs aching and heavy.

Reaching the bank, I pulled myself out of the water and collapsed, my body exhausted and my mind racing. It was lunchtime, and I was the main course. I watched helplessly as the beast approached me. I imagined for a moment what it might feel like to have a bear's teeth sink into my flesh. And yet I was so exhausted, I did not fear dying for once. I just wanted it to be over with quickly. Was this how antelopes felt when the leopard had run them to exhaustion, I wondered? No matter. The bear had won. He deserved the spoils of his hunt.

And then—a hoot, a holler, and a whimper. The bear scampered off, inches away from having a taste of me. Instead of wondering what had scared it off, I just collapsed in relief.

I lay there on the riverbank, a trembling mess, my ears ringing from the relentless roar of the waterfall. A shadow approached, casting a silhouette against the setting sun. I barely managed to lift my head, my vision blurred, but what I saw brought a brief moment of terror: a tall figure with a bow, nocking an arrow. My would-be savior moved closer, reaching out to pull me up from the water's edge. It wasn't until our eyes met that recognition dawned.

"Blue Fox?" I rasped, coughing out the river water.

She laughed heartily and genuinely. "Thank the heavens, I found you!" Her laughter was infectious, and despite my recent brush with death, a small chuckle escaped my lips.

I struggled to find words. "I'm thankful, too."

She grinned, flipping her hair over one shoulder. "Come on, we have to find the others."

My soaked clothes clung to my body, chilling me even further as I tried to catch my breath on the riverbank. My attention was momentarily diverted from the recent bear chase to the woman standing beside me. I gazed up at Blue Fox, utterly amazed.

"I've read about grizzly bears in Lewis and Clark's expedition letters. I never thought I'd see one up close," I said.

Blue Fox laughed. "Oh, Christian. If it were a grizzly, then you'd have a real reason to run."

I stared at her, still trying to piece together what had just happened. "But... you chased it away. With arrows."

She shrugged, her expression nonchalant. "Black bears are skittish. Make enough noise, show them you're not afraid, and they'll keep their distance. And that was just a curious cub."

I recalled the sheer size and presence of the bear and shook my head in disbelief. "It looked pretty big to me."

Blue Fox smirked. "Trust me, you'll know a grizzly when you see one. That was just a curious youngster, wondering what all the commotion was about."

Still shaken, I muttered, "Well, I'd rather not have any more close encounters, be it a curious youngster or a grizzly."

A deep, resounding roar echoed out from the forest above us, sending a chill through my bones. "What was that?"

"That's Momma Bear. We should get moving."

I followed her, still shivering from the icy grip of the river, as we weaved our way through the dense forest. The sound of the river faded, replaced by the chirping of crickets and the gentle rustling of leaves. She seemed to know the area well, each step taken with certainty.

After what felt like hours, we reached a small clearing where Blue Fox dropped her pack. She hung a hide against a sturdy tree trunk, providing a sheltered spot away from the elements.

"I don't think we'll make it back to the group before you freeze to death. Let's get you dried off," she said as she began to gather kindling.

I sat down, eager to warm up, and began removing my boots to empty them of water.

"How far are they?" I asked.

She paused in her fire-making efforts. "They started moving quickly downhill after the ambush. Half a day, maybe, assuming they slow down to wait for us."

I frowned, absorbing her words. "Do you think they will?"

She glanced at me, her gaze sharp. "For you, maybe. They all assumed the fall killed you."

"And you didn't..."

For a split second, her defenses seemed to crumble.

"That makes me happy," I said, my voice tinged with joy.

We gazed into each other's eyes for a long, silent moment. I lost myself in her, drawn in by her beauty, her strength, and her passion. And she seemed to lose herself in me.

In the dancing light of the campfire, as the shadows painted her face, I felt a yearning unlike anything I'd experienced before. From the moment we'd met, Blue Fox had been an enigma—strong, unyielding—yet beneath that hardened exterior, there was a spark, a warmth. Every stolen glance, every fleeting touch had set my world alight. I'd dreamed of a future, one where our paths intertwined, where the weight of the wilderness couldn't touch the bond between us. It was more than just the promise of an alliance or the thrill of shared danger; it was the silent understanding, the way our souls seemed to recognize each other. I believed there was a place for us, beyond our journey and the treacherous paths and relentless enemies.

As night deepened, the mountain air grew colder, biting through our layers and reminding us of the unforgiving frontier that surrounded us. We lay close, the proximity a necessary warmth against the chill. Blue Fox shifted beside me, then reached for my hand, pulling it over her waist and onto her midriff like a protective blanket. Even through the fabric, her skin was warm, her heartbeat a steady rhythm beneath my fingers.

It was a comforting gesture, sending ripples of calm through me. Here she was, showing a level of intimacy I hadn't expected, and my mind found solace in that. Was this my sign to deepen our bond? Or was I misreading her need for warmth and setting myself up for another rejection?

Her breathing was calm, almost rhythmic, but her frame had a subtle tightness. I could feel her muscles tense under my touch, a sign that perhaps she was just as conflicted. Every instinct screamed at me to pull her closer, bridge the gap the journey had created, and lose myself in her embrace. But the hurt, the lingering embarrassment of her rejection at the Mandan village, kept me paralyzed. I remained still, my hand a heavy weight on her, the distance between us wider than the narrow space our bodies occupied.

The night stretched on, the fire dwindling, the tension taut. In the stillness, surrounded by the vast wilderness, two souls grappled silently with their feelings, bound by a connection that was both undeniable and yet, frustratingly, just out of reach.

The warmth of Blue Fox's skin against mine transported me to memories I'd tried to leave behind, revisiting them in only the most vulnerable of moments. I was back in that modest New York apartment, the outside world muffled by the constant hum of the city that never sleeps.

I remembered the soft feel of her skin, much like Blue Fox's now. Sarah had vibrant hazel eyes that always carried a twinkle and flowing brown hair that danced with every movement. We were young and hopelessly in love, the city's rigors only accentuating the intimacy we shared. Sarah was my anchor amidst the urban chaos, my beacon of light guiding me through the city's endless maze.

As the city's symphony played outside one fateful evening, Sarah went into labor. Our excitement was a blend of joy and nervousness, awaiting our first child's arrival. But as the hours passed, excitement gave way to dread. The complications seemed insurmountable. Sarah's grip on my hand tightened, our shared hopes and dreams hinging on every passing moment.

By dawn, New York's relentless pace had claimed two more souls. Sarah and our baby were gone, leaving me to navigate the overwhelming grief. The vibrant city became a haunting reminder of what I'd lost, every street echoing Sarah's laughter and each corner filled with memories. And then the blur of drink. I'd crawled so far down the bottle I was surprised I did not drown.

The fur trade had been my escape, as I sought redemption in nature, far from the city's painful memories. But lying next to Blue Fox, my past was undeniable. The contrast between what once was and what might be tugged at my heartstrings, forcing me to confront emotions I had hoped to leave behind. And yet, my yearning to complete my mission, to return to New York, and to make my fortune did not waver. What future would Blue Fox have in the city?

The distant past and the chilling present collided for a moment, the cold memories of New York fading to the rhythmic sound of water cascading from the nearby waterfall. I became hyperaware of the sensations around me. The crickets chirped their nocturnal symphony, underpinned by the deeper croak of frogs and the occasional hoot of an owl. It was as if nature itself were trying to reassure me, comforting me in my moment of grief.

Beneath me, the cool ground offered a stark contrast to Blue Fox's warmth, the foliage acting as a natural mattress that rustled with every subtle shift of our bodies. Blue Fox had drifted to sleep, but her fingers still flexed in my grip, her nails lightly grazing my palm. It was a simple, involuntary gesture, but it sent waves of sensation up my arm. Each of her breaths came as a gentle puff against my chest, synchronized with the steady beat of my heart. The rhythmic pattern of her breathing, shallow and deep in turn, was like a lullaby, anchoring me further in the present.

A gust of wind rustled the leaves overhead, and the smell of fresh pine filled the air. A lone wolf howled in the distance, the melancholic tone echoing off the mountains, only to be answered by another, then another. It was a reminder of the untamed wilderness we found ourselves in, the unpredictability of our situation.

But as the calls of the wolves faded, the only remaining sound was the crackling of our fire, the occasional popping of embers almost like muted fireworks. The gentle flicker of warmth played upon my exposed skin, leaving a comforting tingling sensation. A stray ember floated above us, its fiery core illuminating the dark like a wayward firefly, dancing and twirling before fading into the obsidian night.

Somewhere in the distance, a twig snapped. My muscles tensed instinctively, and my ears strained for more sounds. There it was again—a soft rustle, like an animal foraging. Likely a deer or raccoon, but the frontier had taught me caution, and I kept one ear attuned to the sounds while soaking in the other sensations.

The cold air stung my nostrils with every inhale, a clean crispness that cleared the mind. A stray droplet fell from our hide shelter and hit my face, its chilly touch startling yet invigorating. The surrounding forest held a dampness, an earthy aroma of decaying leaves mixed with the unmistakable scent of moss. It was a blend of odors that was at once grounding and refreshing.

Beside me, Blue Fox shifted again, her leg brushing against mine. Her hair, which had a life of its own, tickled my cheek. I could smell the natural oils in it, a scent distinctively hers—wild yet familiar. She muttered something in her sleep, the words incomprehensible but the tone unmistakably affectionate. It brought a smile to my face, despite the emotional turmoil within.

A sense of gratitude washed over me. For the second chance at life that this journey had offered, for the raw beauty of the wilderness that surrounded us, and for the unexpected bond I had formed with Blue Fox. Our relationship was complicated, fraught with misunderstandings and different worldviews, but in this moment, lying side by side, I felt a connection that went beyond words.

A shooting star streaked across the sky, its brief brilliance illuminating the canopy above. The vastness of the universe, the ephemeral nature of life, and the fleeting moments of happiness we find along the way—all seemed encapsulated in that single, transient streak of light. The weight of my past and the uncertainty of the future lay heavy on my mind, but for now, surrounded by nature and in the company of Blue Fox, I felt truly present, fully alive in the moment.

As I lay there, surrounded by the hum of the night, I was again acutely aware of the barriers we'd constructed, both self-imposed and shaped by our pasts—the juxtaposition of our closeness and the emotional chasm— one I did not fully understand—that separated us. A whisper of thought traced the edges of my consciousness, filled with hope and vulnerability: if only we could tear down these walls, letting the raw, unfiltered essence of our beings meld and merge, perhaps we'd find a unity that transcended the complexities of our entwined fates.

# CHAPTER 9
## OUT OF THE FIRE

In the early light of dawn, nestled among the dense underbrush, Blue Fox and I lay in silence, each lost in our own thoughts. The close encounter with the bear had left a lingering tension in the air, an unspoken acknowledgment of our growing connection and the precariousness of our situation. Despite the chill of the morning, there was an indelible warmth between us, a flame that had yet to find its full expression.

We rose, shaking off the remnants of night, and set out to find Manuel Lisa and our company. Our steps were cautious, guided by the subtle cues of the wilderness and the unyielding drive to reunite with our companions.

It wasn't as long as I expected before we spotted them, a ragtag group huddled around a series of small fires, their faces etched with weariness and worry. Manuel Lisa stood as we approached, his eyes widening slightly in surprise.

"Christian, Blue Fox!" His voice was tinged with relief. "We feared the worst when we lost you in the chaos."

"We managed," I said, glancing at Blue Fox, whose eyes held a quiet strength. "My company?"

"All here and accounted for," Asher chimed in from off to the side. A quick glance brough them all into view.

"Thank the heavens," I said.

"We're happy to see you, too," Boyd added.

"Listen, Christian, we need to talk about MacBride, MacLane, and Bear." Lisa nodded gravely, gesturing for us to step closer.

Samuel, his eyes shadowed and tired, shifted to make room for us.

"We found them," Lisa began, his voice low. "Down the slope, there's an HBC camp. It's massive, and if your friends aren't there, I don't know where else they could be."

The news hit me like a cold wave. Our enemy's stronghold was the last place I wanted to venture into, yet it seemed our only option.

"We need a plan," I said, meeting the eyes of each member of our diminished group. "A rescue operation."

The air was thick with unspoken fears and doubts, but there was a resolve in each face, a shared understanding that we couldn't abandon our own.

Blue Fox spoke up, her voice steady. "I can scout the camp, get a sense of their numbers, their defenses."

I felt a twinge of fear at her words, the thought of her in danger tightening my chest. But I knew her skills were unmatched, and her offer was our best chance at gaining the information we needed.

"We'll need a distraction," Samuel added, rubbing his bearded chin. "Something to draw their attention while we get our men out."

The conversation turned to tactics and strategies, each of us contributing ideas, building a plan piece by piece. But through it all, my gaze kept returning to Blue Fox, the unspoken words between us hanging heavy in the air.

As the meeting drew to a close, we had a rough plan in place, a daring gamble that hinged on precision and a fair share of luck. We agreed to rest for a few hours before Blue Fox set out to reconnoiter the camp.

As the others dispersed, I found myself alone with her, the pressure of the impending mission mixing with the unaddressed emotions that simmered just beneath the surface.

"Be careful," I found myself saying, the words inadequate to express the turmoil inside me.

Blue Fox met my gaze, her eyes a mirror to my own fears and desires. "I always am," she replied, a ghost of a smile touching her lips.

She turned to leave, but I reached out, my hand closing gently around her arm. The contact sent a jolt through me, a current of longing and concern.

"In all this," I started, my voice barely above a whisper, "don't forget... what we have."

She paused, turning back to face me. For a moment, we stood there, the world around us fading into insignificance. Then, slowly, she leaned in, her lips brushing mine in a kiss that was a promise, a vow made in the face of uncertainty.

As she pulled away, a bond that transcended the dangers we faced enraptured us. With a final, lingering look, she disappeared into the forest, a wraith on a mission that held our friends' lives—and perhaps our own fates— in the balance.

Left alone, I felt our situation pressing down on me, a burden made bearable only by the light of what had grown between us. In the heart of the wild, amidst the looming shadow of conflict, love had found a way to take root. And now, as we prepared to face our greatest challenge yet, it was that love—unspoken, yet undeniable—that gave me the strength to carry on.

Blue Fox returned to camp just as the last light of day faded, her movements silent and swift. Her report was grim but informative: the HBC camp was heavily fortified, with guards patrolling in shifts. But she had identified a weak spot—a less guarded area where the terrain provided cover.

"We strike tonight," I said. "It's our best chance. But it should be a small team. Three or four at most, with cover fire if needed from the hillside."

"I'll go with you," she said.

"I and mine will give you cover for your escape," Lisa added.

I nodded, my heart pounding with a mix of fear and determination. We gathered our scant supplies and our weapons. The air was thick with the weight of what we were about to undertake.

Under the cover of darkness, we made our way toward the enemy camp. The forest was a shadowy labyrinth, but Blue Fox navigated it with the confidence of one born to these lands. Every step was measured, every breath controlled. We were ghosts, moving through the night with a singular purpose.

As we neared the camp, the low murmur of voices and the occasional clink of metal reached our ears. We crouched low, using the underbrush as our shield. The guards were mere shadows, patrolling the perimeter with a casualness that spoke of routine rather than alertness.

Blue Fox pointed to a gap in the patrols, a narrow window of opportunity. We seized it, slipping through the perimeter like ghosts. My heart raced in my chest, each beat a drum of war and fear.

The camp was a sprawl of tents and fires, men moving like specters in the flickering light. We avoided them with meticulous care, every sense heightened to its peak. The location Blue Fox had scouted earlier was our destination —a tent set apart from the others, its isolation a silent confirmation of its purpose.

We reached it, the fabric of the tent the only barrier between us and our captured comrades. I took a deep breath, steadying my nerves, and carefully lifted the flap.

In the dimly lit tent, the silhouette of the bound Scots became clearer. MacBride's usually fiery demeanor was muted, but the flames reignited as soon as his blindfold was removed and his eyes met mine.

"Christ!" MacBride spat with surprise, his voice raspy but filled with hope. "What in the devil's name are you doing here?"

Still dazed from their confinement, MacLane and Bear turned their heads toward me with confusion.

"We came to rescue you."

MacBride scoffed. "Saved by the city lad—how rich!"

"Twice," Bear said.

Ignoring his comment, I continued untying their bonds.

Blue Fox whispered, "We need to get out. Now." As if to emphasize her point, the distant shouts grew louder, and the sound of boots trampling the ground reverberated. "Move!" she hissed as she sliced through the last of the ropes.

After we left the tent and scurried toward the edge of the camp, we spotted a dozen armed HBC men headed our way. In an instant, arrows flew and gunshots rang out. MacLane and Bear instinctively shielded MacBride, pushing him forward and toward the camp's edge. Using her nimbleness and quick reflexes, Blue Fox managed to incapacitate two guards, creating a brief opening for our own escape.

As I tried to help, a stray gunshot whizzed past me, forcing me to dive behind a supply crate for cover. I tried to make a run for it with the others, but an HBC man leaped out of the darkness and tackled me. The shadows of more closed in around me, their shouts a cacophony of excitement and orders.

Blue Fox, seeing my predicament, hesitated for a split second. "Go! I'll get him!" she yelled to the Scots, but MacBride grabbed her arm, pulling her away.

"There's no time! We need to go!" he roared.

The fire in her eyes burned bright, an unwillingness to turn her back on the undeniable bond we had forged.

"Get out of here!" I screamed from the ground, with two more HBC men descending upon me, hoping she would heed my words.

With one last conflicted look in my direction, she allowed herself to be led away, leaving me behind.

I relinquished to my attackers, who pulled me to my feet and dragged me deeper into their camp. Their leader, a tall, imposing figure with a scar running down his left cheek, approached me, his expression a mix of triumph and curiosity.

"Well, what do we have here?" he mused, signaling his men to keep their guns trained on me.

The campfire's glow cast dancing shadows that played tricks on my vision. Yet despite that flickering light, I could see the silhouette of the mountains, imposingly black against the starry night sky. A river roared nearby, serving as a protective barrier on two sides of the camp. They had set themselves up in a sort of mountainous canyon between the pass and the vast Oregon Country beyond. The HBC men took me to a large tent in the center of camp and pushed me through the entrance.

As the tent flaps closed behind me, the quiet ambience inside was only punctuated by the occasional crackling of the nearby campfires and the murmurs of the camp's men. The smell of incense lingered in the air. From behind a low wooden desk, adorned with various maps and scattered papers, a man observed me with dark, calculating eyes. I tried to avoid his gaze, but it was magnetic, pulling me into a dance of recognition and challenge.

"And who might you be?" he asked, breaking the silence. His voice carried a lilting French accent, though he spoke English fluently. He remained seated, fingertips tapping in rhythm on the desk's surface.

"I should ask you the same," I shot back in French, summoning defiance. I knew nothing of this man, but my instincts told me to be wary. There was an unmistakable air of menace about him.

The corner of his mouth curled into a smirk, hinting at amusement. He continued in French, "I find myself in a position of power, so I believe it is you who should answer first."

Determined not to give too much away, I replied tersely, "Christian."

He arched an eyebrow. "Just Christian?"

"That's all you need to know."

He leaned back in his chair, his gaze never leaving mine. "For a man in shackles, you're quite bold."

I shrugged, unwilling to let him see the unease that crept over me. "I've faced worse."

"Oh? And what could be worse than a firing squad?" His smirk widened into a self-assured grin. "Perhaps if we start with introductions, we can build a little trust. My name is Jean-Louis Foucher."

I tried to mask the jolt of recognition, but from the gleam in his eyes, I knew he'd noticed. Jim had mentioned his name and painted it in the colors of blood and revenge. The name now had a face.

Seeing the flicker of recognition in my eyes, Jean-Louis leaned in with smug satisfaction. "It seems you have heard of me."

Deciding to play along, I nodded slowly. "I've heard stories. They paint quite a picture."

His grin grew more pronounced. "Only a picture? Not a masterpiece?"

I took a deep breath, steadying myself. "Depends on who's looking."

That amused him further. "Indeed. And who, Christian, do you look for? Why are you here, far from home, meddling in affairs that are not your own?"

Hesitating for a moment and realizing that some level of transparency might be my best option, I exhaled slowly, admitting, "I work for John Astor's American Fur Company."

His face changed almost imperceptibly, his amusement overshadowed by an inkling of concern. Jean-Louis was well aware of what my admission entailed, and it was clear this conversation was far from over.

He leaned in closer, his face mere inches from mine, his voice dripping with a concoction of mockery and genuine intrigue. "So you were sent to kill me, too, were you?"

I blinked, genuinely taken aback. "What are you talking about? I'm not here to kill anyone."

He chuckled darkly, the sound echoing in the confines of the tent, his fingers drumming steadily against the wooden desk. "You may play coy, Christian, but I have informants. Word is that your esteemed Mr. Astor sent a company out west with a rather particular mission—one that concerns my death."

The confusion must have been evident on my face, for Jean-Louis leaned back with a sigh, rubbing his temples. "It's quite simple. Astor, in his boundless ambition, believes that by removing certain key figures from the board, he can destabilize our operations. And it seems I have been deemed worthy of such attention."

"I don't know anything about that," I said, my mind racing. "I was sent to trade, to establish connections, not to kill."

Jean-Louis studied me for a long moment, his piercing gaze attempting to unravel the truth from the fabric of my words. "You genuinely don't know, do you?"

I met his stare head-on. "Your men shot at us first, not the other way around. I don't want any trouble, just to be on my way to trap fur in Oregon Country, as it's clearly stated in my contract."

"My men had orders to shoot first to prevent Astor's assassins from getting close. Do you have any idea what it's like to know that there are men out there with the sole purpose of finding and killing you?"

"I don't know anything about that," I insisted.

He smirked again, that familiar expression of amusement mixed with something deeper, something I couldn't quite identify. "Perhaps. Or perhaps you're just lying."

"Or perhaps," I retorted, "you're just that paranoid."

He laughed, genuinely this time, the sound rich and full. "Maybe you're right. But in our line of work, a healthy dose of paranoia often means the difference between life and death."

Jean-Louis poured a glass of dark liquor from a bottle on the table, the amber liquid catching the dim candlelight. He took a sip, savoring the taste, before turning his attention back to me.

"You see, Christian—" He swirled the contents of his glass. "—the truce between the Hudson's Bay Company and the North West Company wasn't an accident. It's a delicate dance, choreographed and orchestrated by a few, including myself."

I frowned, trying to piece together what he was getting at. "You're saying you brokered a peace between two competing companies?"

He nodded, setting the glass down with a gentle thud. "Precisely. Do you know the kind of bloodshed that was happening before? The constant skirmishes, the lost profits, the wasted resources? It was senseless. I saw an opportunity for collaboration, for unity. And so, with considerable effort and negotiations, we reached an agreement."

The pieces were falling into place. "And if you were removed from the picture?"

His gaze was sharp, intense. "The peace would crumble. The trust that holds this truce together is personal. My guarantee. Without me, the animosities would resurface, the old wounds would reopen, and chaos would ensue."

"And that chaos," I mused, "would give Astor the foothold he needs."

Jean-Louis smirked, leaning back in his chair. "Ah, you're sharper than you let on. Yes, with the Hudson's Bay Company and North West Company at each other's throats, Astor's American Fur Company could swoop in and capitalize on the disorder."

I was silent for a moment, processing everything. The implications of what he'd said were vast. The fates of entire companies and potentially thousands of livelihoods hinged on this fragile peace and Jean-Louis' life. My mission, which I kept to myself, suddenly made more sense, as did Mr. Astor's plan: MacBride was to take out Jean-Louis, and I was to broker a deal with the North West Company in the aftermath. I then questioned whether we really were the good guys in this situation.

"So you see," Jean-Louis continued, "if Astor sent men to assassinate me, it's because he's playing a much larger game than you realize. He's not just looking for a piece of the tarte. He wants the entire bakery. And he's using you as a disposable pawn."

"Again, I don't know anything about that," I said, my voice barely above a whisper.

Jean-Louis regarded me thoughtfully. "That, Christian, is a lie."

He leaned back in his chair, studying me with a newfound curiosity. "You know, there's something familiar about you. Your accent, your demeanor... You wouldn't happen to have roots in the Vendée, would you?"

I stiffened. "Yes, my father hailed from the Vendée."

A smile broke across Jean-Louis' face. "Ah! I knew it. My home is also the Vendée. The stories, the traditions, the rebellions... it's a place that breeds a unique spirit, wouldn't you say?"

I couldn't help but nod in agreement. "It certainly is. My father was proud of our heritage."

Jean-Louis' eyes gleamed. "Were you there during the War of the Vendée?"

"I was a child. My mother and aunt smuggled me out through Saint-Nazaire. I don't remember much, just that there's nothing left for me to return to there. Everyone we knew was slaughtered."

"I, too, lost family and friends," he said. "I could do nothing for them. I was here, in the wilderness, trapping fur, and never knew what had happened until I read a news report back at headquarters."

"I try not to think about it," I said.

Jean-Louis paused momentarily, rocking on his chair's two back legs. "We're a rare breed, you and I—the last of our people."

There was a moment of shared understanding between us, a connection born of common ancestry and trauma. Seizing the moment, Jean-Louis shifted gears.

"It baffles me," he began, "a man like you, with such a strong lineage. How did you end up here—in the wilds of North America, working for a company like Astor's?"

I hesitated for a moment, weighing my words. "It's complicated. Let's just say I needed the work."

"And how is this line of work suiting you?"

"I hate it. I've enjoyed none of it. If it weren't for Blue Fox, I wouldn't have stuck it out this long, I don't think."

Jean-Louis raised an eyebrow, clearly intrigued. "The young woman who was with you? Ah, matters of the heart. A dangerous game, especially in a land as unforgiving as this."

I sighed, realizing how foolish it must've sounded. "I probably should have stayed in New York."

He nodded thoughtfully. "Indeed, it's a precarious position you find yourself in. But remember, in this land, where loyalties shift as quickly as the winds, where sometimes it's best to forge your own path, you have a chance to do anything you set your mind to."

Jean-Louis leaned forward, resting his elbows on the table. The dim candlelight in the tent danced in his eyes.

"You know, Christian," he began softly, "I like you. I see myself in you. And for that reason, I want to work with you."

"I'm not following."

"Then I shall spell it out. Your company is quite small. Even with the other American company, you are fewer than fifty men. I have hundreds, just in this camp, and more camps all along the river. Given all that's happened, we are poised to hunt you all down like rats and kill every last one of you to rid ourselves of the nuisance that you are. But..."

"But what?" I asked, my heart racing. His sudden change in demeanor, the darkness in his eyes, and the venom in his voice made my skin crawl.

"I might be convinced to let you and your companions live if you can give me MacBride," he said.

The proposition hit me harder than I'd expected. MacBride had perhaps rubbed me the wrong way, and we'd had our disagreements, but I certainly did not want to condemn him to death. The very thought of working against him, against those I'd been traveling with, churned my stomach.

"I can't," I finally managed to say.

Jean-Louis leaned back in his chair again, studying me. "Perhaps not yet. But if you should find yourself surrounded by my men and facing certain death, know that if you can convince that giant Scottish oaf to surrender himself to us, I will let the rest of you live."

Taking a deep breath, I pondered the situation. I did not think for a second that his suggestion would come true, so after a few agonizing moments, I extended my hand. "Fine, Foucher. I'll help you," I said, with no intention of keeping my word.

He shook my hand with a clear sense of satisfaction. As our grip parted, a gnawing doubt settled in the back of my mind. Had he believed my lie? Or would he send me to the firing squad right away?

After our intense conversation, Jean-Louis' eyes lingered on me for a moment, a mixture of evaluation and calculation. He nodded to two of his men, signaling them forward. I braced myself, expecting harsh treatment, but their firm grip wasn't unnecessarily cruel. They led me outside, and the noise of the camp suddenly rushed back to fill my ears. The contrast between the secluded world of Jean-Louis' tent and the bustling life outside was disorienting. Before I could gather my thoughts, they ushered me into another tent. The more humble surroundings and the smell of damp canvas told me all I needed to know. This was where MacBride and the others had been held. Bound and left in dim seclusion, I would have nothing but time and my racing thoughts for company.

Every crease and wrinkle in the fabric of the tent's canvas became intimately familiar over the next two days. The muted noises from the camp outside, shifting footsteps and muffled conversations, painted a vivid picture in my mind. The world outside seemed strangely distant, a stage where I was no longer an actor but merely an observer.

As I counted the days, I reflected on the journey that had led me to this point. From the bustling streets of New York, filled with the cacophony of life, I had ventured into the heart of the wilderness, searching for something I couldn't quite define. Perhaps it was a sense of purpose, a place where I felt I truly belonged, or maybe it was just a desperate attempt to escape the ghosts of my past. My wife, our child—memories that were a weight too heavy to bear.

In the solitude of the tent, every interaction with Blue Fox replayed in my mind. Our first meeting, our challenges, and the burgeoning connection between us.

Her laughter when she'd saved me from the bear, the soft warmth of her touch as we lay side by side, the walls we'd built around ourselves, and the soft kiss she'd given me before running off to scout the enemy camp. And yet our love was still unrequited in some way. The wilderness, the ever-present danger, and the rigors of the road to Oregon Country had created an invisible barrier between us, or at least an excuse for one that created a terrible agony in my heart.

Thoughts of MacBride also crept in—his fiery temper, his vision, his ambition. I'd hated him from the moment I met him. He was a leader who inspired contempt in me unlike any other I had ever met. He had been quick to judge me, too. I felt betrayed by his lack of gratitude after we'd sprung him from his captivity. And yet, given the chance, I had not betrayed him. I wondered then if I was too soft for this land.

In the moments when exhaustion took over and I drifted to sleep, my dreams were haunted by the faces of those I had come to care about. Asher's grief-stricken face when we lost Roarke, Boyd's laughter, Jim's unwavering resolve, and Blue Fox's fiery determination. Their voices mingled in that space between wakefulness and sleep, whispers of hope and echoes of despair.

I remembered Jean-Louis' words, his attempt to sway my allegiance. Was the Hudson's Bay Company really the enemy, or were there deeper, murkier truths to be uncovered? The Frenchman's confidence and assurance had shaken me more than I cared to admit. How many layers of deception and how many hidden agendas were at play in this game of fur, wealth, and power?

Somewhere, somehow, in the bleakness of that tent, I started to consider his offer. If I did find myself in the scenario he described, would I turn over MacBride to save the others? And it dawned on me that perhaps I had not lied to him when I shook his hand. I had believed myself to be a pawn, but Jean-Louis saw something more in me. Potential, perhaps. Would aligning with him free me from this web of backbiting, or would it merely pull me deeper into its tangled depths? And would turning on MacBride turn the others on me, even if I was justified in doing so?

Long nights passed in which my breathing was the only sound; each exhale was a testament to the passing of time. Yet, in this quiet, I began to find clarity. Perhaps I had been seeking a purpose, but it was clear now that I had to forge my own path, regardless of where it led. The ties that bound me, both literal and figurative, could not hold forever.

As another night drew to a close, I felt a renewed sense of determination. Whatever came next, I would face it head-on, guided by my own convictions and the lessons of the past. The wilderness might be unforgiving and the world of the fur trade treacherous, but I would not be broken. The journey had changed me, and though the road ahead was uncertain, I was ready to continue the adventure.

The hours felt endless in the dim confines of the tent. As yet another night settled in and the temperature dropped, just as I started to drift into a restless sleep, a faint scraping noise jolted me awake.

Every muscle in my body tensed. The noise grew closer, becoming more distinct. It was the unmistakable sound of a blade against the canvas. My heart raced.

Suddenly, a slit of moonlight appeared on the tent wall, gradually widening. A silhouette slipped inside, swift and quiet. My initial panic subsided when I recognized her; it was Blue Fox, her face bathed in the soft luminescence.

She quickly approached me, her fingers deftly working at my bindings. "Didn't I tell you to stay out of trouble?" she whispered with a hint of playful rebuke.

Surprise and relief overwhelmed me. "I didn't expect you to come back for me," I admitted in a hushed tone.

Blue Fox raised an eyebrow, a smirk on her lips. "After all the times you've bungled into danger? Honestly, Christian, you're like a puppy chasing its tail. Someone has to keep you out of trouble."

Her jest stung, but there was no denying its truth. "Seems like I'm making a habit of being rescued," I mumbled, flexing my freed wrists.

She shot me a look, her eyes reflecting a deeper concern beneath the teasing. "We need to go. Now." The urgency in her voice snapped me out of my daze.

As we moved toward the opening she had cut, I whispered, "Why did you come back?"

She paused, looking away momentarily. Then, with a deep breath, she said, "Maybe I've grown fond of saving your skin."

My heart skipped a beat. There was more to her words, more than she was letting on, but the moment was interrupted by the ominous sound of footsteps approaching the tent. We shared a worried glance.

Carefully, we pushed through the slit, emerging into the night. The moon was high, bathing the camp in its glow. We crouched low to avoid the pools of light from the scattered torches. Every shadow was a potential threat, every rustle of the wind a potential alarm.

The world seemed to slow as we snuck past tents and supplies, weaving our way toward the camp's perimeter. Just as the dense tree line and our escape beckoned, a shout pierced the air.

"Stop!"

We turned to find ourselves exposed. Dozens of HBC soldiers, their faces illuminated by torchlight, had their guns trained on us. Blue Fox's hand tightened around her knife, and I mentally prepared for a fight.

In the silent standoff, the gravity of our situation sunk in. But amidst the fear, there was a sense of clarity. No matter the outcome, I was grateful not to face it alone.

The unexpected blast of musket fire from behind us momentarily eclipsed the chill air and scent of pine needles. The Hudson's Bay Company soldiers, once so confident in their numbers, scattered in confusion.

"Move!" Blue Fox shouted through the clamor.

As we bolted for the trees, I risked a glance over my shoulder. One HBC man was crumpling to the ground, smoke rising from the place a bullet had just struck. Another cry, and another body fell. The night had transformed into a cacophony of shouts and gunfire.

The dense woods loomed ahead, and familiar faces emerged from the shadows as we crossed the tree line. It wasn't just Blue Fox who had come for me. Jim, ever stoic, gave a nod of recognition, rifle still smoking. Boyd and Asher, their fingers stained with gunpowder, moved to flank us. The two Métis, masters of woodland warfare, guarded our retreat, ensuring none of the HBC men dared pursue us into the dense foliage.

Hulking and powerful Bear stood between MacLane and MacBride. Despite our recent differences, I couldn't help but feel a twinge of gratitude.

A hand clasped my shoulder, and I turned to see Blue Fox. "You think I would let you rot in that camp?" she teased, her usual playful smirk returning.

"Seems I owe all of you," I responded, catching my breath.

MacBride stepped forward, eyes searching mine. "This makes us even." He checked his pocket watch and continued, "We've got a long way to go. Let's move." His voice was gruff, but I detected a hint of relief.

Together, we ventured deeper into the wilderness, each step taking us farther from the clutches of the Hudson's Bay Company. Our reunited expedition traversed the dense forest terrain under the cover of darkness and with an air of focused urgency. The looming trees obscured the moon's soft glow, and the crickets' chorus serenaded our passage. Though fatigue tugged at our limbs, the knowledge that the HBC might still be on our trail kept us moving.

Hours seemed to blend into one another until, just before dawn, the muffled sounds of rushing water hinted at the presence of a creek. As we closed in, the forest thinned out to reveal a camp set up on the banks of a clear mountain stream. Tents, campfires, and the nickering of horses indicated that a sizable group had made this their temporary home.

As we approached, a figure detached from the shadows, weapon raised in a defensive stance. "Who goes there?"

"It's MacBride. We've got Christian."

The figure stepped into the moonlight; it was none other than the stern visage of Manuel Lisa. His piercing eyes scanned the group, lingering on me for a brief moment before nodding in recognition.

"Christian," he said, "it's good to see you free and in one piece."

Lisa's camp was bustling with activity. Men went about their tasks, tending to the canoes and horses, cooking, or sharpening weapons. It was clear that they were preparing for something.

Lisa gestured for us to follow him. "Come, let's talk."

Inside his tent, the warm light of a lantern illuminated the intricate designs on his makeshift table. Lisa was clearly a man of detail and organization, with maps, quills, and other instruments strategically arranged.

As he settled in, his gaze sharpened, the weight of command evident in his eyes. "Now that we've helped you find yours, I need you to do something for me."

"Anything," MacBride said.

"Now I know you didn't come here for a fight. But a fight's what we got on our hands," Lisa said. "I need every friendly body I can find to help me pry out the HBC from this mountain pass, else they kill, maim, or capture every expedition I've got coming through this year. I've got to take them out now, or I'll go bankrupt."

"You want us to fight for you?" I blurted out.

All eyes fell on me. I had even surprised myself. Somewhere, somehow, I had convinced myself now that we had our entire company together, we could leave the HBC behind and move on to Oregon Country, trap, and make that deal with the Northwest Company. It had not occurred to me Lisa would rope us into whatever designs he had. Looking at our men, I could see they itched for a fight. They still wanted vengeance for Roarke. For their sake, I had wanted it, too, but not at risk of us all dying.

"I'm sorry," I said. "Of course we'll help you."

"Great," Lisa said. "Now you and yours have seen the camp up close. What can you tell us that might give us the upper hand?"

Blue Fox, who had done most of the scouting prior to our capture, began. "They've set up their main camp in a natural clearing, protected by a series of ridges and the river. From what I could gather, they've got patrols running day and night along the perimeter. I'd say about two hundred men, maybe more, all well-armed and on high alert."

Lisa traced a location on his map, eyebrows furrowing. "And their defenses? Fortifications?"

MacBride spoke up. "They've dug in. Trenches, wooden barricades and the like. They've also got a few lookout posts on higher ground. If I were to guess, I'd say they're anticipating an attack."

Bear added, "They've got cannons too. Saw them haul in a couple while I was dragged around their camp. They're gearing up for a siege."

Lisa's face darkened at this revelation. "Here in the mountains?" He sighed deeply. "This changes things."

Blue Fox crossed her arms and added, "They might be expecting a fight, but the land is still on our side. These mountains have countless pathways and hidden trails known only to the natives. We could use them to our advantage."

The veteran trapper considered this, his eyes darting between each of us. "That camp is sitting dead center where all the trails from the mountain pass converge at the river. The question is, how do we get around it?"

MacBride crossed his arms and played with his beard, a smirk playing at the corners of his mouth as he joked, "Outnumbered five to one... I think we could take them."

Everyone laughed, except Blue Fox. It didn't seem like she'd even heard him. Instead, she trailed her finger down Lisa's map and said, "There are game trails all up and down these hillsides. If we split into smaller groups, we could sneak by them."

Lisa looked at me, his gaze piercing. "Christian, your encounter with Jean-Louis—did he give anything away? Any weak points?"

His question gave me pause. "How did you know I spoke with Jean-Louis?"

His expression flickered with unmistakable amusement. "Word travels fast in the mountains."

I shifted uncomfortably, sensing there was more to his knowledge than he was letting on. "You have a spy in the HBC camp?"

Lisa chuckled softly, leaning back. "Of course. I always keep an ear to the ground, especially when it concerns the likes of Jean-Louis and the HBC. It's just good business."

MacBride smirked. "You thought Manuel would just sit here and not know what's happening in his own backyard?"

"So what did he say, kid?" Lisa pressed. "Anything we can use?"

"Just that he plans to kill us all," I said solemnly.

Lisa waved away the topic with a casual hand. "The important thing is that you're here now. Jean-Louis might be clever, but he's not the only one playing this game."

I stole a quick glance at MacBride, observing him with fresh eyes. The firelight illuminated his face, casting a dance of shadow and light that seemed to veil more than it revealed. I took a deep breath and considered asking him if Jean-Louis had spoken the truth about his mission to assassinate the man, but it was not the right time. As my thoughts raced from here to there, one idea did sneak between my ears that I thought was worth sharing.

"Supply lines," I said.

"What?" Lisa asked.

"It's a historical principle that strongholds need supply lines, and this camp is no different. They can't sustain two hundred men without a supply line. We don't have to send everyone, but if we send a small group through to disrupt their supply line, they will have to reconsider their position. That could give the rest of us the opening to pass through with our canoes and supplies."

"Smart," Lisa said. "So who's going?"

I looked to MacBride for the final say.

"We'll go," MacBride said.

"I'll send two other small teams behind you in support," Lisa said. "Give them Hell, MacBride."

# CHAPTER 10
## INTO THE FRYING PAN

The predawn mist clung to the mountain slopes, wreathing the trees and blanketing the ground in a soft, ethereal haze. I took a moment to breathe in the cool, crisp air, relishing the bite of it in my lungs. The world was painted in shades of silver and blue, the darkness of night just beginning to give way to the soft glow of morning.

Our journey led us down the mountain's gradual decline, toward the source of the Snake River. As I looked out over the expanse below, I could see the glimmering ribbon of the river winding its way through the valley, a liquid road etched upon the land. The sun began its ascent, casting a golden light over the vastness, turning the mist into a shimmering sea of cloud.

Setting the HBC's stronghold atop the mountain had been a strategic move; it allowed them to block American fur companies, particularly those under Astor and Lisa, from using the pass to cross over the Rockies. The position gave them control over crucial trade routes and allowed them to dominate the region with little opposition. But I had devised a strategy to hit them where it would hurt them most—their supply line. They might have fortified their high perch, but they couldn't sustain themselves without regular shipments of provisions. We aimed to disrupt these, sowing chaos and weakening their advantage so the rest of the trappers could pass through with their canoes and supplies.

As we descended, the forest around us transformed. Tall pines gave way to aspens and alders, their leaves rustling gently in the morning breeze. Small animals, startled by our passing, darted from our path: squirrels, rabbits, and the occasional deer. Sparrows flitted overhead, their songs a harmonious melody echoing through the woods.

MacBride led the group, scanning the terrain with a hawk's precision. Behind him, the two Métis and MacLane kept pace, the horses they led bearing the supplies and provisions necessary for our task. Blue Fox walked beside me, her steps graceful and silent. We exchanged glances now and then, our bond a silent comfort amid the unknown dangers ahead.

The ground grew rockier, with jutting outcrops and an occasional clearing that offered sweeping views of the landscape below. From this height, I spotted smoke rising in the distance, likely from the HBC's supply camps. It served as both a beacon and a reminder of the mission at hand.

Asher, a few paces behind, recounted tales of past skirmishes, his voice a soft rumble that matched the rhythm of our footsteps. His stories were filled with bravery and betrayal, of cunning tactics and narrow escapes. The company listened intently, drawing strength and wisdom from his words.

By midday, we reached a vantage point overlooking a narrow pass. This was the main artery for the Hudson's Bay Company's supply route. Any provisions heading to the mountain stronghold would inevitably have to pass through here. We took a moment to survey the land, strategizing our next move. Bear, ever the tactician, pointed out key positions to hold, choke points to barricade, and areas for potential ambush.

"We have the advantage of surprise," MacBride said, "and this terrain will work in our favor."

Jim, leaning on his musket, added, "They won't know what hit them."

The hours that followed were a whirl of activity. We set up defensive positions and camouflaged our presence as best we could so we could rest for the night before moving on the next day. The anticipation formed a tense undercurrent that permeated the air. The HBC men could be anywhere. Every rustle of leaves, every distant bird call felt like a harbinger of the conflict to come.

I found a quiet spot by the river's edge as evening approached. The water flowed with gentle persistence, nature's enduring cycle in a journey from mountain to sea. I pondered our place in the vast tapestry, the threads of destiny that had brought us to this precipice.

With its surging waters and treacherous rapids, the Snake River stood as both a lifeline and a barrier. We were about to strike at the very heart of the Hudson's Bay Company's operations in this region. The consequences of our actions would ripple outward, affecting the balance of power and the future of the fur trade in Oregon Country.

Nightfall brought silence upon the mountainside. The world seemed to hold its breath, awaiting the clash of wills that would soon unfold. And as the first stars appeared in the darkening sky, we readied ourselves for the battle ahead.

In the cool embrace of the night, I found solace by the river's edge, its gentle whispers a comforting melody amidst the tension of our impending mission. Lost in thought, I barely noticed the deft footsteps approaching until a familiar voice broke through the silence.

"You have a penchant for quiet places," Blue Fox said, her voice tinged with amusement.

The pale moonlight cast her features in a soft glow. Her raven-black hair cascaded in loose waves over her shoulders, and her eyes, those deep pools of mystery, seemed to hold a universe of stories.

"You caught me," I replied, smiling slightly. "Or maybe I'm just drawn to the beauty of nature."

She stepped closer, the distance between us narrowing. "Is that the only beauty you're drawn to?" she teased, her voice a velvety murmur.

Caught off guard, I hesitated for a moment before responding. "Well, nature has its many wonders."

A playful smirk formed on her lips. "Indeed, it does."

We stood there for a moment, neither of us breaking the silence. The air between us crackled with a magnetic pull that had grown stronger over time.

"Thank you for coming for me," I finally said, my voice softening.

A small smile tugged at the corner of her lips. "You have a strange way of showing gratitude, always putting yourself in harm's way."

"It seems to be a recurring theme." I chuckled. "But you, Blue Fox... you always seem to be watching out for me."

She moved even closer, our faces mere inches apart. "Maybe I see something in you worth saving," she said.

Our eyes locked, and for a fleeting moment, the world faded away. The weight of our shared experiences, the challenges faced, and the battles fought all culminated in this singular moment.

"I don't know what the future holds..." I paused to search for the right words. "...but I'm glad you're by my side."

She took a deep breath, her chest rising and falling softly. "And I'm glad you're by mine," she replied, her voice filled with a warmth that spread through me like a comforting embrace.

I leaned in to kiss her, but she pulled away. For the second time, she had denied me. I felt like I was losing my mind. What cues had I missed? Had we not bridged the emotional chasm that had kept us apart?

"I'm sorry," I said.

"It's not you," she explained. "I have a hard time trusting."

"But you kissed me," I said. "Do you regret it?"

"No," she insisted. "It's just that... You've said it yourself—when all this is over, you're on the first boat back to New York. Where does that leave me?"

"I don't know."

And I didn't know. I had given no thought to where a romance between us might lead. With all the danger to our lives swirling around us, it was a miracle to make it to a safe place to sleep at night. She had thought much farther ahead.

"Could you come with me?" I asked.

"I could not survive in a place like New York." She shook her head.

"I don't know what to say, except that I have fallen in love with you, here and now," I said.

"There's no happy ending for me in this," she said. "Except a broken heart."

"You sound like you speak from experience."

Blue Fox glanced at me and then her feet.

"What would it take for you to trust me? To let me in?" I asked.

"If you promised to stay here, with me," she suggested.

I scoffed. "I can't stay here. It's... it's—"

"Fine," she sighed. "It's fine. And that's why."

Saddened, I lumbered off, returned to camp, and set up my own bedding away from Blue Fox's nest. She returned shortly after me, her footsteps as quiet as a cat. I faked snores so she would think I was asleep. She hovered over me a moment, then returned to her spot underneath her hide, alone.

The early morning sun cast long shadows over the terrain as our company mobilized, with the promise of another day's journey ahead. The soft morning light filtered through the dense canopy, creating a dappled pattern on the ground. Everything seemed normal—except for the tension between us.

She kept her distance, avoiding eye contact and speaking to everyone but me. It was evident to anyone who cared to notice, and Boyd, always observant, was the first to approach me about it.

"Something happen between you two?" he asked, casting a sidelong glance toward Blue Fox, who was engrossed in conversation with Asher. Boyd's bushy brows knitted in concern, his voice low so as to remain unheard by the others.

I tried to shrug nonchalantly, but our last conversation weighed on me. "It's nothing," I muttered, though my tone lacked conviction.

Boyd wasn't easily fooled. He raised an eyebrow, giving me a look that said he didn't quite believe me. "You've been different since you got back from that HBC camp. And now this with Blue Fox... What's going on?"

I hesitated, not sure how much to reveal. "Just a difference of opinion," I responded, my gaze drifting toward her.

He followed my gaze. "You know," he began, taking a thoughtful pause, "this life, out here in the wilderness, navigating the politics of the fur trade—it's hard. But relationships? They can be even harder. Whatever happened between you two, figure it out. We need to be united if we're going to succeed."

His words resonated. I nodded, appreciating the wisdom behind them. "I'll try," I promised. "But it's not all in my hands."

Boyd clapped me on the back, his gesture comforting. "That's all anyone can ask for." He returned to his post, leaving me with my thoughts.

The forest had been eerily quiet for the last stretch of our journey. Perhaps that quietness failed to warn us of the impending ambush, or it was complacency from having traveled so far without incident. Either way, we were caught unawares.

Suddenly, the crackling of musket fire broke the serenity of the morning, and bullets whizzed through the air, thudding into tree trunks and the ground around us. Panic set in immediately. Men yelled, horses neighed in fear, and chaos seemed to erupt from all corners.

"To cover!" MacBride's voice thundered over the cacophony. He was already guiding some of the group behind a large boulder, using it as a shield against the onslaught.

MacBride, not one to be outdone, fired a shot back as he organized a defensive line and prepared us to return fire. His sharp eyes darted around, trying to gauge the number of attackers and their positions.

I found myself next to Blue Fox, who had instinctively taken cover behind a fallen tree. Her eyes were alight with focus, scanning the tree line for signs of movement. "How many?" I shouted.

"I can't tell!" she called back. "We need to hold them off and find an exit before they cut us all down!"

As if to emphasize her point, an arrow zipped past, narrowly missing my ear. I took a deep breath, steadying my nerves. This was far from my first firefight, but each time felt like a stark reminder of the constant danger of the frontier. That was when it struck me: an arrow had whizzed past me, not a bullet.

MacLane and Bear, always ready for a fight, began to return fire, the sharp reports of their muskets echoing throughout the forest. The two Métis, agile and quick, began to creep around our left flank, trying to get a better angle on our unseen attackers.

Minutes felt like hours. The scent of gunpowder filled the air, and the sounds of battle reverberated in my ears. Just when things seemed bleakest, there was a rallying cry from the opposite side of the ambush point. Our attackers seemed to be under attack themselves. One of Lisa's teams must have caught up to us amidst the gunfire.

Using this distraction to our advantage, MacBride shouted, "Move! Push forward and out of this death trap!"

With MacBride leading the charge, we surged forward, weapons blazing. Our attackers, now caught between two fronts, faltered. Their once-coordinated assault crumbled under our combined might.

Soon, our attackers' musket fire and arrows lessened, then stopped altogether. The forest grew silent once more, save for the panting breaths of our company and the occasional shout as we regrouped.

"We need to keep moving," MacBride said, his face grimy from the smoke and dirt. "They might attack again."

Nods of agreement rippled through the group, and with that, we continued on, our pace even more urgent than before, the weight of the ambush serving as a stark reminder that the fur trade was a dangerous game and one never truly knew who their enemies were.

Amidst the regrouping and rapid packing of gear, Blue Fox picked up an arrow from the ground, her eyes narrowing as she examined its fletching and the design painted onto the shaft. It was clear she recognized it.

"This is a Snake tribe arrow." Her voice was low, tinged with a mix of surprise and concern.

"Are you sure?" I asked, approaching her side.

She held it up for me to see. The intricacies of the design, its unique patterns in vibrant hues, made it evident that it was unlike any arrow made by the tribes I was familiar with. I trusted Blue Fox's judgment; she had a vast knowledge of the tribes and their customs.

"Absolutely," she replied tersely. "But why would they attack us? My interactions with them have always been peaceful. This doesn't make sense."

"Could the HBC have struck some deal with them?" Boyd pondered aloud.

With MacLane at his side, MacBride joined our small gathering, both men looking at the arrow with furrowed brows.

"That's the game the HBC plays," MacBride commented. "They broker alliances and twist arms when necessary. The Snake tribe might have been offered something they couldn't refuse."

MacLane nodded, deep in thought. "Or threatened with something they couldn't defend against."

Blue Fox looked visibly troubled. "If the HBC has swayed the Snake tribe to their side, our path just became infinitely more treacherous."

MacBride clapped a reassuring hand on her shoulder. "We'll face them together. Whatever alliances the HBC has made, they're not insurmountable."

But even as he said this, the situation hung heavily on us. Knowing the identity of our ambushers was one thing; understanding their motivations and anticipating their next move was another challenge altogether. One thing was for sure—the Hudson's Bay Company's influence in this land was proving more pervasive and formidable than we had ever imagined.

Now that we were ahead of our enemy and heading toward their supply camps, they gave chase. Bullets zipped through the air, and the whoosh of arrows became a constant, threatening presence. The open terrain offered little protection, and we scrambled for cover behind trees, boulders, and whatever scant shield the landscape provided.

Amidst the pandemonium, MacBride's booming voice cut through the noise. "Christian! You need to push forward! Take our company and head downstream to the supply camps!"

My eyes darted between the ensuing battle and MacBride, the weight of the decision clear on his face.

"And what of you?" I asked.

He gave me a wry smile. "We'll be right behind you!"

"No," I said, my voice choked with urgency. "We all go together!"

He locked eyes with me, his gaze unwavering. "Christian, this is the best chance we have. It's a strategic move. With the HBC focused on us, you can strike where it hurts them the most."

Clutching his rifle tightly, Boyd said, "Kid's right. We can't split up—it's suicide."

MacBride looked at us both, then nodded, a grim determination settling over his features. "All right. We'll head downstream. But MacLane, Jim, Bear, and I will take the rear to cover our escape."

MacBride gave a mock salute, the action contrasting with the seriousness of the situation. "Just make sure you take us down the right path."

MacBride, MacLane, Bear, and Jim formed a protective perimeter at our rear, aiming at the advancing HBC forces and Snake tribe warriors. Blue Fox charged forward, her movements effortless and swift and her eyes peeled for danger ahead. She and I exchanged a lingering look, as if she might say something about the previous night.

"Keep your eyes on where we're headed," she said instead.

Our group began a hasty retreat downstream, each step a testament to the trust we placed in Blue Fox and her ability to navigate the wild. The sounds of gunfire echoed behind us.

The rush of the Snake River was a constant backdrop to our swift march downstream. Every so often, the rustling leaves or a distant bird's cry put us on high alert, fingers instinctively going to triggers or arrow nocks. We all knew that the HBC men were still close, but we had not expected them to give chase so soon.

And then, without warning, it began again. The sharp crack of muskets shattered the forest's relative calm. We ducked, scrambled, and took cover behind trees and rocks. More gunshots followed, and it felt like the forest was closing in on us.

"It's a trap!" yelled Asher. "Christ, there's dozens of them!"

Amidst the chaos, a voice boomed out. "MacBride! I call for a parlay!"

The voice was unmistakable.

MacBride, taken aback, peeked out from behind his cover. "Jean-Louis?!"

From the other side, Jean-Louis Foucher, the enigmatic Hudson's Bay Company captain, stepped forward, his hands raised. "It's me, MacBride. Let's talk."

The two men approached each other with a wary tension. The rest of us held our breaths, unsure what to expect. I felt a pang in my chest, remembering our last encounter. And yet, I felt relieved that Jean-Louis' prediction had not come true.

The two spoke in hushed yet intense tones. I strained to hear, but their words were lost in the distance. All I could make out was their body language—a mix of animosity and reluctant respect.

Finally, MacBride returned, his face a mask of uncertainty.

"What did he want?" Boyd questioned, his voice barely above a whisper.

MacBride hesitated. "Jean-Louis is offering terms of surrender. He claims he has us surrounded and is willing to let you all go if I surrender myself."

Bear growled. "That's outrageous!"

"It's not as simple as that," MacBride retorted. "He's got men crawling up and down this countryside. If we fight, we'll most certainly die."

Jim's outburst abruptly cut short the murmurs that swept our ranks. "He's right there! We can kill him now if we're smart about it!" His voice quivered with angry disbelief.

All eyes turned to him. A burning intensity had replaced the usual playful glint in his eyes. "The entire reason we're here, the entire mission, was to kill Jean-Louis. After what he did to my brother, I won't rest until I have my vengeance."

His confession echoed loudly in my ears, a stark admission of our objective. Assassination. The realization gnawed at me. They were here to kill Jean-Louis, to destabilize the region, and I was to make a deal with the North West Company from that turmoil. They kept calling Jean-Louis shrewd and ruthless, but we were no different.

With every step taken in this wilderness, I had tried to decipher right from wrong and find a path of honor amidst the shadows. But the lines had blurred. Who were the heroes? Who were the villains? Jean-Louis was most certainly not in the right. But neither were we. Jean-Louis watched on as we deliberated, confidence written on his face.

Boyd chimed in, his tone thoughtful, "MacBride, Jean-Louis is a shrewd man. How can we be certain he won't just kill us all anyway?"

MacBride hesitated. "We can't. But if there's even a sliver of truth in what he's saying, I have to consider it."

I could see the internal struggle in Jim's eyes. The thirst for vengeance was strong, but neither did he want to see his comrades slaughtered.

"It's not just about my brother," Jim spat bitterly. "It's about every life Jean-Louis has taken, every family he's torn apart. How many others have suffered because of him? How many more will suffer if we let him go now?"

I felt torn. A part of me sympathized with Jim's pain, while another part recognized the futility of our resistance.

"We should try to kill Jean-Louis," Blue Fox said, giving every man in our group pause. "Jim, you spoke of families torn apart—he tore mine apart and ruined my mother's life. I've been searching for him all my life, to tell him, to show him, to make him understand."

"Make him understand what?" I asked.

"He raped my mother and abandoned the child that came of it—and that vengeance will find him," she said through gritted teeth.

Her admission stopped me in my tracks. "Blue Fox, I had no idea."

Jim laughed bitterly. "Then it's vengeance for two of us!"

"All right," MacBride finally said. "Jim, Blue Fox, we try it your way. We make a go of it and aim straight for Jean-Louis."

"That's what I wanted to hear," Jim said.

"It's suicide!" I scoffed.

"We're with you, MacBride," MacLane said. "We're with you to the last."

"We're all going to get killed!"

"We fight to the last," Bear said.

There I was, sitting in the middle of a group decision to commit suicide. MacBride was about to order us to charge into the HBC's line of fire with no plan and a minuscule chance of success. Our mission was sure to fail, and I had no desire to die that day. I could still make a deal with the North West Company if I could just make it to their fort on the Columbia River.

At that moment, when I felt I had exhausted all other options, I remembered what Jean-Louis had said. How had he known that he would put us in this position? Had we played so blindly into his hands?

Acting on instinct more than reason, my hand darted to the hilt of my knife. In a swift movement, I had it pressed against MacBride's throat, securing him as my captive. Gasps of shock resonated through the air, and eyes wide with disbelief stared back at me.

"Jean-Louis!" My voice echoed amidst the trees, the French words demanding attention. "I have the man you wanted."

The faces of my comrades mirrored their betrayal. Boyd looked shattered, his trust visibly broken, while Blue Fox's icy glare pierced through me. Jim's fury held me, the raw intensity of his anger undeniable.

"Christian! After all we've been through!" His voice was filled with incredulity.

"It's not just about what we've been through, Jim. It's about what's right, about finding a way to end this without more bloodshed," I tried to explain.

As I retreated towards the HBC men, MacBride in tow, Jean-Louis emerged, his calculating gaze appraising me with newfound respect. The path ahead was uncertain, but I believed I had made the right choice at that moment.

Blue Fox's eyes tracked me, the warmth they'd once held replaced by a cold fury, burning with an intensity I hadn't seen before. It wasn't just anger; it was a feeling of deep betrayal, a raw hurt that seemed to emanate from her very core. The contours of her face, usually relaxed and carefree, tightened into a mask of disbelief.

She had trusted me, confided in me, and now it must seem like I was undoing all the progress we had made together. Our shared moments, our quiet conversations by the fireside—everything was now tainted by my actions. Every step I took backward, a knife pressed against MacBride's throat, was a step away from the bond we had formed. It was as if an impenetrable barrier had suddenly risen between us.

At that moment, amidst the chaos of the standoff, her reaction cut deeper than any knife ever could. An immense weight of regret pressed upon my chest, and it took everything in me to keep my composure. As I moved farther away, her image imprinted itself in my mind, a stark reminder of the personal cost of my decision. Even though I knew I was saving her life, she felt betrayed.

Jean-Louis' men, quick and efficient, closed in on MacBride, binding his wrists with a rough rope. MacBride glared defiantly at Jean-Louis, then at me, but said nothing. To my dismay, the HBC men tied my wrists up, too. The air grew thick with tension, punctuated by the distant sounds of the river flowing past us.

Jean-Louis met my gaze briefly before saying, "You and your friend will face justice at Fort George under the Hudson's Bay Company laws. The rest of your company may leave. Our quarrel is not with them."

"You said I could go, too," I growled.

He grinned and turned his back to march back up the hill. While anger surged through my body, I also felt a profound relief I had saved the others, tempered with guilt and uncertainty. But that fleeting moment of calm was abruptly shattered.

Jim, driven by vengeance and an unwavering sense of duty, sprang into action. From the edge of my vision, I saw him dive toward his dropped rifle, retrieve it, and pivot to aim at Jean-Louis in one fluid motion. The world seemed to slow as his finger squeezed the trigger.

The shot rang out, echoing in the wilderness. But it went wide, missing Jean-Louis by a hair's breadth.

In a heartbeat, a barrage of musket fire responded. Multiple shots from Jean-Louis' men converged on Jim's position. He didn't stand a chance. His body crumpled to the ground, the life swiftly draining from him.

The sharp, acrid smell of gunpowder hung in the air, but all I could focus on was the lifeless form of Jim Schmidt. The world around me seemed to blur. In that split second, I'd betrayed MacBride and indirectly caused the death of a man who, despite his mission, had been a steadfast ally.

I felt a cold numbness start at my fingertips, slowly creeping its way up my arms and into my core. They would blame me. Even though they'd been ready to die for MacBride, Jim might still be alive if I hadn't taken that leap of treachery.

"Damn you, Christian!" Boyd's voice sliced through the heavy silence. He was kneeling beside Jim, rage and sorrow painting his face. "This is on you!"

The murmurs of agreement from the others felt like knives cutting deep into my very being. The faces around me—Boyd, Asher, Blue Fox, Bear, even the two Métis—were masks of betrayal, hurt, and anger.

I wanted to speak, explain, apologize, but the words seemed trapped in my throat. Every fiber of my being screamed at the injustice of it all, at the realization that my actions had set off this tragic sequence of events. A deep chasm of guilt yawned wide within me, threatening to swallow me whole.

The Hudson's Bay Company men were organizing themselves, preparing to leave with their prisoners. Jean-Louis shot me a glance that wasn't unkind, but lacked warmth. It was clear that while I might have momentarily aligned with him, I was no ally.

Bitter reality settled in as the HBC party led us away. Not only had I changed the course of events irrevocably, but I had also shifted the dynamics of trust within our group. Jim was gone, and with his departure, our unity and purpose had shattered.

# CHAPTER 11
## JEAN-LOUIS

The dense woods closed in around us, the trees' knotted branches creating a veil of shadows obscuring the sunlight. The rhythmic crunch of leaves underfoot and the distant cries of birds provided a poignant backdrop to the mounting tension between MacBride and me as we marched with the HBC party.

We walked in silence for a while, each absorbed in our own thoughts. The creak of leather and the murmur of voices floated back from the HBC men leading the way. Finally MacBride turned to me, his hands bound and his gaze piercing.

"Why, Christian?" he demanded, his voice taut with a mixture of anger and bewilderment. "Is this revenge for how I treated you? I thought I'd made amends."

His words angered me, and I struggled to formulate a response. "You were going to get us all killed." My voice was a mere whisper amid the rustle of the forest.

He frowned, his lips pursing in determination. "I never won you over, did I?"

I remained silent. MacBride kept his eyes on me, studying me, his brow furrowed low over his eyes. Some of the HBC men looked over their shoulders to check that I still had ropes around my wrists, chuckling at us while taking long puffs from their pipes. Their laughter unnerved me. It spoke of a lack of respect, and after what I'd done, the stakes at play, it stoked a fire inside of me. I had never considered myself an angry man, but I boiled with rage beneath my calm exterior in that moment.

"You didn't think they'd rope you, too, did you?" MacBride asked, breaking the cycle of thoughts that had sent my heart aflutter.

"No."

We walked in silence for another moment before he said, "You know, I haven't taken much time to get to know you on this trek."

"What would you like to know?"

"How you learned French, for example?" he asked.

"Oh, well, my father is French, and my mother American. They smuggled me out of the Vendée when I was a kid, back to my mother's family in New York."

"The War of the Vendée? You were there?" MacBride asked, mouth agape. "You're too young."

"I was seven years old." I paused, summoning the strength to delve into memories long buried. "I grew up in New York because we were escaping. Escaping a past stained with blood and betrayal. The War in Vendée... It wasn't just a war; it was a slaughter." My words seemed to hang in the air between us, heavy with the pain of remembrance.

MacBride's brows knitted in concentration as he tried to piece together the puzzle of my life. "Go on," he urged more gently.

I took a deep breath, and my shoulders slumped forward. "The French revolutionary government executed my grandfather. They paraded him before the townsfolk, denounced him as a traitor. They killed him right in front of me."

MacBride's eyes, already holding a depth of shared pain, widened in shock. "Christian, I had no idea."

I gave a mirthless chuckle. "It wasn't just the loss of my grandfather. It was why they killed him. He believed he was doing the right thing, saving lives. He switched sides, thinking they would spare our countrymen if he allied with the revolutionaries. But they betrayed his trust and slaughtered everyone anyway. Friends, neighbors, and people I grew up with all died because they chose the wrong side. And my grandfather's misguided attempt to save them only brought them swifter to the executioner's blade."

MacBride launched into his own childhood tale. "My family was part of the MacBride clan in southern Scotland. My father and grandfather joined a rebellion against the English that got them killed as well. So I understand how you feel, in a way. I was orphaned, as was MacLane, and no sooner than we turned sixteen the English enlisted us in the army. It was terrible fighting against the French. The scars of war never truly heal."

For the first time, I felt a connection to the Scottish oaf. I had not imagined we could have had similar childhoods, or at least with similar themes. Perhaps that was why we'd butted heads when we first met. We were more alike than we wanted to acknowledge, and we saw those things that we did not like about ourselves in each other.

"I haven't managed well," MacBride muttered. "This expedition has gone sideways from the start, and I..."

His eyes softened. The towering, proud, and boisterous man I had met in St. Louis melted away before me. All that remained was the lumbering carcass of a defeated man.

"...I have my own demons to wrestle with," he finished.

I took a moment, breathing in deeply. When I spoke again, my voice was softer, the abrasive edges worn down by the depth of my sincerity. "MacBride," I began, staring straight into his eyes, "we've had our differences, that's undeniable. There's been anger and resentment between us. But right now, our quarrels and personal animosities have to be put aside."

I watched him warily, taking note of the desperation in his gaze.

"I agree," he said.

"Listen," I continued, "I don't care if, once this is all over, we go our separate ways and never speak again. But right now, at this moment, we need to work together. Finish what we started. We were tasked with a mission, and we both know what's at stake."

"If we survive this, I don't think we'll go our separate ways."

His words struck a chord deep within me. He had expressed his first vote of trust in me, and I did not let it pass unnoticed. The shift between us gave me a glint of hope.

MacBride tugged at my rope, his voice nearly a whisper. "Mark my words; before we reach the fort, Jean-Louis will ask you for a demonstration of your loyalty. He'll hand you a gun and tell you to kill me in exchange for your release."

My steps paused. "And how do you know that's what he's going to do?"

"Because that's what he did to me," he growled.

I stared at MacBride for what felt like an eternity, the forest around us a silent witness to our confrontation. As the seriousness of what he'd said sank in, I felt the sharp edges of my anger and resentment begin to dull.

"What do you mean by that?" I asked.

MacBride let out a heavy sigh. "I used to work for Jean-Louis. He played the same games then as he does now. He's a madman and gets a thrill out of watching people kill each other."

The column came to a sudden halt, the murmur of conversations and the shuffle of feet quieting down. Standing slightly elevated on a ridge, Jean-Louis turned back and scanned the men. His eyes, piercing and deliberate, locked onto MacBride and me.

"Christian! MacBride! To the front!" His voice echoed through the trees, leaving an air of anticipation in its wake.

MacBride and I exchanged a brief look of uncertainty, then started weaving our way through the HBC men. As we climbed, the forest floor grew rockier, the incline steeper, and the canopy above thinned out.

As we reached the ridge, the view opened before us. Jean-Louis stood with a few of his closest men, looking out over the vast expanse of territory. Below, a meandering river gleamed in the sunlight, its banks dense with trees and vegetation. But what took our breath away was the sight on the opposite bank. A sprawling encampment, with tents and fires scattered around, and the familiar emblem of the Hudson's Bay Company flying high above. Seeing their camp from this new vantage point gave us the clearest view of just how large a force they had brought into the mountains.

Jean-Louis remained silent for a moment, allowing the scene to sink in, then turned his gaze upon us. "You know, Christian," he began, his voice dripping with a measured calm, "I have ears everywhere."

I felt a jolt of panic, and MacBride's already tense face tightened further. Our conversations had been full of doubts, plans, and secrets. How much had Jean-Louis learned?

Jean-Louis continued, "I understand your history, your reasons. But trust is a rare commodity in this world. MacBride here—" He tilted his head toward the Scot. "— his loyalties are clear. But you... you seem to be at a crossroads."

I swallowed hard, my heart pounding. "What do you want?" I asked cautiously.

"A demonstration," Jean-Louis said. "A show of loyalty. You've turned in your own man, and that's a start. But if I am going to trust that you will not take up his cause if I set you free, I need you to prove that you're willing to do what it takes to demonstrate your loyalty to me."

MacBride's eyes darted toward me, a mix of anger and desperation. He raised his eyebrows as if to say *I told you so* without voicing it.

Jean-Louis, seeing my hesitation, stepped closer, his voice a whisper. "This is the moment, Christian. Where do your loyalties lie?"

In the distance, the sprawling camp stood as a reminder of the greater game at play. But at that moment, on the ridge, it felt as if everything had narrowed down to just Jean-Louis, MacBride, and me.

Jean-Louis reached into his coat, producing a gleaming, well-maintained flintlock pistol. He extended it towards me, the dark wood and polished metal a stark contrast against the paleness of my skin.

"Kill him," he murmured, a challenging edge to his voice.

One of his men unbound my hands. My fingers brushed against the pistol's cold grip. It felt like a chain pulling me into the darkest depths of my ability to tell wrong from right. My gaze shifted from the weapon to MacBride. His eyes, once filled with anger and spite, now bore a hint of fear, yet there was a silent plea there, an unspoken understanding.

"Christian," MacBride said, his voice strained, barely above a whisper, "do it. Save yourself. I forgive you."

The decision in front of me consumed every fragment of my being. A sickening realization dawned on me, tying my stomach in knots. The scene eerily mirrored the horrors of my past—the horrors I had tried so desperately to escape. Jean-Louis was no better than those revolutionaries, trying to force my hand, just as they had forced my grandfather's against our own people in Vendée.

Jean-Louis grew impatient. "Kill him!"

The wind howled across the ridge, carrying with it the weight of my past and the looming specter of my future.

And with the vast expanse of the encampment before me, the sun glaring down, and the world seemingly waiting with bated breath, I made my choice.

I turned the pistol and discharged it at the HBC man aiming a rifle at me. The air, already thick with tension, filled with the acrid smell of gunpowder. Jean-Louis' face twisted in rage, and the ringing in my ears almost drowned out his shout: "Seize him!"

But in that split second, as HBC soldiers lunged toward us, I locked eyes with MacBride. There was no need for words. Everything we had been through, every disagreement, every clash—it all condensed into a singular understanding between us.

MacBride, his hands still bound, launched himself with unexpected force at Jean-Louis. Using the element of surprise, he managed to wrestle a blade from the man's belt. Meanwhile, I tackled another HBC man, using his body as a shield from the others. I sent two soldiers sprawling with a determined shove, creating a temporary path toward the ridge's edge.

Seeing my intent, MacBride clutched at Jean-Louis' suspenders and joined me, and together we lurched for the slope. Just as we reached the edge, MacBride and I thrust forward in tandem, our combined force sending all three of us tumbling down the side of the ridge.

The last snows of winter proved an unexpected ally. We slid, bumped, and rolled down the icy slope, propelled by gravity and adrenaline. The world became a blur of cold, wet snow, and sharp rocks. We did our best to control our descent, trying to avoid the worst of the obstacles.

With a final splash, we found ourselves submerged in the cold waters of the river that ran at the base of the ridge. Gasping from the shock, I kicked to the surface, grasping at the current-battered reeds to pull myself to the shore.

Coughing and spluttering, I collapsed on the riverbank. I was battered and bruised but alive. MacBride wrestled in the water, still clinging to Jean-Louis, the river roaring around them. The men on the ridge took aim, but the next man in command shouted at them to stand down out of fear of hitting Jean-Louis. Just when I thought MacBride had the upper hand, Jean-Louis turned him around and smashed his head into the rocky riverside. I dashed to his aid, and seeing me, Jean-Louis released him and dove into the river.

The frigid water shocked my lungs as I plunged into the river after MacBride. The roaring current immediately swallowed us, its grip iron-tight, pulling and pushing from all directions. My earlier resolve wavered, the freezing temperature seeping into my bones, threatening to cripple me.

The river was unrelenting. Tall, shadowy trees blurred as we were carried downstream, their branches reaching out like skeletal fingers. My heart raced at the jagged rocks lurking beneath the surface, just waiting to catch an unsuspecting foot or hand.

Beside me, MacBride battled the water with fierce determination, using his legs to steer and propel himself forward. I locked eyes with him briefly, sharing an unspoken pact: we would get through this together. We would catch Jean-Louis.

I tried to take a breath but was met with a mouthful of water, its icy bitterness choking me. Panic threatened to overwhelm me, but a voice in my head reminded me of all I had survived to that point and the choices that had led me to this moment. This wasn't my end.

We struggled to maintain a sense of direction, and the frothy chaos made it near impossible. The sun's glimmer, our only guide, was quickly fading beyond the treetops. My body screamed in protest, every muscle burning from the effort of keeping myself above water.

Up ahead, the river seemed to narrow, the sound of rushing water growing louder and more ominous.

"Waterfall!" MacBride's shout barely reached my ears over the deafening roar.

Desperation fueled my limbs as I tried to swim to the riverbank. But the current was a monstrous force, dragging us closer and closer to the precipice. My heart hammered in my chest, images of my life flashing before my eyes.

And then, with one final heave, MacBride and I managed to grab on to a jutting rock, using the last of our strength to pull ourselves up and away from the river's deadly embrace. The ground was cold and hard beneath me, but I hardly noticed, gasping for breath, my lungs on fire.

"Jean-Louis!" I called out, pulling MacBride to his feet.

He was making a run for it not twenty yards away from us. MacBride and I looked at each other, both drenched and shivering but alive. The deafening rush of the waterfall echoed, reminding us of our narrow escape.

"After him!" he panted, a trace of grudging respect in his eyes.

I nodded, realizing that our alliance, born out of necessity, had solidified in the heat of the moment. We might not be friends, but we were survivors. And in this wilderness, that bond meant everything.

We gave chase. MacBride sprinted off to the left, and I to the right. Jean-Louis zigzagged, glancing over his shoulder, and leaped over rocks and downed trees with surprising agility. He had fresher legs than we, but he was fatter and slower. MacBride and I were starved wolves on our fifth wind, our prey so close we could taste his desperation in the air. And then it dawned on me that we were, in fact, hunting another human being. I had made such a fuss over MacBride's ease with taking a life and hesitated more than once in the heat of battle. Would I have the courage to kill Jean-Louis if the task fell on me?

I did not have to answer my own question. As we ran after him, Jean-Louis glanced back at us, desperation written on his face. He attempted a bold leap over a rocky crag, but tripped. His leg bent under him, and he plunged head first into a pile of rocks with a hoot and a loud thwack. MacBride and I caught up to him at the same time, and we both grimaced at what we saw. His head had struck a sharp stone protruding from the earth. Its pointed end had cracked open his skull like an egg, revealing the fresh yoke inside.

"Do you think he's dead?" I asked in shock.

MacBride leaned his arm against a tree to catch his breath. "I'm willing to bet all my wages that he is."

"You got what you wanted, right?"

MacBride nodded, still heaving. "Aye. And so did you."

"What do you mean?"

"You've had your knickers in a twist this entire trip about fighting and killing. You got what you wanted. Mission accomplished, and we didn't actually have to kill him."

"I suppose you're right," I said.

We both started to laugh through our heaving breaths, the sound cutting through any remaining tension. We laughed at the absurdity of it all—the hang-ups we had brought to the table and the powerlessness we ultimately faced. We had fought over ethics, and in the end it did not matter.

Finally MacBride sobered. "We should get moving if we don't want to end up like him."

We set off, our wet clothes clinging uncomfortably to our bodies, but the danger of the river was now behind us. Ahead lay the vast unknown and the promise of a future where old grudges could be forgotten and new alliances formed.

The forest around us seemed to close in as the last remnants of daylight dwindled. The air grew colder, a chill that bit through our drenched clothes and sent shivers down my spine. Every rustling leaf, every snapping twig, felt like the approach of an unseen enemy. But what worried me more was the cold and the onset of darkness.

"We can't continue like this," I panted, the weight of my soaked clothes dragging me down. "We'll freeze if we don't find shelter or start a fire."

MacBride shot me a look, his eyes shadowed but resolute. "We need to find the others. But you're right. First, we need to warm up, even if it's just for a bit."

The woods loomed large around us, the trees standing like silent sentinels. The night was slowly coming alive with the chirping of crickets, the distant call of an owl, and the soft rustle of wind through the leaves. But any warmth the day had offered was quickly seeping away.

"We need dry wood," I stated, scanning our surroundings.

The dense canopy above limited our visibility, but a glimmer of hope appeared when MacBride, with his sharp eyes, spotted a fallen tree partially shielded from the snow by a dense cluster of pines. We hurried over, breaking off branches and feeling for dry wood beneath the dampened outer layers.

"We also need something to light it with," MacBride mused, a hint of frustration edging his voice.

I fumbled in my pockets, finding the flint and steel I always carried. They were wet but not entirely useless. "This might work," I said, holding them up.

With the wood gathered, we cleared a small area on the forest floor, scraping away the wet leaves and setting up a tiny mound of twigs and branches. I struck the flint and steel together again and again. Sparks flew, but they died just as quickly, unable to catch on the damp tinder.

Time seemed to stretch, and every failed attempt gnawed at our patience. But with persistence, a tiny spark finally caught, smoldering and growing as we gently blew on it, feeding it with the driest bits of our collection.

The fire grew, its warmth a balm to our chilled bones. We inched closer, stripping off our wettest garments to hang nearby, absorbing the fire's heat, and trying to dry out.

"We can't stay here long," MacBride murmured, his gaze fixed on the dancing flames. "But we've bought ourselves some time."

I nodded in agreement. "We'll rest a bit, warm up, and then move. The others could be anywhere. We need to find higher ground, signal them somehow."

MacBride looked at me, and for the first time since our ordeal began, I saw a hint of gratitude in his eyes. "You've done well, Christian. I might not have agreed with your choices, but I'm glad you're with me right now."

The fire's glow cast an orange hue over his face, bringing into sharp relief the lines of worry and fatigue etched into his features. We sat in silence for a few moments, the crackling of the fire the only sound breaking the stillness of the night.

Finally, MacBride broke the silence, his voice hesitant, as if choosing each word with care. "You know, Christian, from the moment we first met, I took a disliking to you. I can't exactly pinpoint why, but something about you just... riled me up."

I glanced at him, my brow furrowing, not sure where he was going with this.

He continued, "When I fired you and left you to fend for yourself, I was proving a point to myself in many ways. But seeing the choices you made, understanding your past... it's become clear why you chose the path you did."

I looked down, feeling a surge of anger, resentment, and understanding. "So you're saying you understand why I joined Jean-Louis?"

MacBride nodded, a hint of regret in his eyes. "In a way, yes. I pushed you away, perhaps even drove you to it."

His words settled between us, creating a thick tension. But MacBride wasn't done. "I want to apologize, Christian. Not just for my treatment of you but for everything. Especially about Jim."

I looked up sharply, surprised. "What do you mean?"

"If I had been a better leader, more understanding and less rigid, maybe our company wouldn't have had the cracks it did." He swallowed hard, his voice quivering with raw emotion. "Jim's death... it weighs on me. I can't help but feel that if things had been different—if I had been different—he might still be alive."

A heavy silence enveloped us. The gravity of his confession and the weight of the guilt he carried were palpable.

I took a deep breath, letting the pain and resentment I'd felt towards MacBride wash over me before letting it go. "I acted rashly, and I apologize for that. We both made choices, and we both have to live with the consequences. Jim's death weighs on me, too. I feel like it was my fault. If I had done something different—"

MacBride nodded slowly, his eyes filled with both sadness and relief. "We're two flawed men, aren't we?"

A hint of a smile played on my lips. "Aren't we all?"

The fire crackled and popped, the comforting warmth a stark contrast to the cold truths we had just confronted. But in that moment, amidst the vast wilderness, two men found understanding, forgiveness, and a path forward.

MacBride shifted slightly, stretching his legs and looking around at the dark forest surrounding us. "We've been through a lot today," he began, rubbing his temples as if to ward off a headache. "I reckon we won't get much farther tonight, not with the darkness setting in like this."

I nodded, feeling the weariness in my own bones. "Yeah, it's best if we stay put. We need our strength if we're going to find our way back to the others."

MacBride looked over at the fire, its flames dancing and sending sparks into the night air. "We should stoke the fire, make sure it burns throughout the night. It'll keep us warm and ward off any animals."

I reached for a nearby log and placed it on the fire. "Sounds like a plan." The warmth of the flames caressed my face.

MacBride settled back, his gaze distant, as if lost in thought. "Tomorrow's a new day. We'll figure out our next move then."

He reached into his pocket and pulled from it the time piece he had looked at dozens of times a day. "This was my best friend's watch. He gave it to me before he died fighting at Waterloo. I want you to have it."

"I can't," I said. "

"You can. He gave it to me for saving his life once, and I want to give it to you for saving mine."

"I don't deserve it."

"You deserve it plenty," MacBride said, nestling a bit deeper into his nest.

"But I betrayed you," I insisted.

"And you saved all our lives again."

"Yeah," I murmured, feeling a deep exhaustion creeping over me. "I guess so."

And with that, I took the watch, and the two of us settled in, the flickering fire our only company in the vast, silent night.

# CHAPTER 12
## MAKING AMENDS

The sun peeked over the horizon, casting a golden hue over the snow-laden trees. The forest's shadows receded, but the weight of our situation did not. Every rustling leaf, every distant bird call, felt like potential danger. I trudged behind MacBride, my boots sinking into the mud and muck of the forest floor with every step. He seemed certain of his path, leading us to a rendezvous point in the hopes of finding our company, his eyes trained on some distant point, but the more we walked, the more I felt we were aimlessly wandering.

"MacBride," I began, my voice hoarse from the cold and fatigue, "are you sure we're heading in the right direction?"

He didn't break his stride, though he did shoot me a sidelong glance. "We need to head south and slightly west. If my bearings are correct, and they usually are, we should reach our rendezvous point by nightfall."

I frowned, scanning the vastness around us. "It all looks the same to me. Trees, mud, more trees."

He paused for a moment, turning to face me, his breath visible in the chilly air. "Christian, in these lands, it's the subtleties that guide you. The moss on the trees, the direction of the rivers, the position of the sun. You need to have faith."

I stared back at him, trying to muster that faith. Our newfound camaraderie from the previous night still felt fragile.

"I just want to regroup with the others," I admitted. "And get out of this damned cold."

MacBride nodded, understanding etched on his face. "We both do. But for now, we must keep moving."

With that, he turned back to his course, and I followed, still unsure but clinging to the hope that we were headed toward safety and not further into danger. I did wonder then how the others might receive me.

The terrain gradually shifted as we descended from the high mountains into the valleys and glens below them. The trees began to thin out, giving way to clearer patches of land. The Snake River was our landmark, a natural pathway we hoped our companions would also head towards. Its winding course was both a beacon of hope and a tactical advantage. If we could find it, we could find our way back to civilization, or at least back to our group.

Our footsteps were synchronized, the squelching of mud beneath our boots the only consistent sound accompanying us. In these dire circumstances, words were superfluous. A gesture, a glance—they communicated more than spoken language ever could. We had become finely attuned to each other's movements, alerting one another of potential hazards with a nudge or a subtle point.

I noticed the stillness of the woods around us, a stark contrast to the frenzied escape we'd made from the HBC camp. It was an uneasy stillness, a silence hinting at potential danger lurking beyond our perception. Every so often, I would hear a twig snap or the rustling of leaves, and my heart would race, but then silence would engulf us once again.

Hours seemed to pass in this state of heightened alertness. Then, as we neared a clearing, a faint, distant sound reached our ears. Gunfire. My head whipped in its direction, my eyes meeting MacBride's. The sound wasn't close, but it wasn't too far either. It echoed eerily through the trees, a chilling reminder of danger.

MacBride motioned for us to crouch, pressing a finger to his lips for silence. We hunkered down, trying to determine the direction and distance of the gunfire. Was it an altercation? Were our comrades involved?

The seconds stretched into minutes. We listened intently, waiting for another volley, but the woods returned to their unsettling silence. No more shots rang out.

Taking a deep breath, MacBride whispered, "It could be anything. Hunters, perhaps, or…"

"Or our men," I finished for him, hope and fear mingling in my voice.

MacBride nodded slowly, weighing our options. "We need to get to the river. It's our best shot at regrouping. But we should approach with caution."

With renewed urgency, yet moving as stealthily as ever, we continued our trek, the threat a constant presence in our minds, urging our steps forward.

The distant echo of gunfire began sounding off at regular intervals once more. The need to act was clear, but the course of action itself was shrouded in uncertainty.

"We should follow the gunshots," I blurted, my eyes scanning the trees in the direction of the sound. "It could be Lisa. It could be our party."

MacBride's experienced eyes betrayed a hint of worry. "Or," he began slowly, weighing each word, "it could be the Hudson's Bay Company. And if it is, then marching straight towards them would be akin to walking into a trap."

I exhaled loudly, my impatience evident. "But we can't just ignore it, can we? Our fellows could be in danger!"

He nodded in agreement. "I know, Christian. I share your concern. But we need to think this through. Rushing in without a plan could get us both killed."

His words, though true, only added to my frustration. "What's our alternative? Continue wandering aimlessly in these woods, hoping to miraculously stumble upon our group?"

MacBride's jaw tensed as he regarded me, his gaze unwavering. "Listen," he began, his voice firm, "I've been in situations like this before. Our priority is to avoid capture. If it is the HBC—and given the proximity, I believe it is—we'd be playing right into their hands by heading towards the gunfire."

His logic was hard to refute, but the thought of leaving our comrades potentially in peril was almost too much to bear.

"So we just abandon them?" I challenged.

His expression hardened further, the weight of our circumstances evident in his eyes. "No," he replied resolutely. "But we need to be smart about this. We'll circle around and approach from a different angle. If it is our men, we'll find a way to help. If it's the HBC, we'll cross that bridge."

My instincts told me to push forward, but MacBride's wisdom and experience held me back. I took a deep breath, trying to calm the tempest of emotions within. "All right," I conceded, "we'll take the long way."

He clasped my shoulder reassuringly. "We'll do everything in our power to help them, Christian. I promise."

MacBride gave a wry smile, his eyebrows rising in playful mischief. "And besides," he added, "if I remember correctly, the last time you thought Blue Fox needed rescuing, it was you who ended up being saved by her. Perhaps, if we're lucky, she'll do us both the favor again."

I couldn't help but chuckle. "You just had to bring that up, didn't you?"

His grin widened. "Just trying to keep your spirits up and your pride in check."

Laughing, I shook my head. "Let's hope she's around then. It seems I have a habit of needing saving."

Our momentary levity had provided a much-needed break from the tension, but we refocused on the task at hand, moving cautiously through the damp and muddy terrain. I soon learned that I should have trusted MacBride from the start, as we arrived mere moments later at the Snake River.

The river greeted us with its wide expanse and rhythmic murmurs, casting a gleaming reflection of the fading sunlight. In the encroaching darkness, the riverbank was alive with flickering campfires. A smattering of distant figures could be seen—trappers setting up their tents, adjusting their snares, and conversing over the dancing flames.

"The whole river's lit up," I remarked, taking in the numerous fires. "It's like a festival."

"That's good news for us," he said. "It means the HBC is letting them all through. Our gamble paid off."

"A fish rots from the head down, as they say," I mused. "I just can't believe how many there are out there."

MacBride gazed at the multitude of encampments. "It's trapping season. The Snake River always lights up like this in the spring. Like you, thousands of men try their luck at the trade every year."

"Are they part of the HBC?" I asked.

"A few, I'm certain," MacBride conceded. "Most of the men who travel west have no affiliation with the main companies. They're freelancers. They come out here, trap, and sell to the companies at the rendezvous."

"So that's what we're really fighting over. Not direct control of the land, but the men who trap within it and what they catch," I thought aloud.

"Aye." MacBride chuckled. "With so many here, we won't stick out. We should set up our own camp. Just two more trappers, as far as anyone's concerned."

"I could use a rest," I conceded. "But where would our company head without us?"

He pointed south, where the river meandered its way into the distant horizon. "If I were leading them, we would've headed to the camping grounds in the southern part of Oregon Country. It was the plan."

I nodded, digesting the information. It felt odd, being detached from the group, with only a general direction to guide us. The company had become family, and the thought of them in the wilderness without us was unsettling.

"We should get a fire going," MacBride said, pulling me from my thoughts. "Keep our strength up, blend in, and when dawn breaks, we continue our search."

With that, we set to work, gathering wood and stones. Tonight, we were just two among many trappers seeking refuge and warmth by the Snake River. But as the stars peeked out from the canvas of the night sky, I couldn't help but wonder where our company was and whether we'd be reunited soon.

As I helped MacBride gather sticks for our campfire, my thoughts wandered to her. Blue Fox. The memories of our moments together swirled through my mind, as vivid as if they had occurred only yesterday. The intensity of her gaze, the strength of her spirit, and that enigmatic aura that always surrounded her.

With every rustle of the leaves, every distant laugh from another camp, I half expected to see her step out of the shadows, to surprise me as she often did. There was something composed and resolute about her, a fierce independence that had drawn me to her from our first encounter. I felt an unspoken connection with her—a bond that transcended our different worlds.

I missed the way she challenged my perspectives, the conversations that meandered through the night, and the comfort of her presence beside me. There were so many unsaid words between us, emotions yet unexplored. The way we had parted, the abruptness of it all, felt like a wound that had yet to heal.

As I sat down, my gaze fixed on the river's shimmering surface, I allowed myself a moment of vulnerability, thinking of how it would feel to hold her close once more. Would she be searching for me too? Did she feel the same pull, the same longing? Or had I broken the bond forever by betraying her trust? Was there a path to redemption for me?

I shook my head, trying to dispel the whirlwind of emotions. The priority was to regroup with our company and ensure everyone's safety. But deep down, I held on to the hope that our paths would cross again and that when they did, the universe would grant us the time we needed and deserved to mend our relationship.

And yet, so far as we had tried, our romance could never be. She could not live in New York, and I refused to stay out West if given the chance to return. Or could I stay? Could I give up the luxuries of the city, the promise of a job, reputation, and social status for her? The thought grew on me. There was a serenity to nature, a detachment from the hum and buzz of city life. I had longed so much for redemption in New York, had I missed it when it looked me in the eye?

With the ease of someone well-versed in the wild, MacBride arranged some mushrooms he'd picked from the base of nearby trees to warm them up beside our campfire. I watched, intrigued but also cautious.

"Are you sure about those?" I nodded towards the mushrooms.

MacBride chuckled softly. "You think I'd poison us after everything we've been through?"

"I just... haven't had the best luck with forest food," I admitted.

He glanced at me with a teasing smirk. "That's because you probably didn't know what to look for." He picked up one of the mushrooms, holding it out for inspection. "See this one? Notice the gills underneath? They're free from the stem, not attached. That's one good sign."

I leaned in, examining it. "All right, what else?"

He pointed to the top. "The cap is convex, not concave. And it's smooth, not slimy. Also—" He sniffed it. "—it has a pleasant smell. Not something you'd turn away from."

I raised an eyebrow. "And if it were slimy?"

He shrugged. "Then it'd be firewood, not food."

I chuckled, settling back against a log. "So, you learned all this from your trapping days?"

MacBride nodded, rotating another mushroom to dry its other side on the rock. "Among other things. The forest can be a bountiful provider if you know where to look and what to look for. But one wrong move, and it can be deadly."

I took in his words, realizing how much I had yet to learn about the wilds around us. "Thank you for the lesson."

He grinned. "Anytime."

Sitting by the fire, watching the mushrooms sizzle, I sighed heavily. "Sometimes I think I'm just not cut out for this forest life. The city, the streets, the chaos... that was my domain. Here, everything feels foreign, treacherous."

MacBride shot me a look, his face illuminated by the flickering firelight. "Do you remember the first time I met you?"

I chuckled softly. "Yeah. I couldn't even shit in the woods."

"And look at you now," he said, his tone earnest. "You've traveled thousands of miles through the uncharted wilderness, faced down HBC men, wolves, and bears, swam down rivers, and made campfires while soaking wet. That's not the work of a city man, Christian. That's the work of someone who's learning and adapting. Someone who's becoming part of this wilderness."

I looked into the fire, watching the flames dance. "I've made so many mistakes, though."

He nodded. "Yes, you have. We all do. But you've also shown courage, resilience, and a will to survive that many seasoned trappers lack. The forest has a way of bringing out the best and worst in people. And in you, I've seen a lot of both."

His words warmed me more than the fire ever could. "Thank you, MacBride. It means a lot."

I awoke to a rustling sound, followed by a distinct and methodical chewing. My eyes fluttered open, adjusting to the soft light filtering in. Beneath the canopy of trees, the morning sun gently touched the ground, its rays struggling to break through the dense foliage above. The source of the sound was just a few paces away.

Blue Fox stood leaning against a nearby tree, one hand clutching a piece of jerky and the other casually holding a long bow. She chewed with a deliberate exaggeration, her eyes twinkling with mischief as she caught my confused gaze.

I blinked a few times, wondering if I was still caught in the remnants of a dream. MacBride stirred awake beside me, his expression equally perplexed.

"Good morning," Blue Fox said, her voice dripping with amusement. She took another obnoxious bite, her cheek bulging as she continued to chew.

"Blue Fox?" I exclaimed, pushing myself up. "How did you—when did you—?"

She grinned, taking her time before answering. "Found you two while you were sleeping. Figured I'd give you a morning wake-up call."

MacBride chuckled, rubbing the sleep from his eyes. "Of all the ways to be woken up in the wilderness, I must say, this was the least expected."

She winked, finishing her jerky. "I've been tracking you two for a day now. You're not as quiet as you think."

I smirked. "Well, one of us isn't."

She laughed, her eyes meeting mine. The relief I felt at seeing her safe was immeasurable. There were still so many questions, so much to discuss, but gratitude filled the air for that moment.

Blue Fox tossed a small pack of jerky toward us. "Eat up. We've got a long day ahead."

"I want to say—"

She cut me off. "Don't." She looked at me squarely, her face betraying nothing, but her eyes shimmered with emotion. "Not now."

I opened my mouth to argue, wanting to apologize, to explain, but she was right. The moment wasn't right. We had too much ahead of us, too much uncertainty. Apologies would have to wait.

Sensing the tension, MacBride jumped in, attempting to break the ice. "Well, since you've been trailing us, any news on the others? What's happened?"

Blue Fox adjusted her stance, pulling the rifle closer to her side. "Asher, Boyd, Bear, MacLane, Georges, and Jean-Baptiste are camped downriver. After the two of you split from us, the HBC left our path wide open. We backtracked to Lisa's camp, picked up our canoes and supplies, and headed downriver. As for Lisa, he and his company turned south toward California."

MacBride's brows knitted with concern. "And the HBC?"

She shook her head. "They've been moving groups downriver. Dozens of them. It looks like they're abandoning the mountain camp."

"So it's over?" I asked.

She shot me an icy glare. "I wouldn't want to run into the HBC again, if that's what you mean."

I shrank, embarrassed by the stupidity of my question. MacBride stood, brushing off the forest floor's detritus, and reached out a hand to help me up, too. Blue Fox noticed.

"You've made friends again, I see."

"Aye," MacBride said. "Christian saved my skin, and together we managed to kill Jean-Louis."

Her jaw dropped. "You—"

"Well," I interjected. "A rock killed him. We merely led him to it."

MacBride bent over laughing. "I can't—" he tried to say.

I grimaced, wondering if MacBride had even made the connection between Jean-Louis and Blue Fox. Given his laughter, I hoped he hadn't. We had just told her that her father was dead.

Blue Fox did not laugh. Her eyes wide with shock, she was at a loss for words.

"Are you all right?" I asked her.

"I'm fine," she said, so suddenly that both MacBride and I jolted. "I just wish I could have... I wanted to... tell him. Tell him everything. Explain to him the harm he caused."

MacBride stepped toward her and touched her shoulder. "It would have fallen on deaf ears, lassie. He was not a moral man."

"MacBride's right. There was no soul in those eyes to plead with," I added.

Blue Fox shifted as she held back tears, her eyes darting from place to place and her fingers fiddling with her bowstring. "It's over, then."

I gazed at the river, its waters reflecting the first rays of light breaking over the mountains. "With each end, a new chapter begins."

She forced a smile and nodded. "All right, then. Eat some jerky. We leave in ten minutes."

The trail along the Snake River meandered gently, the sun casting its warm glow over the landscape. As we moved with a deliberate pace downriver, the sound of water lapping at the riverbanks was a constant companion. The serene beauty all around us contrasted the angst I felt as we walked.

MacBride led the way, his confident strides setting the pace, while Blue Fox purposefully lagged behind. My heart thudded against my chest. Though I was physically walking at a steady pace, I felt tethered in place emotionally, the weight of past decisions holding me back.

She allowed the distance between us and MacBride to widen until we were isolated in our own pocket of the forest, buffered by the sounds of rustling leaves and chirping birds. Then, in a soft voice that carried a power I had come to associate with her, she broke the silence.

"I understand why you did what you did." Her tone was neutral, but every word was laden with significance. "But it still feels like a betrayal. I'm angry, Christian. I'm angry with you."

A sinking feeling settled in my stomach. Her words stung, not because they were meant to hurt but because they were raw, genuine.

"Blue Fox," I began hesitantly, my throat dry, "I regret hurting you—it was not my intent. I wish I had a way to convey how deeply sorry I am. But I understand if words aren't enough."

She halted, her posture erect, eyes piercing mine. They were eyes I had lost myself in countless times before, finding comfort and strength in their depths. But today, they were stormy, filled with a myriad of emotions that I struggled to comprehend.

"Trust is a fragile thing," she whispered. "Out here, in the wild, where dangers lurk at every corner and alliances mean survival, trust is our lifeline. And you severed that lifeline."

We stood like that for a few moments, the world around us seeming to blur into the background. Every word she uttered felt like a physical blow, each syllable a reminder of the gravity of my missteps.

"I understand," I replied, my voice quivering. "And I would do anything, anything at all, to mend what's been broken. Please tell me, Blue Fox, how can I make this right?"

She took a deep breath, her chest rising and falling slowly, deliberately. The intensity in her gaze never wavered. "It's not about grand gestures or hollow promises, Christian. It's about the small, everyday choices we make. The decisions that define who we are and where our loyalties lie. Words are fleeting, but actions... actions echo long after they're made."

The truth of her words settled heavily on me. "Every day, then," I said, my voice barely above a whisper. "For you, for the company, for myself. I want to earn back the trust I've lost. But I know it's a long road."

She seemed to contemplate my words, her eyes searching mine for any hint of insincerity. "It's going to take time."

"I will," I vowed, the weight of the promise settling in my core. "I'll do everything in my power to prove myself to you, to everyone. I understand what I've done and am ready to face the consequences."

The moment stretched between us, but MacBride's voice rang out, cutting through the tension.

"Blue Fox!" He'd paused up ahead, turning to face us, his gaze unwavering. "If you're holding any man accountable, hold me as much as Christian."

She looked up, surprise in her eyes. "MacBride?"

He approached, his usually calm demeanor replaced by one of rare vulnerability.

"I failed Christian as a leader," he said. "I pushed him and cornered him, did nothing to win him over. I paved the path for him to make the decision he did. If there's blame to share, a fair chunk of it lies with me. And let's not forget that his decision saved your skin and mine. The HBC would have cut us down had we tried to charge at them."

The forest seemed to hold its breath, waiting. The three of us stood there, a silent understanding passing between us.

"I respect you, MacBride," Blue Fox said after a pause. "I've seen your leadership, your strength. And if you say you had a hand in all of this, I agree with you." She glanced back at me, her gaze softening ever so slightly. "But trust, as you both know, isn't something given lightly. Since you're both responsible, then you both must atone."

MacBride nodded. "I understand that. I'll walk that path of redemption right beside him, making amends for my own part."

I felt a surge of gratitude toward him, tempered by the prospect of the long road I had ahead. A journey of rebuilding trust, of proving myself, of making amends felt more daunting than a thousand westward treks into Oregon Country.

Blue Fox exhaled slowly. "Time will tell." Her gaze lingered on me a moment longer, a mix of hope, caution, and something deeper I couldn't quite decipher.

And with that, we resumed our journey down the Snake River, each step forward a promise of commitment to the challenges and reconciliations the future held.

The dimming light filtered through the trees as we approached the familiar encampment. Tents and small campfires stretched out in a modest clearing, and our company's emblem hung from a nearby branch. A few heads turned our way, some expressions revealing surprise, others wariness, but all had a hint of curiosity.

Boyd and Asher were seated together, skinning some game. Their knives paused momentarily as their eyes met mine, their expressions hardening instantly. A chill ran down my spine, but I stood tall, ready to face the consequences of my actions.

MacBride took a deep breath, standing at the front and acting as the shield he had become for me. "I know what many of you may be thinking, especially after everything that's happened," he began, his voice commanding the attention of all around. "I want to make it clear: Christian and I have had a long talk. I understand his choices and the circumstances that led to them. I've forgiven him and want him here, with us."

Murmurs rippled through the gathered men. I could feel eyes measuring me, gauging whether MacBride's trust was misplaced or not.

Boyd stood up, his face a mask of barely contained anger. "Forgiven? After what happened to Jim? After he sided with those bastards?"

MacBride's gaze never wavered. "I hold as much responsibility for what happened as Christian. We've lost and erred, and now we must move forward. For Jim and for ourselves."

Asher's gaze was equally cold, his voice dripping with bitterness. "You may be willing to forgive and forget, MacBride, but some wounds don't heal that easily."

"I understand," I interjected, stepping forward, my voice firm but filled with remorse. "I'll live with my choices for the rest of my life. The weight of Jim's loss is on my shoulders, and it's a burden I'll carry. I'm not asking for immediate trust, but I'll do everything in my power to make amends."

Silence descended upon the camp. Everyone seemed to be in deep thought, weighing their feelings against MacBride's command.

As the camp settled into an uneasy quiet, MacLane, his angular face taut with concern, stepped closer to MacBride. He had always been one of MacBride's closest allies, a trusted voice in the company. But even trust had its limits.

"MacBride." His voice was just above a whisper, the kind that carried weight in its hushed tones. "You've always been our rock. Have you gone soft?"

The camp, already on edge, went still. Everyone knew the bond between the two men, and the boldness of MacLane's question was not lost on any.

MacBride's ice-blue eyes bore into MacLane's. There was a moment, just a breath of time, where it looked as if he might explode with fury. But when he spoke, it was with that calculated, measured strength that had made him a leader.

"Soft?" MacBride's voice rang out, the dangerous edge clear. "You think forgiving a man, understanding his choices, makes me soft? It's easy to hold on to anger, Lucas. It's easy to let hatred and vengeance cloud our decisions. But true strength, the kind of strength I've spent years cultivating, is knowing when to let go. Knowing when to rebuild."

MacLane held his ground, but there was a flicker in his eyes, a hint of regret at questioning MacBride so openly. "I just wanted to make sure you weren't losing your edge, especially now when we need it the most."

MacBride stepped closer, his towering figure dwarfing MacLane. "I haven't lost anything," he growled. "But mark my words, moving forward, if anything jeopardizes this company, even if it's from one of our own, I will deal with it. No matter the cost."

MacLane nodded slowly. "Understood."

The firelight danced on their faces, painting a picture of two formidable men, both shaped and hardened by the challenges they'd faced. Their conversation, though brief, was a stark reminder of the fragile balance of trust, leadership, and survival on the frontier.

MacBride had one more thing to say. "If any of you doubted our chances for success, then hear this: Jean-Louis is dead. And with him, hope for our mission's success has been rekindled. We head to Oregon Country now. We soldiers have done our part—it's time for the trappers to do theirs."

The night settled around us, a reflection of the dark atmosphere. There was much to be done, relationships to mend, trust to rebuild. But for now, we were together, a fractured company finding its way through the wilderness of both the land and the soul.

# CHAPTER 13
## PETER SKENE OGDEN

The rhythmic splash of paddles against the water of the Snake River was a familiar sound that brought a semblance of normality to our journey. After traversing the grueling mountains, being back in a canoe felt almost like a return to simpler times. The forest, with its tall pines and hidden dangers, had receded, revealing the sprawling expanse of the high desert. Its dry landscape was peppered with hardy shrubs, contrasting the vast, cool waters we now navigated.

We had bought our canoes from the Snake tribe, whom we encountered in the flesh soon after descending from the mountains. They were a peaceful tribe interested in trade. We learned from them that the HBC had stolen some of their weapons and used them to scare off other trappers. That explained why we saw their arrows when the HBC had attacked us. They mentioned we had not been the first company to pass by complaining of a Snake attack in the mountains. How awful, I thought, that the HBC had made such a concerted effort to malign these peaceful people.

Asher, paddling a few yards ahead, suddenly alerted, his hand coming up to shade his eyes against the sun's glare. "Canoes ahead!" he warned, pointing downstream.

Without hesitation, MacBride commanded, "Into the reeds! Quickly!"

My heart raced. I was still inexperienced, and every unexpected turn in our journey felt like a test I wasn't prepared for. We steered our canoes towards the bank, looking for cover. Soon, the entrance to a ravine became visible, its mouth guarded by a grove of cottonwood trees.

It was the perfect hiding spot. Pulling the canoes ashore, we camouflaged them with reeds and brush.

Huddled together, we listened as the sound of paddling grew closer. We'd been cursed on this journey. I waited in anxious silence, wondering who was out there: friend or foe?

As the canoes approached, it was evident that these men were fur trappers. The sun reflecting off their tools, the rugged gear stacked in their canoes, and the familiar weariness in their posture were telltale signs. But they didn't bear the Hudson's Bay Company emblem nor their red caps, which was a relief.

Boyd, crouching next to me, stiffened. "Hey, I know that man." He whispered with growing excitement, "That's Pete! From the rendezvous two summers ago!"

Before anyone could stop him, Boyd emerged from our cover, waving his hands wildly and calling out. "Pete! Hey, Pete!"

The group in the canoes, startled by his sudden appearance, immediately ceased paddling. Hands moved to muskets, eyes scanning the bank warily. But then a rugged-looking trapper with a thick beard and sunburned skin stood. He squinted in our direction, shielding his eyes with one hand.

"Boyd? Bobby Boyd? Is that really you?" he shouted back, disbelief in his voice.

MacBride looked ready to strangle Boyd for his impulsiveness. We all held our breath as Boyd and Pete continued their exchange.

"It's been years, mate!" Pete called out, motioning for his men to relax. The rest of the canoes followed suit, and a collective sigh of relief rippled through our group.

"Well, don't just stand there! Come on over!" Boyd beckoned them enthusiastically.

As the canoes reached the bank, hearty laughs and loud greetings filled the air. Boyd and Pete shared a rough embrace, slapping each other's backs.

"I never thought I'd run into you out here," Pete exclaimed, a wide grin on his face. "What's the occasion?"

Boyd quickly introduced MacBride and the rest of us, briefly explaining our expedition. In return, Pete introduced his crew, all trappers from various parts of the West.

Boyd, with the broadest grin I'd seen on his face in days, turned to MacBride, gesturing animatedly to the man now standing beside him. "This here's none other than Peter Skene Ogden! One of the finest trappers I've had the honor of meeting."

There was a collective murmur among our group. Even for someone like me, inexperienced and new to the intricacies of the fur trade, the name held weight. Ogden was a legendary figure in the trapping world, and the tales of his expeditions were the stuff of campfire stories.

Given his reputation, Ogden was a slightly smaller man than I would've imagined, with sharp eyes that seemed to miss nothing. His face, weathered from years in the wilderness, broke into a smile, revealing teeth stained from tobacco.

"Boyd, you old scoundrel! It's been a while. Never thought I'd find you hiding in the reeds!" The men laughed.

MacBride stepped forward, extending his hand. "Mr. Ogden, it's an honor. I've heard much about you."

Ogden's grip was firm. "All good, I hope," he replied with a wink.

In a teasing tone, Boyd jabbed, "Last I heard, Pete, you were causing a ruckus up in Saskatchewan. What're you doing so far down here in Oregon Country?"

The legendary trapper chuckled, his eyes gleaming with mischief. "Ah, Boyd, always one for gossip. Well, let me fill you in. There was a… minor disagreement, let's call it, up north."

"We always called them 'Ogden's flare-ups' back in the day." Boyd laughed, slapping his back.

"Ha! This flare-up led to one fella being a little more dead than he probably should've been." The group shifted uneasily, unsure how to react, but Ogden continued, his tone light. "You see, the chap belonged to the HBC, and they weren't too pleased with me. Word got out, and there were whispers of charges—murder, to be specific."

Blue Fox raised an eyebrow, impressed despite herself. "And you're just wandering around freely?"

Ogden winked. "Well, the North West Company, my dear employer, decided it'd be best for everyone— especially me—if I found myself on an 'exploratory expedition' in the middle of nowhere. Less chance of me causing further diplomatic incidents, you see?"

MacBride, trying to suppress a grin, interjected, "A smart move on their part, if you ask me."

"Indeed." Ogden nodded sagely. "But you know, Boyd, Oregon's not too shabby. Wide-open spaces, plenty of game, and most importantly, a distinct lack of HBC men looking for my head."

Sensing the opportunity, MacBride leaned forward, resting his hands on his rifle's pommel. "Speaking of HBC men, Pete, you should know we've got our own little chase with them."

Ogden raised an eyebrow, his jovial demeanor turning serious. "Oh?"

"Aye. They've got a bounty on my head and Christian's." MacBride motioned in my direction. I felt a sudden chill run down my spine. "They knew we were coming. The whole of the upper stretches, closer to the mountains, is swarming with Hudson's Bay men. We barely got out."

Ogden's face darkened. "That's where I was headed." He turned his gaze upstream, taking a moment to absorb the news. "What happened?"

MacBride recounted the events, from the ambush in the mountains to Jean-Louis' attempt to make a spectacle out of us. The atmosphere grew tense as he spoke, the gravity of our predicament becoming all too real.

"And now?" Ogden asked.

"We're trying to find our original trapping grounds further south in Oregon. Salvage what's left of this expedition."

The trapper rubbed his chin thoughtfully. "This changes things for me. My men and I don't have the numbers to face the HBC head-on, especially if they're out in force like you've said."

Blue Fox spoke up. "It might be wise to join forces, at least for a while. There's safety in numbers."

Ogden considered it, looking from face to face, weighing his options. "Tell me more about these trapping grounds of yours. Might be we can find a way to make this work for all of us."

"Bear," MacBride called. "Get me one of our maps."

Bear ruffled through his belongings and produced a roughly drawn map from his leather-bound cartographer's chest. He spread it out, and everyone gathered around. The parchment was weathered and stained from countless river crossings and rainstorms. The map was not perfect, but it provided a solid overview of Oregon Country.

MacBride, leaning over the map with one hand resting on his knee, pointed. "Here." He indicated a southern region of the territory. "This is where we're headed. If the intel we got from St. Louis is right, it's prime beaver territory."

Squinting, Ogden scanned the area he'd indicated. "That region? The word is it's mostly a desert. Barely anyone's ventured out that far. They say it's just barren land with no water."

"We've heard there are rivers and lakes we've yet to chart, hidden among the wastelands," MacBride countered. "If we find them, they could be teeming with beavers, untouched by trappers."

Ogden studied the map, his fingers tracing imaginary paths. "It's a gamble," he mused, "but if it pays off, the reward could be significant."

Rolling up the map, Bear added, "It's also away from the main HBC operations. We can lie low and trap in peace, at least for a while."

Ogden met MacBride's gaze. "If we combine our forces, share the risk, and the rewards...well, it might just be a plan worth considering."

MacBride grinned. "Thought you might see it that way."

Leaning forward, Ogden pointed to a region even further west on the map. "Over here," he said, drawing his finger across the area, "beyond where you've marked, right up against the mountain ranges, there's territory still largely unknown. We've only heard snippets from native tales and the occasional adventurous trapper."

Curiosity bloomed within me. "And what have they said about that land?"

Ogden shrugged. "Stories vary, but there's mention of vast forests, hidden valleys, and more. Some speak of a paradise, others of treacherous landscapes resembling the moon's craters. Either way, it's uncharted. But most importantly," he said with a smirk, "definitely no HBC men out that far."

MacBride, folding his arms, replied, "Sounds like a fine place for someone looking to get away from... let's say, workplace disagreements."

Ogden chuckled. "Yes, that's one way to put it. So, here's my proposal. We join forces as we navigate downriver. When you and your group find a spot that looks promising, you can set up and start your trapping. My group and I will continue on, heading for that uncharted territory. We're explorers at heart, after all."

MacBride nodded. "It's a good plan. We can support each other until we split, share intel, and increase our chances against threats. And if either group runs into trouble, we know we've got allies not too far off."

Ogden extended a hand. "Agreed. Here's to new partnerships and the great unknown."

MacBride shook it firmly, sealing our new alliance.

As days blended together, our motley group of trappers paddled downstream. The rhythm of our strokes became a sort of mesmerizing song, occasionally interrupted by the splash of a fish jumping or the distant call of a bird. The Snake River sparkled, its waters dancing with reflections from the overhead sun, making the surroundings a canvas of light and shadow.

A week into our journey, the river began to bend conspicuously to the north. As we approached the curve, the wilds to the west beckoned. I could see the untamed land that Ogden had described, a world untouched and waiting for our footprints. MacBride squinted into the distance before declaring his decision.

"We're leaving the river behind," he said, his voice carrying a hint of finality. "From here on, we venture west on foot. Those canoes won't be much help where we're going."

Everyone seemed to accept the decision with a resigned nod. The flurry of preparation was almost instinctive. We checked our supplies, hid our canoes in the thick reeds to ensure they'd be waiting upon our return, and hoisted our packs onto our backs.

As we shouldered our packs and prepared to step into the wilderness, Ogden, with an authoritative tone I'd quickly become familiar with, called out, "Make sure you've packed plenty of water! Don't expect to find any for a long while in this terrain."

A murmur of agreement spread through the group as everyone double-checked their water skins and canteens, ensuring they were full. As we did so, Boyd, staring out into the vastness before us, said wistfully, "Wish we had some horses right about now."

I could see why. The expanse before us was seemingly endless. Walking through it without the aid of horses would be grueling.

"It would make things easier," MacLane agreed.

MacBride smirked. "Think of it as a chance to stretch your legs."

From the banks of the Snake River, we began our journey into southeastern Oregon Country, and with every step, this untamed territory unveiled itself to me. As we moved away from the river, the verdant foliage gave way to a sweeping high desert, a tableau of browns, tans, and muted greens. The horizon was a ragged edge where the earth met the sky, with distant mountains casting their stoic silhouettes against the azure canvas. My feet crunched on a mix of soft sand and hard-packed earth, and with every gust of wind, I could smell the distinctive sharp scent of sagebrush. The land was like nothing I'd ever seen, an expanse that seemed to stretch into infinity, defying all my expectations of what the Wild West was supposed to look like. I quickly realized that tales and maps could never capture the raw essence of this place.

The days were fiercely hot, and it wasn't long before my skin took on the same tanned hue as our new friend Pete. But despite the sun's relentless assault, the land thrived in its own peculiar way. Rabbitbrush and resilient juniper trees dotted the desert plateaus, standing as living testament to nature's ability to endure in the harshest conditions. Intermittently, outcroppings of volcanic rock jutted out, telling tales of ancient eruptions and nature's volatile temper.

In this vastness, a profound silence enveloped us. The usual chirrups and calls of familiar woodland creatures were conspicuously absent. Instead, the occasional cry of a hawk or eagle high above punctuated the quiet, each cry echoing through the wide-open space. This was a place of few words, where even our own conversations were hushed, as if out of respect for the land's deep-rooted tranquility.

But what truly amazed me were the unexpected bursts of life we encountered. Every so often, a pronghorn antelope would spring from the brush, its graceful legs eating up the ground with surprising speed. Jackrabbits, their long ears alert, would dash across our path, and I spotted ground squirrels skittering in and out of their burrows.

Water, that most precious resource, was a rarity, and its scarcity was a constant weight on all our minds. But nature, in her wisdom, had ways to signal its presence. Clusters of dense green vegetation hinted at hidden springs, and every once in a while, we came across a stream, its waters a lifeline in this parched realm. At those moments, we would all rush forward to quench our thirst and refill our canteens.

When the sun dipped below the horizon, the desert underwent another transformation. The heat of the day gave way to a surprising chill, and I found myself drawing my jacket tighter around me. But the night's true gift was the sky. The heavens above southeastern Oregon Country were a spectacle to behold. Stars, so many they seemed like grains of sand, lit up the night. Shooting stars streaked across the firmament, and I lay on my back, watching, feeling both small in God's grand creation and connected to something much larger than myself.

One evening, as we sat around the campfire, its flickering light casting long shadows, I shared my thoughts with Blue Fox. "It's beautiful," I whispered, "in a haunting sort of way. There's a spirit here, something ancient and indomitable."

"This land," she said softly, her voice imbued with reverence, "speaks to those who listen. And Christian, you listen."

It was then that I understood. I was not alone in my reverence amidst the beauty and challenges. Blue Fox, in her own way, had been guiding me, showing me the deeper layers of this world, and in doing so, revealing layers of herself.

The silvery hue of the moonlight cast a glow upon the landscape, turning the desert into a mystical realm of soft shadows and muted colors. The fire crackled behind me, but its warmth and light seemed distant as my gaze fixed on the night's beauty. An impulse to be closer to the land under the moon's watchful eye overcame me.

I hesitated for a moment before voicing my request. "Would you walk with me? There's something... magical about the desert under the moon. I thought you might appreciate it too."

She looked up, the pale light making her eyes seem even more mysterious and deep. After a heartbeat, she nodded, standing gracefully. We began walking, side by side, moving further from the camp's glow. The soft sand crunched beneath our feet, and the night's sounds—the whispering wind, the distant call of a night bird— serenaded us.

The vast expanse felt even more profound in the dim light. Without words, we both seemed to understand the gravity of the moment. We were mere specks, wandering amidst an ancient realm that had seen countless moons rise and set.

After what felt like hours, we reached a vantage point that overlooked a valley. Sitting down, we watched as the moonlight played on the sands below, turning them into a sea of silver waves. The world seemed hushed, as if holding its breath.

"It's beautiful," I whispered, almost afraid to break the spell.

Blue Fox turned her gaze to me, her eyes reflecting the moon's glow. "The land has many stories. Each grain of sand, rock, and plant holds memories of times gone by. But those stories come alive under the moon, if only for a fleeting moment."

I pondered her words, lost in thought. "I feel a connection," I admitted, "like the land is speaking directly to my soul. Do you feel it too?"

She nodded, her fingers absently tracing patterns in the sand. "It's an understanding. The land knows those who respect it. Those who see not just its surface but its spirit."

We sat in companionable silence for a while, letting the moonlight wash over us. It was a moment of pure connection, not just with the land but with each other. The boundaries between us seemed to blur, and I felt a profound sense of belonging in that quiet, sacred space.

Soon I found myself inching closer to her, and this time she did not push me away. Our heads hung low, and we looked up together, into each other's eyes. Hers were whirlpools of mystery and desire, her lips an inviting siren, calling me to sail in. There, in the glow of the endless night sky, we shared a long, tender kiss.

The morning sun was just beginning to paint the sky in warm hues when the first shouts rang out, alerting the camp to an unusual sight. We all scrambled out of our tents, squinting against the dawn light, our gazes following the pointed fingers of the sentries.

On a distant ridge, silhouetted against the rising sun, was the unmistakable figure of a mounted warrior. He sat motionless on his horse, a spear resting by his side and a feathered headdress adorning his head, its plumes fluttering gently in the morning breeze. The horse, an impressive beast with a shiny, dark coat, stood tall and still.

A murmur of uncertainty ran through the camp. While we had been cautious of potential threats, we hadn't expected a lone figure, especially not from high ground where he had a clear view of our camp.

Blue Fox, with her keen eyes, was the first to identify the figure. "Paiute," she declared, her tone a mix of respect and caution. "They're skilled horsemen; that ridge is part of their territory."

MacBride stepped forward, shielding his eyes from the sun. "One warrior doesn't pose a threat, but he's a sign that there are likely more nearby. We must be cautious."

Ogden, leaning on his rifle, added, "He's making no move to approach or signal. Likely, he's just observing, maybe even sending a message of his tribe's presence. We see it all the time."

"It's a warning," MacLane muttered.

Boyd, always the optimist, chuckled. "Maybe he's just admiring our camp setup."

Despite his joking, everyone knew the gravity of the situation. In unknown territory, the dynamics with the local tribes were unpredictable. An ally one day could become a foe the next, depending on circumstances.

Blue Fox, her gaze still fixed on the distant figure, spoke up, "It's customary for the Paiute to watch newcomers. It's their way of assessing intentions. They're proud people, protective of their lands."

I nodded, remembering her reverence of this land the previous night. "Then we respect their customs. We continue as planned, making no aggressive moves."

As the morning wore on, the lone Paiute warrior remained a sentinel on the ridge, watching the camp's every move. His presence was a lingering reminder of the complexities of the land and the many narratives that had played out upon it long before we had arrived.

As I was checking over the supplies, Boyd ambled over, a wide grin plastered across his rugged face. Asher followed closely behind, a mischievous twinkle in his eye. Given the events of recent days, their playfulness was a surprise.

"So, Christian," Boyd began, slinging an arm around my shoulder and pulling me into a mock headlock, "seems like you and Blue Fox had quite the moonlit rendezvous last night."

I struggled free, my cheeks burning. "What are you on about?"

Asher snickered. "Oh, don't play coy with us. The whole camp noticed the two of you wandering off together. And returning together. Connected some dots, have you?"

I tried to brush them off. "We just talked, that's all. About the land… and things."

"About the 'land'?" Boyd smirked, nudging Asher. "That's a new one. Haven't heard that excuse before."

"Must be some 'land' to keep you out all night," Asher added with a wink.

I rolled my eyes, pushing past them. "You two have too much free time."

Boyd chuckled. "You're a good kid, Christian. You don't kiss and tell." He grabbed my arm gently to stop me. "Look, Christian," he said, his expression turning more serious, "we're giving you a hard time, but Lord knows you've made mistakes that cost us. You deserve a few lickings. And it makes us feel better, too."

Asher sighed, running a hand through his hair. "It's hard to forget what happened. Though, you did save our hides, and we won't forget that, either."

I swallowed, their words hanging over me like a hangman's noose. "And I'll regret my mistakes every day. But thank you. Both of you. For giving me a chance. I hope to earn your forgiveness."

"We'll get there, kid." Boyd clapped my shoulder. "And we're happy you and Blue Fox are getting along. Makes for good camp gossip."

The three of us stood there for a moment, a newfound understanding bridging the distance between us. We had a long journey ahead, but at that moment, it felt like we were on the path to healing.

The sun was still just a suggestion in the sky when we began our day, its weak light only gradually illuminating the expansive stretch of southeastern Oregon Country. As the hours stretched on, my thoughts returned to Blue Fox. Our moonlit encounter, that intimate moment we'd shared, still hung fresh in my mind. The depth of what I felt was new and exciting, yet at the same time, a creeping unease accompanied it. The land that had facilitated our bond seemed to be shifting, holding a new mystery.

It wasn't just the stark landscape that had me on edge; it was a feeling that was hard to shake, a sensation of being watched. I glanced around, trying to catch sight of anything unusual, yet nothing stood out. But the feeling persisted.

Blue Fox noticed my restlessness. "It's the Paiute," she murmured, sidling up to me during one of our short breaks. "Ever since we spotted that warrior, they've kept an eye on us."

Questions swirled in my thoughts. "Do you think they mean us harm?"

She pondered for a moment, eyes scanning the horizon. "Not necessarily. But this is their land. We are guests, and not all guests are welcome. Especially if their intentions aren't clear."

Overhearing our conversation, MacBride said, "They're just curious. As long as we keep to ourselves and respect their territory, they won't bother us."

Days turned into nights, and nights back into days. The routines of travel became automatic: setting up camp, breaking it down, rationing supplies. Yet, through it all, the feeling of unseen eyes never left. Our murmurs around the campfire grew more frequent as everyone, not just me, felt the invisible presence of the Paiute.

One evening, MacLane shared a story of a previous expedition when they'd encountered a different but similar tribe. They'd felt watched for days, until one evening the tribe had revealed themselves, merely wishing to trade. It was meant to be a comforting tale, but the tension lingered.

The land around us began to change, the stretches of barren desert giving way to patches of greenery, with wetlands occasionally dotting the horizon. Birds of various kinds flitted in the sky, their songs a welcome respite from the eerie silence we'd grown accustomed to.

Finally, after what felt like an eternity of walking, we reached a vantage point. Below us stretched an immense body of water, shimmering under the late afternoon sun, its edges blurring into marshlands. From our elevated position, the shallow lake appeared as a vast mirror, reflecting the sky's soft hues, interrupted only by the sporadic movement of waterfowl.

MacBride broke the silence. "This is it, the heart of Oregon Country. Uncharted, unknown."

Beside me, Blue Fox inhaled deeply, her gaze lost in the distance. "It's beautiful."

The breathtaking view momentarily made us forget that we were being watched. But as the sun began its descent, casting long shadows behind us, I couldn't help but feel that our journey into the unknown was just beginning.

# CHAPTER 14
## THE HIGH DESERT OASIS

The morning air was cool, and a mist hung over the shallow, swampy lake, giving it an ethereal, almost dreamlike quality. The calmness of the scene was broken only by soft paddle strokes as our canoes moved slowly through the water.

"We'll start with the tributaries. If my instincts are correct, we should find a good population of beaver here," MacBride declared, his voice carrying over the still water. His eyes were alight with excitement and hope. This was what we had come for, after all.

As we moved closer to where the lake's waters mingled with the incoming streams, signs of beaver activity became evident: freshly gnawed tree stumps, the telltale slides leading into the water, and the occasional slap of a beaver tail echoing in the distance. Boyd had taught me along the way what to look for, and it felt satisfying to see them.

With her keen eyesight, Blue Fox was the first to spot one. "There," she whispered, pointing to a ripple in the water. And then, as if on cue, a beaver surfaced briefly before diving down again.

Boyd let out a low whistle. "Looks like you were right, MacBride. This place is teeming with them."

Asher, ever the skeptic, chimed in, "One beaver doesn't mean—"

Before he could finish, MacLane interrupted, "Look there! And there!" Multiple ripples and the occasional dark silhouette gliding through the water made it clear that this was not just one or two isolated beavers. We had stumbled upon a thriving habitat.

"We'll set up traps along this stretch," MacBride decided, his voice full of satisfaction.

We had barely begun to set up camp when Blue Fox began crafting tall poles from sturdy tree limbs. She worked efficiently, her hands deftly stripping away any excess twigs or foliage. Before long, she was erecting her teepee. Her movements had a certain grace and rhythm, and I found myself watching, captivated.

MacBride called out, "This isn't just a stopover. Settle in for the long haul—we've struck brown gold!" His voice echoed with authority, and we all sprang into action.

Ogden's men moved past our clearing and set up their own camp on the western side of us. They made their camp quickly and set about resting, watching us as we worked.

Boyd and Asher marked out an area to dig earthworks. With the potential threat of the Paiute and other unknown dangers, these fortifications would provide some protection against any unexpected attacks. As the dirt flew, MacLane and a couple of others headed into the trees with axes in hand. The rhythmic thuds of felling trees soon filled the air.

I joined Bear and a few men who were tasked with cutting logs into suitable lengths for building. The sharp scent of freshly cut wood tickled my nostrils, and the sound of axes biting into timber became a sort of rustic melody.

As dusk approached, the camp began to take shape. MacBride supervised the construction of a central fire pit, outlining a spot right in the heart of our encampment. Following Blue Fox's lead, some men set up their tents while others built nests using our prepared logs. Every structure was erected with an eye for durability, as we knew we'd be here for some time.

I took a moment to step back, surveying our progress. The camp was a hive of activity, a well-organized chaos.

Men moved with purpose, each contributing to the effort. Tools clinked, voices chattered, and the ambience of a community coming together grew stronger with each passing hour.

At one point, MacBride approached me, clapping a heavy hand on my shoulder. "You've done well, lad," he said, his eyes taking in the sprawling camp. "We're turning this wilderness into something that resembles home."

I smiled, warmed by his praise. "It's all hands on deck, MacBride. We're all doing our part."

He chuckled. "True, but don't sell yourself short."

"I'm just glad we made it," I said, feeling my confidence in our expedition rising. After all we had survived to get to this place, it felt as if we had made it home, in a sense.

"Aye. The hard part's over, I think," MacBride said. "At this rate, we'll be in Fort Nez Perce in no time, negotiating that deal Astor sent you for, and then you'll be on your way home to New York. It must feel good."

"Hm," was all I could reply.

It should have felt good, but it didn't. I still had so much ground to make up with Blue Fox, and the land, the wilderness, and the serenity of God's grand creation had started to win me over. For the first time since our journey had begun, I resisted the thought of returning to the city.

Night had fully settled by the time we sat down to eat. Around the central fire, the glow painted a picture of camaraderie. Stories and laughter flowed freely, and for a few hours, the challenges of our journey melted away.

As the night deepened and the stars glittered overhead, I lay back on my makeshift bed, reflecting on the day. We had transformed an untouched piece of wilderness into our temporary abode. And while the campfires burned brightly, signaling our presence, the vast darkness above reminded us how small we truly were in the grand scheme of things.

As dawn's light pierced the canvas of my tent, I could hear the distinct sound of activity outside. Emerging, I noticed Ogden's crew busily packing their belongings, loading up their bags, and preparing for departure.

Walking over to their camp, I found Ogden overseeing the preparations, his demeanor focused and purposeful. He glanced up as I approached. "Morning," he said with a nod.

"Leaving so soon?" I inquired, though I knew the answer.

His gaze lingered on the horizon. "As promised," he said. "We're pushing farther. There's uncharted territory out there, and I intend to see it."

A part of me admired his relentless spirit and his desire to venture into the unknown. "Any idea what you'll find?"

He grinned, the corners of his eyes crinkling. "That's the thrill of it, isn't it? No idea. But whatever's out there, we'll face it."

I looked over to his crew, a hearty bunch who seemed ready for any challenge. It was evident from how they worked together, moving with a sense of unity, how much they respected Ogden.

MacBride approached us, offering him a firm handshake. "Safe travels," he said. "If you find a river of gold or a mountain of diamonds, remember us."

Ogden chuckled. "I'll send word, don't you worry."

They exchanged a few more words about possible routes and potential dangers. Despite their brief time together, the two leaders had clearly formed a bond of mutual respect.

As Ogden's company began their march westward, the rest of our crew gathered to see them off. There were handshakes, backslaps, and a few hearty laughs. Amid the farewells, Boyd shouted, "Remember us when you're famous, Pete!"

Ogden turned, raising a hand in acknowledgment, his company illuminated in orange hues by the rising sun. "Will do!"

And just like that, they were gone, disappearing into the vast expanse of Oregon Country. Our paths had converged for a brief moment in time, and now they diverged once more, each group carving its own trail in the annals of exploration.

The usual morning clamor of our camp—the clinking of cooking pots, the occasional call of someone seeking a misplaced tool—was interrupted by the sudden and urgent thudding of heavy footsteps. Georges burst into view, dirt and sweat streaking his face. It took me a moment to realize he was alone. Where was Jean-Baptiste?

"MacBride!" Georges shouted, his voice laced with unmistakable panic. Camp activities abruptly stopped, and all eyes turned to the Métis scout.

MacBride was by his side in an instant, his seasoned eyes scanning Georges' face for an explanation. "What happened? Where's Jean-Baptiste?"

Georges was panting heavily, trying to catch his breath. I translated as he spoke. "We were scouting up north, near that ridge. Jean-Baptiste slipped. Fell down a damn ravine. His leg… It's broken. Snapped clean."

A wave of murmurs coursed through our camp. I could feel a cold knot forming in my stomach. The wilderness was as beautiful as it was brutal. One wrong step and the land could claim you.

"We need to get to him fast," Blue Fox said, already grabbing her medicine pouch and a length of sturdy cloth.

MacBride nodded, his face a mask of determination. "Georges, take us to him. Boyd, Asher, gather some supplies and follow. We'll need ropes, blankets, and water."

The camp sprang to life as everyone scurried to gather the needed supplies. I grabbed my own kit, ensuring I had everything I might need. But as I moved to follow the group, MacBride's commanding presence halted me.

"Christian," he began, his tone firm, "I need you here. The Paiute are an unknown factor, and the camp can't be left bare. We need trusted men to hold it down."

I hesitated, glancing in the direction the others had headed. "Of course," I finally agreed. "We'll secure things here."

The rescue group departed in a rush, leaving the camp eerily silent. MacLane, with his always-alert eyes, and Bear, whose size was only dwarfed by his gentle nature, remained with me. To pass the time, the three of us set to work, continuing the construction of the shed. We'd flattened a good section of ground, and a few sturdy logs had been felled. Now it was a matter of piecing it all together.

MacLane threw a sideways glance at Blue Fox's tepee as we worked. "She's quite something, isn't she?" he remarked casually.

Bear chuckled. "That she is. You ever seen a woman quite like Blue Fox?"

MacLane smirked. "Not in all my years. Those eyes... sharp as an eagle's and twice as fierce."

As they continued, sharing a laugh and reminiscing about other women they'd encountered in their travels, I grew increasingly tense. The playful banter felt like a sharp sting. Was I so transparent that even they noticed my budding feelings for her?

"I've seen the way Christian looks at her," Bear teased.

MacLane turned to me, his eyebrows raised. "Oh? Is that so?"

I grimaced, my ax suddenly feeling heavier in my hands. "Can we focus on the task?" I snapped, more harshly than I intended.

Bear held up his hands in mock surrender, but his eyes showed a glint of seriousness. "Just making conversation, friend. No harm intended."

We worked in relative silence for a while, the rhythmic sounds of our tools echoing. Yet I couldn't shake off the burning sensation in my chest, a mix of embarrassment and jealousy.

By the time the sun began to dip, casting long, slanting shadows across the camp, we'd made significant progress on the shed. Exhausted but satisfied, we sat around the fire. The night darkened around us as the orange glow from the fire flickered across our faces. MacLane, his face partially shadowed, kept shooting me side glances. I pretended not to notice, keeping my eyes on the fire, my hand tight around my mug.

"You know, Christian," he began, his voice dripping with contempt, "it's quite interesting how you've found a place among us after what you did."

Bear stiffened beside me, but he didn't intervene. The atmosphere thickened, only the crackling flames punctuating the silence.

I took a deep breath. "MacLane, I've paid for my mistakes. MacBride trusts me—so should you."

His sneer became more pronounced. "Trust? Why would I trust someone like you? It's quite amusing that you think you belong here."

I clenched my jaw, trying to maintain my composure. "Enough. We all have our pasts. Let's leave it at that."

But he was relentless. "You think because MacBride might have a soft spot for you, for whatever reason, that you've earned your place? Don't kid yourself."

His words were tinged with a dangerous edge, as if his resentment had been building for a while, and I felt my patience slipping. "MacLane, drop it."

He leaned forward, eyes narrowed. "Or what? You'll make another mistake?"

The insult stung. I could see his eyes glittering with malevolence in the fire's glow. It was clear that this wasn't just about past mistakes; it was personal.

"I don't want any trouble," I responded, voice low, "but I won't be your punching bag."

"Oh, brave words," he mocked. "Must have picked them up from our Indian harlot."

That was it. My blood boiled. "Careful, MacLane. You might not like what happens if you keep pushing."

His laughter was cold. "What will you do? Have your harlot defend you?"

The fire seemed to roar louder in my ears. "Say one more word," I warned, "and you'll regret it."

His eyes glinted. "At least when I make a mistake, I own it. Not hide behind others or pretty faces."

His words cut deep, and a part of me wanted to unleash my frustration right then and there. The air was electric, each of us waiting for the other to make the next move.

I closed my eyes for a moment, taking a deep breath to calm my racing heart. When I opened them, I looked directly into MacLane's challenging gaze. "It's not about hiding," I said evenly. "It's about knowing when a fight is worth it."

His smirk was infuriating, but I wouldn't give him the satisfaction of losing my cool. "You might want to take a leaf from my book," I continued, "instead of always hiding behind MacBride's shadow like a cowering lapdog."

Bear gasped, and we both looked at him. He placed his hand over his mouth laughing and motioned for us to look away.

MacLane's face turned a shade darker, his jaw clenching. "What did you just say?"

I tilted my chin up, a defiant gleam in my eyes. "You heard me. Maybe if you stopped being his lackey for once, you might actually earn some respect around here."

For a split second, there was a tense stillness. But it was quickly shattered when MacLane lunged at me with a guttural roar. The calm restraint I'd been so desperately holding on to slipped away in the face of his attack.

Before I could react, his weight was on me, the two of us crashing into the dusty ground. The fire illuminated our faces as we grappled, mud splattering and fists flying. My focus narrowed; my only thought was defending myself.

But just as quickly as it had begun, a strong pair of hands grabbed us both, pulling us apart. Bear's large frame stood between us, his arms outstretched, forcing distance.

"Enough!" he roared, his voice echoing through the campsite. His eyes, usually calm and collected, were now filled with a rare anger.

MacLane and I were both panting hard, the adrenaline still coursing through our veins. Bear pointed at me, then at the ground opposite the campfire. "Sit," he commanded. Then he pointed at MacLane. "You sit over there."

Neither of us dared argue. We took our designated spots, eyes never leaving each other. The camp was eerily silent except for the crackling of the fire and our labored breaths.

After ensuring we were settled, Bear took his place by the fire, casting a watchful eye over the both of us. "Now," he said, his voice more controlled but still stern, "I suggest we all keep our mouths shut and our hands to ourselves until MacBride and the others return."

The night seemed to stretch on endlessly. The sounds of nature, the chirping of crickets, and the distant hoot of an owl only emphasized the uncomfortable tension between us. Every so often, I snuck a glance at MacLane, who stared intently at the fire, his features shadowed but his anger evident.

The moment MacBride and the others entered the camp, I could sense the heavy air of despair surrounding them. Georges, usually an energetic man, was silent, his face wet with tears. His comrade's absence was a void that weighed on all of us.

Bear approached MacBride, offering a nod of understanding before retreating back to his place by the fire. MacLane laid a hand on Georges' shoulder, attempting to provide some form of comfort.

"What happened?" I asked.

"Christian." Exhaustion lined MacBride's voice. "We couldn't find Jean-Baptiste."

I swallowed hard, the lump in my throat growing. "But... Georges said he was injured. How did he just disappear?"

Blue Fox, her face a mask of stoicism but her eyes betraying her sorrow, took a deep breath before answering. "Jean-Baptiste must've tried to find his way back after Georges left him. I tracked him to a patch of wood up north."

She paused, taking another steadying breath. "When I got there, it was clear that wolves had taken him."

The weight of her words settled over the camp like a suffocating blanket. Though we all knew the harsh realities of this land, its cruelty never ceased to sting. I could feel my chest tightening. Jean-Baptiste, the younger of the Métis, was gone, taken by nature in its rawest, most unforgiving form.

As the night deepened, we gathered closer together. Because the Métis had kept to themselves, we had no stories of them, but we did share memories of Jim and Roarke, celebrating their lives as we mourned their untimely ends. In the heart of the wilderness, we were reminded once again of the fragility of life and the strength of our bonds.

As the campfire embers glowed dimly, most of the company began retreating into their tents, the weight of the day's events weighing heavily on their shoulders. I caught Blue Fox's gaze from across the fire, the soft light casting shadows over her face. I motioned towards the wilderness beyond, a silent invitation for another of our moonlit walks.

She hesitated, her eyes searching mine for a moment. It wasn't the usual fiery determination I was accustomed to seeing, but rather a vulnerable uncertainty.

"Christian," she began, her voice soft, "I… I cannot."

I felt a pang of disappointment, but I tried to hide it. "Is something wrong?"

She sighed, drawing herself up with the same pride and strength I had always admired. "The others are talking," she admitted. "And as much as I would like to think it doesn't matter, the perception of our companions holds weight."

I furrowed my brows in confusion. "Talking? About what?"

"Us," she whispered. "They see us, and as flattering as it is to have their attention, it's not the attention I want. I've worked hard to earn my place, to show that I am just as capable as any man, if not more. I fear that this… whatever it is between us will overshadow that. I don't want to be reduced to the woman in love."

A lump formed in my throat, the weight of her words settling heavily. It was a perspective I hadn't fully considered, a side of the coin I hadn't seen. The world we inhabited, the rough and rugged world of fur trapping and wilderness, demanded strength and respect. For a woman, especially, it was a tightrope walk.

"Blue Fox," I whispered, "my admiration for you, my feelings—they don't stem from a desire to weaken you, but because I'm in awe of your strength."

She smiled faintly, the moonlight catching the glint of a tear in her eye. "I know, Christian. And I value that. But right now I can't risk anything that might disrupt my place with the expedition."

I nodded, feeling a pang of sadness. "All right."

She placed a hand on my arm, her touch warm and comforting. "Thank you, Christian."

And with that, she retreated to her teepee, leaving me alone with the embers and my thoughts.

The morning sun peeked over the horizon, casting the camp in a soft golden hue. I was adjusting a trap when MacBride's gruff voice called out, "Christian, MacLane, with me."

MacLane and I exchanged a glance, both of us clearly aware of what was to come. As we followed MacBride, I noticed he was leading us farther from the camp, ensuring our conversation remained private. Finally, after we'd walked for what felt like an eternity, MacBride stopped and faced us, his imposing silhouette framed by the rising sun.

"I heard about the scuffle last night," he began, his voice low and simmering with anger. "Bear told me everything."

I took a deep breath, bracing myself for the onslaught. MacLane's gaze remained fixed on the ground, but I could see the defiance in his expression.

"I brought you both out here," MacBride continued, "not just to discuss what happened but to remind you of our goal. We have a mission to complete, and I'll not have petty squabbles or old grudges getting in the way."

I nodded. "I understand."

MacLane muttered something under his breath, which only seemed to infuriate MacBride more.

"Look at me when I'm speaking to you," he snapped. MacLane slowly raised his head, his wounded look evident, but there was also a stubborn resistance.

"We're in the heart of the wilderness," MacBride continued, his voice stern. "Any mistake, any discord, can cost us our lives. I've seen it happen too many times. Men torn apart by beasts—or worse, by their own stubborn pride."

Silence hung heavily between us. I swallowed hard, his words sinking in.

"I won't have any more disruptions," MacBride warned. "If you two can't find a way to work together, then by God, I'll make sure you do."

I nodded again. "Understood, MacBride."

MacLane took a moment longer, showing rebelliousness against his leader for the first time, before he finally nodded in agreement.

"Good," MacBride said, his tone softening just a fraction. "Now, let's get back to work."

And with that, he turned and headed back to the camp, leaving us in an uneasy truce. MacLane waited a moment before storming off, his anger visible even from a distance. A momentary stillness settled over the landscape, interrupted only by the distant sound of the camp coming to life. As I made my way back, a shimmer on the horizon caught my attention.

There he was. The Paiute warrior, the sentinel on the hilltop. My heart raced. I glanced at my camp, but no one else appeared to have spotted him. When I looked back in his direction, he began to turn his horse, as if to leave. I hardly knew what came over me in that moment—I just sprang into action, marching toward the warrior to make contact with him before he vanished once more.

Every step I took was deliberate over the rough terrain. As I ascended the hill, the warrior stilled, not giving away any hint of his intentions. He sat astride a sturdy horse, both seeming one with the landscape.

Drawing closer, I raised my hand in a gesture of peace. The Paiute studied me intently, his eyes sharp and assessing. I stopped a few feet away, close enough to see the intricate patterns painted on his face and the feathered adornments of his attire but far enough to allow him space.

"Hello." The word felt clumsy and out of place. In case he understood French, I followed it up with, "Bonjour."

He responded with a series of words unfamiliar to my ears. Clearly, he spoke neither English nor French, and my knowledge of the Paiute language was nonexistent. Communication would be a challenge. I regretted not seeking out Blue Fox. But if I had, the warrior would have disappeared again.

Drawing a deep breath, I decided to employ the universal language of gestures. Pointing to the camp and then to myself, I tried to convey that we meant no harm. In response, the warrior gestured to the land, sweeping his hand in a wide arc, perhaps indicating the vastness of his tribe's territory or questioning our intentions.

Thinking quickly, I knelt and drew a simple map in the sand. I depicted the river, our path, and the lake, trying to show our journey and our plans to trap and trade. I hoped it would indicate that we intended to stay temporarily.

The Paiute watched, his expression unreadable. After a moment, he dismounted and knelt, then etched symbols and patterns around my rudimentary map. He drew a series of interconnected circles among the symbols, possibly indicating the various Paiute bands or settlements. He pointed at one circle, then to himself, and then drew a line connecting it to our camp.

I took this to mean his tribe or band was close by, and our presence might impact them. I nodded in understanding, trying to convey empathy and a willingness to cooperate.

He pointed at the interconnected circles and then at the camp, making a gesture of coming together. I surmised he was suggesting a potential meeting or collaboration between his people and ours. I nodded eagerly, hoping to forge a positive relationship.

The warrior pointed to the horizon, where the sun was gradually climbing, and gestured for me to follow. I hesitated for a moment, considering the implications, but the prospect of understanding and bridging the gap between our worlds was too tempting to resist.

As we descended the hill, the Paiute led me to a hidden grove by the lake, where a clear stream flowed. He bent down, scooped water into his hands, and drank. I followed suit, the cool water refreshing against the morning heat.

A sense of tranquility settled between us, a shared moment of respect. As the gentle ripples of the stream caught the morning light, a rustle of footsteps from behind shattered the stillness.

I turned to see Blue Fox emerging from the tree line, her eyes scanning the scene. As she approached, her gaze shifted from me to the Paiute warrior, who watched her with mild curiosity.

"Christian," she began, her voice a mixture of relief and reproach, "you wandered off without a word. Do you realize how dangerous—"

"Blue Fox," I interrupted, gesturing towards the Paiute. "He's been watching our camp. I thought it was best to speak with him and establish a connection."

She sighed, shaking her head, then turned to the warrior, exchanging a few words in Paiute. The conversation was punctuated by gestures, with Blue Fox often pausing, seemingly trying to decipher his meaning.

The Paiute pointed towards the distance, where the silhouette of a village was faintly visible against the vast horizon. He gestured to both of us and then himself, drawing a line in the sand connecting our position to the village.

Blue Fox nodded, turning back to me with a raised eyebrow. "It seems you've made an impression. I think he's inviting us to his village. He's impressed by your courage to approach him without arms, without fear."

I blinked in surprise. "I… I just wanted to understand, to make a connection."

"And you have," she said. "But it doesn't change the fact that you should've been more cautious."

I lowered my head, acknowledging her point. "I'm sorry, Blue Fox. It was impulsive."

She sighed, her stern demeanor softening. "Just... next time, let me know. Especially with everything that's happening in the camp."

The Paiute mounted his horse gracefully, waiting for us. Blue Fox and I exchanged a glance, a silent agreement passing between us. We would visit the village together, hoping to bridge the vast chasm of misunderstanding and build a foundation of trust.

With one last look at the stream, I followed Blue Fox and the Paiute warrior, the three of us moving in unison toward the horizon and the promise of newfound alliances.

As we trailed behind the Paiute warrior, the landscape shifted familiarly, the details of each rock, tree, and shrub eerily reminiscent. Soon the outlines of our camp came into view, and I felt utter confusion. How had I managed to get lost so close to our base?

Blue Fox shot me a look, her eyes amused. "I think I misunderstood him."

The Paiute stopped just before the camp's perimeter, turning to regard us with a serious expression. Blue Fox approached him, attempting to converse once more. Their exchange was a dance of mismatched steps, Blue Fox trying to interpret the gaps in their shared language while the warrior watched her with growing impatience.

"Christian," she finally said, turning to me with a chuckle, "it seems I did misunderstand him after all. He wasn't impressed with your bravery. He was concerned for your safety." She smirked. "He thought you had gotten lost and led you home."

My cheeks reddened. "So much for forging new alliances," I murmured.

She sighed. "Well, at least we've established a connection, albeit not the one we hoped for."

The Paiute warrior, observing our exchange, motioned towards the items at our camp—the pelts, tools, and provisions. It became evident he was curious about trade.

Seizing the opportunity, Blue Fox began gesturing at various items she was carrying, attempting to communicate their value. She pointed towards the beaver pelts, tools, and food, then made a swapping motion, trying to gauge his interest in a barter.

The Paiute warrior watched carefully, his face giving away little. His gaze settled on certain items for a few moments but then flitted away, neither confirming nor denying his interest. The tension of the negotiation lingered in the air.

After what felt like hours, he pointed to a few pelts and tools in particular, making a gesture that clearly indicated trade.

Blue Fox nodded slowly, then pointed towards his belongings, trying to decipher what he was willing to offer. The warrior, understanding her query, unveiled a collection of items from his pack—beautifully crafted arrowheads, woven feather bracelets, and other intricate jewelry.

Blue Fox picked up an arrowhead, admiring the craftsmanship. The Paiute nodded in acknowledgment, then picked up a steel hunting knife, running his fingers over its surface.

Their silent barter continued for a while, each item's worth weighed and measured, not just in material value but in the effort and skill behind its creation.

As the sun crept higher in the sky, it became apparent that they had reached an agreement of sorts. The Paiute warrior, collecting his new acquisitions, gave us a nod— not exactly warm but acknowledging our trade.

Blue Fox, cradling the arrowhead in her hand, turned to me. "It's not the alliance we expected, but it's a start. Trade is a universal language, and through it, we might find common ground."

I nodded, still embarrassed by my earlier blunder. "Thank you, Blue Fox, for bridging the gap."

She smiled faintly. "Next time, just ask me to go with you."

Blue Fox and I returned to camp under the inquisitive gaze of our companions.

# CHAPTER 15
# THE PAIUTE

The cool morning air was alive with anticipation as we prepared for the Paiute's arrival. In the days since our first meeting, the warrior had returned to trade several times until Blue Fox convinced him to return with his village elders for a feast. The camp had been tidied up, and a central space was cleared for the cultural exchange. She warned us to be on our best behavior; these Paiute had never seen white men before.

While the rest of us buzzed about camp to prepare for our guests, MacLane sat alone on the far side of camp, pouting. Though he and I had not seen eye to eye from the start, I felt compelled to approach him. I had to make sure everyone played their part, even him.

"What's the matter, MacLane?" I asked him.

He kept his back toward me and said, "This whole thing's a mistake."

"What makes you say that?"

"We know nothing about these Paiutes, and they of us. For all we know, they'll rob us blind and slit our throats. Plenty of tribes like the Blackfoot out there," he explained.

"If that's who they are, don't you think they would have done us in by now?" I asked.

"Hard to say," he scoffed. "MacBride thinks it's a mistake, too."

"He didn't say anything," I said.

"'Cause he's had a right stauner for you since you helped him kill Jean-Louis," he growled.

I sensed his resentment toward me more than ever. "We are on the same side, MacLane. We need allies out here."

"You're going to get us all killed. But who am I to stop you? No one in this company listens to me anyway."

His words gave me pause. I stepped away with a strange feeling in my gut. Something was building inside of him that frightened me. He had proven himself to be a dangerous man more than once, and there he had the look of a broken man. It was a dangerous combination. But before I could discuss it with MacBride, the Paiute made themselves known.

In the distance, a series of soft chants broke the tranquility of the morning, growing steadily louder. From the hill's crest, the Paiute delegation appeared, led by the warrior who'd first made contact with us. Their rhythmic singing, combined with the soft thudding of their feet on the earth, brought a magical resonance to the atmosphere. They carried tools, baskets, intricately woven blankets, and pots, showcasing the handicrafts of their people.

Blue Fox stepped forward, her posture radiating confidence. She began humming a soft melody, an inviting tune from her heritage. As the song ended, she greeted the Paiute leader with a gentle nod. "Welcome," she began. "Today, we hope to share stories, traditions, and hopes for the future."

The Paiute leader, adorned in a long tan beaded robe, nodded back. His sharp features and eyes seemed to penetrate time. Through a series of gestures and a few words that Blue Fox seemed to comprehend, he conveyed their appreciation for this gesture of friendship.

The day unfolded in a beautiful tapestry of experiences. I watched in awe as a Paiute craftsman showed Boyd how to fashion a tool using just stone and bone while another demonstrated the intricate art of basket weaving to a group of captivated onlookers, including myself.

In one corner, Paiute children played a game that involved tossing small pebbles into a hole. Their laughter and shouts filled the air, the universal language of joy.

Blue Fox had gathered a circle around her. With animated gestures and infectious enthusiasm, she shared legends of her people—stories of brave warriors, cunning tricksters, and lessons from nature. The Paiute listened intently, and when she finished, one of their elders stepped up. With Blue Fox translating snippets, he spun tales of their ancestors, the vast deserts and the mysteries they held, the spirits that watched over them, and the sacredness of the land.

As the sun descended, casting a warm golden hue, I sat beside the Paiute warrior. Our conversation was limited, given the language barrier, but through simple gestures, smiles, and nods, we forged a silent bond.

Bear showed him his sketches of the land, the animals, and of their tribe from a distance. He seemed impressed, pointing to a sketch of a coyote and then to himself, letting out a soft chuckle. I assumed it was some inside joke or perhaps a shared myth.

Looking around, I realized that this day was about more than just sharing traditions and tools. It was about finding common ground, about understanding that despite our differences, at the core, we were all just people trying to make sense of the world and find our place in it.

The day concluded with a shared feast. Both groups contributed, creating a spread that was as diverse as the stories we'd shared. As we sat under the canopy of stars, breaking bread together, I felt a profound sense of gratitude.

This was what it meant to truly explore—not just to traverse lands but to delve deep into the heart of cultures, to understand and be understood. The world felt a little smaller that night, and our journey's purpose a little clearer.

Laughter echoed from one end of the clearing to the other, mingling with the aroma of roasting meat and the smoky tendrils rising from the fires. Between mouthfuls of food, men from both parties exchanged stories, gestures, and even songs, attempting to bridge the chasm of language with shared human experiences.

Sitting at the head of the gathering, MacBride took in the scene, his mind seeming to work overtime. Beside him, Blue Fox translated snippets of conversation, her voice soothing and rhythmic. MacBride nodded occasionally, his gaze never wavering from the group of Paiute leaders sitting across from him.

Clearing his throat, he stood up, drawing the attention of everyone present. The murmurs died down as MacBride began to speak, his voice firm yet laden with respect.

"Friends," he began, his voice echoing through the clearing, "we came here as strangers, seeking new lands, new resources. But friendship is what we have found, a value more than furs or gold."

The Paiute leaders exchanged glances, their expressions unreadable. MacBride continued, "We understand the significance of this land to you. It is not just dirt and trees but history, ancestors, and spirits. We wish to respect that. But we also hope for a future here, a place where our people can live side by side, reaping the benefits of this bountiful land together."

There was a moment's pause. The weight of MacBride's words settled over the gathering, the air thick with anticipation. Blue Fox began translating. As she spoke, the Paiute leaders nodded in understanding, their faces softening.

MacBride took a deep breath. "I propose a treaty, an agreement between our people. We promise not to overhunt, to respect the sacred grounds, and in return, we ask for your guidance, your wisdom about this land, and the opportunity to trade fairly."

A hush fell over the gathering. The Paiute leaders whispered amongst themselves, their expressions contemplative. One of the elder Paiute, distinguished by intricate tattoos and an air of wisdom, slowly stood up. He spoke at length, his voice calm but firm. Blue Fox translated for MacBride as he spoke, her voice barely above a whisper.

"He says they do not know us nor how many of us there are still to come. They cannot make an alliance until they know us better."

MacBride nodded, understanding the elder's reservations. "Tell him that our word is our bond. We are trappers, not conquerors. And to prove our sincerity, we will honor their customs and rituals and offer gifts as a sign of our commitment."

Blue Fox conveyed MacBride's words. The elder listened intently, his eyes searching MacBride's face for any sign of deceit. Finally, after what felt like an eternity, he nodded slowly and deliberately.

"He invites you to do so, though his decision is unchanged," Blue Fox said.

The atmosphere around the campfire shifted after the Paiute elder's refusal. The joviality of moments before seemed to evaporate into the cool night air, replaced with an uneasy tension. As Blue Fox finished translating, I caught a fleeting glimpse of frustration in MacBride's eyes. The warmth in his eyes looked momentarily replaced by a man affronted, a man challenged.

For a few moments, nobody spoke. The festive ambience that had pervaded the camp was gone, replaced by a stifling silence punctuated only by the crackling of the fire and the distant hooting of an owl. It felt like the world held its breath.

MacBride finally cleared his throat, attempting to salvage the situation. "We respect your decision," he began, his voice strained. "We came here with the best of intentions, to establish a relationship of trust. But we understand your concerns."

The Paiute elder nodded in acknowledgment but did not speak. Around them, the gathered tribe members exchanged glances, their expressions guarded. I could see that the balance had shifted. The warm openness from earlier in the evening was replaced with an air of wariness.

The feast continued, but the atmosphere had changed irrevocably. Conversations were muted, the laughter less hearty. Everyone seemed acutely aware of the looming divide between the two groups. As I passed around the food, I could feel the coldness, the hesitation. Bear caught my eye from across the fire, his expression one of concern. MacLane, for once, was silent, watching the scene unfold with a grimace.

As the night deepened, I noticed MacBride increasingly withdrawing into himself, a deep furrow marking his brow. He ate little, his gaze distant. Blue Fox, ever the diplomat, tried to maintain the conviviality, speaking animatedly with the Paiute members, laughing at their stories, but the strain was evident in her eyes.

Hours passed, the fire dimmed, and the Paiute members began to drift away one by one. With a final nod towards MacBride, the elder retreated into the darkness, his departure marking the end of the gathering.

MacBride stood up abruptly. "Pack up," he ordered, his voice clipped. "We leave at first light."

Confused murmurs spread through our group. Asher approached MacBride, questioning the sudden decision. "Why? We've barely been here. The beavers—"

MacBride cut him off. "It's not safe. We overstayed our welcome."

Bear stepped forward, his eyes scanning the area. "We can handle ourselves, MacBride. Let's not be hasty."

"No." MacBride's voice was final. "We've been here long enough. It's clear they don't want us. We'll find another location."

"Let's get the hell out of here," MacLane echoed. "I don't want to stay an instant longer with those redskins skulking about."

I approached MacBride, who was busy overseeing the packing, the lantern's glow accentuating the lines of worry on his face.

"MacBride," I began, choosing my words carefully, "is leaving so suddenly the best course of action? We could try to mend relations, to understand their hesitations."

He paused, took a deep breath, and looked at me squarely. "Christian," he said, his voice heavy with concern, "this isn't the first time I've encountered a situation like this with the tribes. Years back, we met a tribe up north. They behaved just the same: warm at first, then cold and distant. We thought nothing of it, decided to stay, believing that time would mend any unseen rifts."

I listened intently—this was a piece of MacBride's history I hadn't been privy to.

"We were wrong," MacBride continued, his eyes distant. "They weren't just being cautious; they were measuring us, gauging our strength, testing our vulnerabilities. One morning, not long after, we were ambushed. We lost good men that day. I won't make the same mistake twice."

I nodded, realizing the depth of his concern. "I understand your caution, but perhaps the Paiute are different."

MacBride sighed, putting a hand on my shoulder. "Every leader carries the weight of his past decisions, Christian. I can't risk the lives of our men on a hopeful 'perhaps.' Not again."

I looked into his eyes and saw the burden of leadership, the heavy responsibility of lives entrusted to him. Here was a man who, hellbent on carrying out his mission a few weeks prior, had put us all at risk. Now that he'd recognized the error of his ways, he was trying to do things differently to keep us safe. Our journey had changed him. Gone was the boisterous, arrogant man I had met in St. Louis. This new MacBride felt more measured and considered—and I felt a greater trust in his judgment.

"Very well," I replied. "Tomorrow we pack out of here."

We returned to our tents for one last rest on the shores of that bountiful lake in the middle of the desert. The sky was draped in a canopy of stars, and a soft wind rustled the trees, but beneath those natural sounds, a faint irregularity pricked at my senses. I pushed aside the flap of my tent and carefully stepped out, my eyes scanning the darkness for any sign of movement. The campfires had reduced to smoldering embers, casting a dim glow over the campsite. Everyone seemed to be in their tents, resting peacefully in anticipation of the early morning journey.

Then a soft voice whispered my name. I turned toward the sound, squinting into the dimness. It was Blue Fox, beckoning me from the entrance of her teepee.

I hurried over, trying to make as little noise as possible. As I ducked into her tent, the scent of herbs and the warmth of the space enveloped me. She was sitting cross-legged with a look of alertness that matched my own.

"I heard it, too," she said in a low voice, her eyes glinting with concern.

"Footsteps," I whispered, my heart rate quickening. "But I couldn't see anyone."

She nodded slowly, her fingers playing with a small pouch hanging around her neck. "The night can play tricks on our senses, but these... these were not tricks. Someone or something was out there, watching."

Her words settled over me, deepening my unease. "Do you think it's the Paiute?"

She pondered for a moment, her face inscrutable. "It's possible, but I can't say for certain. They could be curious or cautious, or perhaps they're seeking an advantage should things go awry."

I felt a shiver crawl up my spine. "What do you suggest we do?"

"For now, we should stay vigilant," Blue Fox replied. "Let's take turns keeping watch. It's crucial that we are prepared for anything."

I nodded in agreement, grateful for her wisdom. We settled into a routine, alternating between watching the camp and resting, always alert to the whispers of the night.

Hours passed, and as dawn began to break, the nocturnal sounds gave way to the chirping of birds. The threat, real or imagined, seemed to have passed. Yet my unease lingered, a silent reminder of the unknown dangers that surrounded us.

The first rays of morning light had barely stretched across the horizon when a loud, guttural cry ripped through the camp, jolting everyone awake. As I scrambled out of the tent, squinting against the sunlight, I saw MacBride, his face contorted in rage, standing beside the area where we'd stored the pelts.

They were all gone.

Every single one of the beaver pelts we had painstakingly gathered over the last weeks had disappeared. The ground bore the unmistakable signs of multiple footprints. There was no doubt about it; we'd been robbed.

Men spilled out of their tents, uttering curses and exclamations of disbelief. MacLane immediately took charge of examining the tracks, tracing them into a nearby thicket.

Blue Fox joined me, her face pale but composed. "It had to be the Paiute," she murmured, keeping her voice low.

Bear strode over, his face grim. "They played us. The feast, the dance—it was all a diversion to measure us up, and while we slept, they took what they wanted."

MacLane reemerged from the thicket, frustration evident in his stance. "The tracks split up in several directions. We won't be able to trace them all."

MacBride, seething, took a deep breath, trying to contain his rage. "This is exactly what I feared," he growled, his voice laced with fury. "While we sat and hoped for peace, they took advantage of our trust."

I interjected, "We don't know that for sure, MacBride. It could've been another group, another tribe—even outsiders."

He fixed me with an icy stare. "This is Paiute land. Who else would dare? And do you still believe in coincidences after what happened last night?"

An uneasy tension filled the camp as MacBride, Bear, and MacLane busily prepared their weapons. I could sense the anger and the call for retaliation, and I knew I couldn't stand by and let things spiral further.

I moved closer, addressing MacBride directly. "We need to think this through. We have no idea how many Paiute there might be. They know this terrain far better than we do."

He stopped and looked at me, eyes hard and cold. "And? Should we just let them steal from us?"

I tried to keep my voice even. "It's not about letting them get away with theft. We need to see the bigger picture. We've been trapping on their lands. Maybe, in their view, they're just taking back what was taken from their territory."

Bear grunted, gripping his rifle tighter. "This is business, Christian. They took our property. It's theft, no matter how you spin it."

Ever eager to contradict me, MacLane sneered, "Maybe if you hadn't tried so hard to be their friend, they wouldn't have seen us as easy targets."

I exhaled deeply, fighting to keep my frustration in check. "This isn't about pointing fingers, MacLane. We're in a dangerous spot, and we need to be smart about our next move."

From the corner of my eye, I caught Asher and Boyd stepping forward, their expressions resolute. Asher spoke first, voice laced with contempt. "MacLane, don't act all high and mighty now. Weren't you the one who wanted to hightail it outta here last night?"

Boyd joined in. "Yeah, one moment you're a scared rabbit, the next you're the big brave wolf. Make up your mind."

MacBride's eyes darted between the men, weighing the arguments. "Enough," he said finally. "Christian's right. We need to leave, but we also can't let ourselves be pushed around. We'll pack up and—"

A sudden loud bang interrupted him. I flinched, looking around frantically to find the source. MacLane, face twisted in rage, was lowering his rifle, smoke still wafting from its barrel. Before any of us could react, Blue Fox rushed past us toward a small shape just beyond the clearing.

My heart sank as I approached the fallen form. A young Paiute boy, no older than fourteen, lay in the dirt, an alarming red stain spreading across his chest. His wide eyes stared blankly at the sky, his breaths shallow and erratic.

"MacLane! What have you done?!" I shouted.

He sneered back, unapologetic, "He was watching us! Probably the one who stole from us!"

I knelt beside the boy, feeling helpless as Blue Fox murmured soft words in his language, her fingers pressing against the wound in a desperate attempt to stem the flow of blood.

Tears stung my eyes. "This… this was a child, MacLane. He was unarmed! What were you thinking?"

MacLane shrugged, his cold eyes not even glancing at the dying boy. "He shouldn't have been spying."

The camp was in chaos. MacBride looked torn between rage and disbelief while Bear clenched his fists, holding himself back from lunging at MacLane.

Asher's voice, dripping with contempt, broke the tense silence. "You've just put a price on all our heads, MacLane. We should've been long gone, and now we might not even make it out of here."

We all knew the reality. Our relationship with the Paiute had deteriorated irreparably, and this tragedy was the final straw. The chances of us walking away from this land unscathed had just diminished significantly.

The atmosphere in the camp was thick with tension. Every rustle in the bushes, every distant birdcall, felt like a warning. The enormity of MacLane's action weighed heavily on us all.

Asher broke the heavy silence. "We can't stay here. Not now."

Bear nodded, rubbing his gruff chin. "We need a plan, a direction to head."

It was Boyd who finally spoke up. "We were supposed to head to the rendezvous fort on the Columbia, Fort Nez Perce. Might as well head there. They'll offer us some protection."

MacBride shot him a wary glance. "And what? Trade with what, Boyd? Our stolen pelts?"

"I'm just saying it's a place with walls, and right now, we're sitting ducks out here," Boyd retorted.

I stepped forward, fingers brushing the dirt from my palms. "Maybe Boyd's right. Not about the trade but the safety. We're deep in Paiute territory, and I doubt they'll let us be after… what just happened. But our first step should be to get back to the Snake River. Once there, we can figure out our next move."

Bear looked thoughtful. "It's a long trek back to the Snake, and with the state we're in, it's bound to be treacherous."

I took a deep breath. "It's true. We're low on supplies, and God knows what the Paiute might be planning. But the Snake River is familiar territory; at least it gets us out of immediate danger."

MacLane piped up. "But what about supplies? We'll run out before we even get there."

"We might find some game on the way," Asher countered. "And berries, roots… We've survived on less."

There was a collective nod of agreement.

MacBride seemed deep in thought, the weight of the group's fate heavy on his shoulders. Finally, he said, "All right, the Snake River it is. But we move quickly and keep a low profile. No fires during the day, and low fires at night. We'll take turns keeping watch. No more mistakes."

The group nodded again, understanding the gravity of our situation.

Bear took charge. "Let's break camp. Everyone, grab what you can. Leave anything that will slow us down."

I looked over at Blue Fox, who was whispering a prayer over the lifeless body of the Paiute boy. Our eyes met, and I saw sorrow and determination in her gaze. The road ahead was uncertain, filled with unknown challenges. But at that moment, I knew we would face them together.

We set off, walking briskly through the wilderness, every sound magnified, every shadow a potential threat. But as the hours turned into days, our resolve grew. We were a unit, moving with a single purpose—survival.

As we moved farther away from the tragedy, memories seemed to weigh heavy on all our minds. The stolen pelts, MacLane's recklessness, the death of the young Paiute boy

—all these events seemed to converge into a single point of tension that hung over us like a storm cloud.

Yet, amidst the trials, there were moments of beauty. The Oregon Country landscape, with its vast high desert plains and majestic painted hills, offered a constant reminder of the wonders of the world. And as we trudged along, there were times when the sheer magnificence of our surroundings took our breath away.

But the further we journeyed, the more apparent it became that our supplies were dwindling at an alarming rate. Every meal was a careful calculation, with each member rationing their portions to ensure that we had enough to last until we reached our destination.

One evening, as the sun set behind the distant peaks, casting long shadows across the valley, we made camp by a small stream. The soft babbling of the water was a soothing contrast to the harsh realities of our journey.

I was sitting by the fire, lost in thought, when Blue Fox approached. She sat next to me, her eyes reflecting the flames.

"We have come a long way," she said quietly. "I'm surprised the Paiute haven't caught up to us yet."

I nodded, taking a deep breath. "Perhaps they decided not to chase us."

We sat together in silence, lulled into a sense of calm by the soft trickling of the water in the stream. I had wanted so much out of our journey to that place. There had been hope for peace and prosperity. So much of our journey had been marred by bloodshed and revenge. I could not blame the Paiute for wanting the same. It had all escalated out of my control, and yet again, my actions had landed us in trouble.

She smiled, placing a gentle hand on my arm. "Let's hope."

The tranquility of our moment was shattered by a series of eerie, high-pitched cries. They echoed through the valley, sending a chill down my spine. Blue Fox's eyes grew wide, her face filling with alarm.

"Paiute," she whispered.

The camp was immediately thrown into a frenzy. Bear, with his always-ready attitude, barked orders. "Pack up now! We need to move fast!"

MacBride, despite the shock, was quick to take charge. "No fires, no torches. We move in the dark."

As we prepared to leave, MacLane's face was ashen, his earlier bravado nowhere to be seen. Asher and Boyd worked in tandem, ensuring that no necessary supplies were left behind.

The cries grew louder and closer. The eerie resonance of the war calls hung heavy in the night air.

With everything packed, we began our swift trek, moving as silently as the night would allow. The cool air bit at our faces, but the adrenaline pumping through our veins kept the chill at bay.

Blue Fox took the lead, her keen sense of the land guiding us through the dense underbrush and rugged terrain. The nearly full moon provided just enough light to see our way.

The war cries seemed to follow us, a haunting refrain that kept our pace quick and our nerves on edge. Every rustle in the bushes, every snap of a twig, made us jump.

Hours seemed to drag on as we pushed forward without rest. Fatigue began to set in, but the fear of being caught was a powerful motivator. Every so often, I glanced back, half expecting to see Paiute warriors on our trail. But the darkness concealed all.

As dawn began to break, the terrain around us changed, opening up to a vast plain. The cries had faded, either lost in the distance or silenced by the approaching day.

Bear, panting heavily, looked to MacBride. "Do we rest now, Captain?"

MacBride scanned the horizon, his brow furrowed in thought. "We'll push on for another hour, put more distance between us and them. Then we'll find a place to rest."

At that moment, Blue Fox pointed behind us. "Look!"

Paiute warriors galloped toward us with all the speed they could muster. As we began to run, the terrain beneath our feet shifted from soft earth to the gravelly crunch of rocky ground. With every step, our anxiety mounted as the echoes of pursuing hooves grew ever closer. Blue Fox led us through a maze of rocks and vegetation, her expertise evident in every turn she took, every shortcut she found.

Suddenly, a hiss zipped through the air, followed by a thud, as an arrow lodged itself into the ground right next to me. The silhouettes of Paiute warriors on horseback were cresting a nearby hill, bows drawn.

"Run!" Bear shouted, pulling his rifle from his shoulder. He fired a shot, more to deter than to hit, and the echo reverberated through nearby canyons.

The arrows came faster now, raining down around us. I heard MacLane cry out, but a quick glance showed he was unharmed, merely startled by an arrow that had passed too close for comfort.

Asher and Boyd fired back, the distinct cracks of their guns providing a fleeting hope of deterrence. But the Paiute warriors were relentless, their horses closing the distance at an alarming pace.

Blue Fox suddenly veered us left toward a rugged incline thick with shrubs and boulders. "Up there!" she yelled, pointing. "Horses can't follow easily!"

We scrambled upward, our boots slipping on the loose stones. The horses' whinnies and the enraged shouts of the Paiute echoed behind us. MacBride stationed himself at the back, ensuring no one was left behind. I huddled behind a stone and watched as he helped Bear, MacLane, Asher,

Georges and Boyd up a particularly challenging stretch of the climb.

But just as he was about to follow, there was a cruel hiss of an arrow cutting through the air. Time seemed to slow, every detail sharpening in excruciating clarity. The arrow struck MacBride squarely in the back, its force knocking him forward onto the rocky ground.

I wanted to rush to his side, pull him with us up the rugged incline to safety. But as if reading my thoughts, MacBride stood with the ferocity of a wounded bear, the arrow jutting from his back, and shouted, "Go! Now!"

MacLane hesitated, glancing between his leader and the approaching Paiute. "We can't just—"

"GO!" MacBride roared, his voice echoing across the valley, drowning out even the war cries of the Paiute.

Turning toward the advancing warriors, MacBride squared his broad shoulders and roared a battle cry of his own, imbued with all the wrath and fury he could muster. It was a deafening, harrowing sound that seemed to challenge the very fates. With his rifle in hand, he aimed and fired at the closest Paiute, sending the warrior off his horse. The shock in the warrior's eyes was evident even from where I stood.

Every step we took away from MacBride felt like a betrayal. He had been the driving force behind this journey, the firebrand leader who'd rallied us, fought with us, frustrated us, and in some moments, inspired us. All our disagreements and angry words melted away in that moment. MacBride was stubborn and proud, but he also had a fire in him that could light up the darkest nights. That fire was burning now in his final stand.

Asher and Boyd tried to provide cover fire, sending a hail of bullets toward the warriors to keep them at bay. But MacBride shouted at them with that characteristic flare of bravado, "Save your bullets for the journey ahead!"

He wrestled with the arrow in his back, grimacing as he tried to pull it out, but the pain seemed to be too great. Instead, he used his pain and anger to fuel his resistance. Every shot he fired found its mark, sending one Paiute warrior after another sprawling to the ground.

But the numbers were against him. Arrows whizzed toward him, and more found their mark, one piercing his leg, another his shoulder. But still he fought, roaring challenges, his red hair shining like a beacon under the sunlight, every ounce of his being defying the warriors to come closer.

MacBride rushed forward, charging into the horde of Paiute warriors with a fearsome roar in a move of desperation, or perhaps just a desire to take as many of them with him as he could. It was a sight I would never forget—the tall, imposing figure of a man I had once thought invincible meeting his end with the valor of a true warrior.

We watched in stunned silence, unable to tear our eyes away from the tragic spectacle unfolding before us. With every fall MacBride took and every rise he made, he seemed to embody the spirit of defiance and resilience. His foe kept their distance. They knew what awaited them if they drew too close.

A whirlwind of emotions coursed through me. MacBride had been so many things to me—an adversary, a mentor, a confounding puzzle, and in some odd moments, a friend. Despite our differences, there was no denying his passion, his love for the land, and his indomitable spirit that refused to be tamed. It was that spirit I saw now in his last moments.

And then, after what seemed like an eternity, MacBride fell. The Paiute warriors closed in on him, but he didn't give them the satisfaction of a final cry. Instead, he lay there, a silent testament to the fierce spirit that had driven him all his life.

The Paiute let out a single triumphant war cry before withdrawing, leaving behind a landscape marked by the scars of battle and the fallen body of our leader.

# CHAPTER 16
## A LAKE NAMED MALHEUR

The vast expanse of the Snake River greeted us as we trudged along, each step weighed down by the memory of MacBride's valiant sacrifice to save our lives. The shimmering water reflected the crimson hues of the setting sun, a poignant reminder of the blood that had been spilled just days before.

Our canoes lay hidden among the tall reeds, right where we'd left them. But the relief of finding them intact was short-lived, as tensions began to rise. With that characteristic air of confidence bordering on arrogance, MacLane stepped forward.

"Christian, I'm relieving you of command," he declared, eyes scanning the group for any signs of dissent.

I stepped forward, my resolve firming up. "What is the meaning of this?"

"It's your fault we're in this mess. It's your fault MacBride is dead. And you know it. You're not fit to lead us," he barked.

"How dare you?!" I yelled, my heart bleeding from the loss of our leader. "You killed the Paiute boy. They exacted revenge on us because of your carelessness!"

Asher, trying to play peacemaker, intervened, "Both of you, calm down. We've lost enough. Let's not turn on each other."

MacLane's face contorted in anger. "This isn't a democracy. Someone needs to lead, and I say that's me, not a sniveling traitor."

Boyd spoke up, "MacLane, you're not thinking straight."

Bear grunted in agreement. "We have our orders. Christian is next in line, and he's done more than enough to prove himself to us."

MacLane's gaze flitted around the group. It was clear the majority favored me to lead them. But he wasn't one to give in easily.

The atmosphere was thick with tension, every eye darting between MacLane and myself. His breathing grew more labored, and his hands clenched into fists, his knuckles white. Everyone present sensed the storm brewing within him, but no one could've predicted the sudden tempest that was about to erupt.

In a swift, unexpected move, MacLane lunged at me, his momentum catching me off guard. Before I could react, we both went tumbling down the riverbank, the rough gravel scraping at our clothes and skin. The sharp scent of the river, mixed with the metallic tinge of blood, filled my nostrils. I tried to rise as we hit the bottom, but MacLane was faster. He pinned me down, eyes wild, face contorted in rage.

Before I could utter a word, I felt the cold steel of his rifle's barrel press against my lips, forcing its way into my mouth. His fingers twitched on the trigger, and every tiny movement sent a chill down my spine, the acrid taste of gunpowder overwhelming me with fear.

"Do you have any idea what you've done, Christian?" His voice, usually so assertive, now wavered with emotion. "You think you can just swoop in and take charge? You think everyone will follow you blindly?!"

I tried to speak, but the gun's presence muffled my words. My eyes pleaded with him, searching for a shred of sanity of the Lucas MacLane I had known, however briefly.

From the top of the bank, shouts echoed. "MacLane, get off him!" Bear's deep voice boomed. Asher and Boyd started to scramble down the bank, their hurried footsteps sending small showers of pebbles down.

MacLane's focus, however, remained locked on me. "You think you're better than me? You think these people respect you more?" Tears of frustration and rage formed in his eyes, making them glisten dangerously. The gun wavered slightly, and for a split second, I thought it might be my chance to act.

There I was, knee-deep in the mud, with a gun barrel shoved halfway down my throat. I was a dead man. Oregon Country had not been kind to me, not kind at all. They'd said the Indians would cause trouble. They were trouble enough, but it was one of my own who had turned his rifle on me; it was one of my own with his finger on the trigger. We were supposed to trailblaze and push out the Hudson's Bay Company so that Americans could enter the fur trade. To that point, we had mainly turned on ourselves.

Blue Fox's voice pierced the tense silence, her tone icy and commanding. "MacLane. Remove. The gun."

His head snapped to the side, meeting her fierce gaze. Their eyes locked in a battle of wills. Seconds felt like hours. The river's soft babble was the only sound breaking the silence.

And then, ever so slowly, MacLane withdrew the gun, removing it from my mouth and letting it hang limply by his side. No sooner had he done so than an arrow struck him in the heart. He looked up at Blue Fox, her graceful figure silhouetted by the evening sun, holding her bow at her hip.

From the moment the arrow hit its mark, time seemed to stretch and distort. MacLane's eyes, fierce and filled with rage moments ago, now looked at Blue Fox with a mixture of shock and realization. As he crumpled to the ground, a hush settled over the group.

Blue Fox's gaze, unwavering, didn't move from MacLane. Her face was a mask of cold determination, and no one dared challenge her actions. It was as if, in that instant, the fragile line between self-preservation and retribution had been blurred.

Asher was the first to move, breaking the paralyzing silence. "We need to get moving. Now."

I nodded, my own voice coming out steadier than I felt. "Gather what you can, quickly. We're getting on the canoes."

There was a flurry of activity as the group rushed to collect their belongings, but notably, no one moved toward MacLane's fallen body. It wasn't out of disrespect—rather, the harsh reality of our situation had sunk in. Everyone recognized that lingering might lead to more danger. HBC men might show up at any time. And with MacLane's recent erratic behavior, it was clear that he had pushed himself away from the group, making any sentimental attachment to him almost nonexistent.

As we launched the canoes into the water and began our descent down the Snake River, the rhythmic paddle strokes and the gentle lapping of water against the canoe provided a soothing contrast to the chaotic events that had just unfolded.

Sitting in the stern of one of the canoes, I glanced back at the receding shoreline where MacLane's body lay. An odd pang of guilt washed over me. For all his flaws, MacLane had been a product of the challenging environment and circumstances we all faced. But he had allowed his insecurities and jealousy to get the better of him.

Bear, paddling beside me, looked defeated. He was the only Scot left, and I worried about his allegiance. I knew he and MacLane were close.

"I'm sorry for your friend," I said.

"Don't be," he said. "MacLane made his own bed. I cannot blame you for that."

Suddenly, Blue Fox's sharp eyes scanned the canoes, her face contorting in confusion. "Where's Georges?" she called out, her voice cutting through the gentle splashing.

The group paused, each person looking around, realizing that Georges was nowhere to be seen.

I frowned, scanning the receding shoreline as if expecting to spot Georges hiding in the shadows. "He was with us when MacLane and I fought. Did anyone see where he went?"

It was Asher who finally spoke, his face grim. "Last I saw him, he was running off toward that mountain." He pointed to a distant peak, its silhouette barely visible in the dimming light. "Looked like he was in a hurry. Maybe he's decided the HBC is a safer bet."

Bear grunted. "Wouldn't be surprised. After everything that's happened, some might think the devil you know is worse than the one you don't."

No one looked visibly distressed. Of everyone in the company, the Métis had kept to themselves so much that they had remained virtual strangers to us the entire journey. It was a shame, really. Was it my fault? As the only other francophone in the company, had I somehow failed to bring them into the fold? I felt responsible, somehow, but I couldn't quite say how in the fog of all that had happened.

I sighed. "We can't go back now. It's too risky with the Paiute and potentially the Hudson's Bay Company on our tail."

She nodded, the lines on her face deepening with concern. "I understand, but it doesn't make it any easier."

I placed a reassuring hand on her shoulder. "We've lost too many already. We have to move forward and ensure the safety of those we still have."

The sun began to dip below the horizon, casting a soft orange and pink hue across the sky. A somber mood settled over us as the night darkened and the first stars appeared. With the river's swift current propelling us forward, we all silently hoped for safer shores and the promise of a fresh start. But the scars of the past, both visible and hidden, would stay with us, shaping our journey ahead.

The weeks following MacBride's death were both somber and strenuous. Our group, significantly reduced in number and grappling with shadows of the past, found solace in the monotony of the journey. We traveled downstream, our canoes slicing through the waters of the Snake River, stopping at various tributaries along the way. Trapping beaver became our primary concern—our survival depended on it. Boyd had somehow made it back with three traps, allowing us to gather some furs on our way.

The mornings began early, with dawn painting the skies in hues of pink and gold. Blue Fox and Boyd took the lead, determining the most lucrative spots to set our traps. Asher and Bear, with their knowledge of fur trading, ensured the pelts were cleaned and prepared to the highest standard, and I helped where I could. Every evening, our collection of beaver pelts grew, their sleek furs glistening in the firelight. Our shared purpose bonded us, and as the days passed, we started to rebuild the camaraderie that had once defined our group.

During these weeks of trapping, the landscape began to change—the rugged terrain of the Rockies gradually transitioned into the sprawling expanse of the Columbia Plateau. The waterways teemed with life, and the dense forests flanking the rivers echoed with the calls of birds and distant animal cries. The air grew milder, signaling our approach to the verdant valleys of the Pacific Northwest.

In a little over three weeks, we'd managed to trap and skin about fifteen beaver pelts. While it wasn't a fortune, it was a decent haul, and we hoped it would be enough to secure supplies and lodgings at Fort Nez Perce. The anticipation of reaching a place of refuge, of civilization, kept our spirits high, even as we remained vigilant against potential threats.

One crisp morning, as the fog still clung to the water's surface, the dense forests gave way to reveal our destination: Fort Nez Perce. The journey that had begun in the heart of the Rockies, filled with challenges, confrontations, and losses, was finally leading us to a semblance of safety.

With renewed energy, we paddled onward, eager to explore the promises that lay behind the fort's imposing walls.

As we approached the main entrance to Fort Nez Perce, the palisade walls towered over us, the hand-hewn logs bearing the marks of ax and saw. Sturdy bastions protruded at the corners, likely filled with men ready to fend off any threat. Torches flanked the entrance itself, their flames flickering in the midday sun. A guard clad in a simple cotton shirt, leather pants, and a tricorn hat appeared above the gate. His gaze was sharp, eyes scanning each member of our party before settling on me. "State your business," he called down, voice echoing off the wood.

Gathering my thoughts, I stepped forward, clearing my throat. "We're from the American Fur Company. We've been... let's just say, a little roughed up by the HBC out there. We're looking for a place to rest and trade."

There was a pause as our words hung in the air. Then the guard gave a brief nod.

"Hold a moment." He disappeared from view.

My heart pounded in my chest. We had finally arrived at the place where I would carry out the mission I had been given. Success meant a return to New York. Success meant leaving this new world, and all the people in it, behind.

Whispers filled the space around us. "Think they'll let us in?" Asher mused, nervously adjusting the straps of his pack.

"They have no reason not to," Blue Fox replied. "But one never knows."

The creaking of heavy wood disrupted our speculations. The grand gates of the fort began to swing open, revealing a bustling courtyard beyond. The guard from earlier gestured for us to enter. "Welcome to Fort Nez Perce."

Stepping inside, it was as if we had been transported to another world. The interior of the fort was a hub of activity. Men and women went about their duties, some hauling pelts, others bartering at makeshift stalls. Sounds of laughter and conversation filled the air, blending with metal tools clinking and hammers rhythmically pounding.

To our left, a series of wooden cabins stood in neat rows, likely accommodations for trappers and traders. Each had a small garden plot in front, some filled with herbs, others with blooming flowers. The scent of freshly baked bread wafted from a larger building, probably the fort's communal kitchen.

To our right, a pen held animals—goats, chickens, and a few pigs—that would provide sustenance to the fort's inhabitants. A little farther off, a blacksmith's forge sent sparks flying, the smith himself, a burly man with a thick beard, shaping a piece of metal with practiced ease.

In the center of the courtyard was a flagpole bearing the flag of the North West Company: a red flag with a Union Jack in the upper left quadrant, and the letter "NWC" in the lower right. Next to it, a well-trodden path led to what looked like the main trading post, a larger building with wide double doors. As we approached, traders spilled out, pelts in hand, either satisfied with their dealings or in heated discussions with companions about the value of their catch.

Beyond the immediate structures, the palisade walls encased the entire establishment, their height ensuring protection from any external threat. Walkways lined the upper levels, allowing guards a clear view of the courtyard below.

"This place is something else," I muttered, taking in the sights and sounds.

Boyd clapped me on the back, grinning. "Told you it'd be worth it. Now, let's see about getting those pelts traded and finding a place to lay our heads."

As we moved deeper into the fort, it became clear that, despite our previous hardships, a new chapter was unfolding. A chapter filled with the promise of trade, rest, and perhaps a fresh start.

We fetched a mighty good price for our pelts at the trading post, enough to resupply, redeploy, and then some. We secured lodging near the tavern, and he mentioned a bathhouse while concluding the negotiation with the clerk.

The idea of a bathhouse was akin to an oasis in a desert. While the ruggedness of the frontier had its allure, there was something deeply comforting about the luxuries of urban life.

"A bathhouse, you say? I'd give all my pelts for a good soak right now," I remarked with a chuckle.

The clerk grinned, showing a row of yellowed teeth. "Ah, city roots, I presume? You'll find our bathhouse on the western edge. Fresh water's drawn every evening."

I nodded my thanks, feeling a lightness in my step as I made my way there. The others seemed less inclined to indulge, the wild having become their second skin. But I was adamant about washing away months of grime and sweat.

The bathhouse was a simple wooden structure with separate stalls containing a large tub. Steam rose from the warm water, carrying with it the inviting scent of cedar. Stripping down, I sank into the water with a contented sigh, letting it envelop me, dissolving the tension in my muscles.

After what felt like hours, I emerged, feeling rejuvenated. I'd traded for some fresh linens at the post, and the sensation of clean fabric against clean skin was invigorating. With a renewed sense of purpose, I headed to the tavern, where I was to meet the others.

The tavern was a lively establishment, its wooden beams resonating with the sounds of laughter, conversation, and the clinking of mugs. Finding my group wasn't hard; they'd secured a large table near the window. Much to my surprise, all of them had also taken the opportunity to clean up. Their faces were free of the layers of dust and dirt that had become a regular feature over the past weeks.

Taking a seat next to Asher, I caught Blue Fox's gaze from across the table. There was a hint of amusement in her eyes and something else I couldn't quite place. "What?" I asked, self-consciously adjusting my new shirt.

She tilted her head, her mysterious smile tugging at her lips. "It's just… it's good to see you like this. All civilized."

I chuckled, rolling my eyes. "Some habits die hard."

Boyd raised his mug in my direction, smirking. "To civilization and its small comforts." The toast was met with a chorus of agreement, and as we drank, I felt a sense of camaraderie enveloping us.

The tavernkeeper, a portly man with a ruddy complexion and a full beard, approached our table with an affable grin. His eyes glinted with curiosity. "Quite the motley crew we've got here tonight," he observed jovially. "Where do you all hail from?"

We exchanged awkward glances. How could we distill the complexity of our journey, with its myriad challenges and experiences, into a concise tale? Asher cleared his throat, taking the lead. "Started from St. Louis, aimed to head into the Rockies. Things… didn't quite go as planned."

Bear added, "Got a bit lost, encountered resistance from the Hudson's Bay Company. It's been a long trek."

The tavernkeeper's eyebrows shot up in genuine surprise. "From St. Louis, you say? How long have you been on the road?"

I shrugged, the days having blended into one another. "Months, but I'm not exactly sure how many."

"Nine," Boyd chimed in quietly.

"NINE months out there?!" the tavernkeeper exclaimed, drawing the attention of a few neighboring tables. "Bless my soul! A babe could've been born in that time. That's no small feat, traversing these wilds for so long."

I paused, a thought striking me. "Wait, what's today's date?"

The tavernkeeper looked puzzled but responded. "It's September 4th. Why?"

A strange feeling washed over me, and I felt a wistful smile forming on my lips. "It's… it's my birthday. I completely lost track of time."

Asher chuckled. "Well, what are the odds?"

Bear clapped me on the back, a playful grin on his face. "Happy birthday, city boy! Who'd have thought you'd be celebrating it in a place like this?"

Blue Fox's eyes softened, her earlier teasing replaced with genuine warmth. "Happy birthday, Christian."

Seizing an opportunity, the tavernkeeper said, "Well, in that case, a round of drinks on the house for the birthday boy and his crew!"

A cheer went up at our table, and I couldn't help but laugh. In the midst of all the trials we had faced, it was these small moments of unexpected joy that kept us going.

My revelation had been met with joy, but the weight of our journey, our trials, and our losses hit me all at once. As the merriment continued around me, I felt a deepening melancholy. I looked down into my cup, swirling the dark liquid.

"What a journey." My voice was low, almost drowned out by the laughter and chatter of the tavern. "Here we are, on the eve of succeeding at my mission, and it tastes of ash on my tongue. I can't help but feel as if I've failed."

The table grew quiet. Asher was the first to speak, his usually playful demeanor replaced by genuine concern. "Christian, we've been through hell and back. It's understandable how you're feeling."

Bear nodded. "Aye. And you of all people should feel proud for getting this far. Most men would've turned tail and run after the first month. You kept on."

Blue Fox leaned forward, her eyes piercing mine. "When I met you at that fort just north of St. Louis, you had that look. You know the one I'm talking about—the look of an uncertain man. I gave you a week. A week before the wild or its creatures took you. But here you are, nine months later. Not only did you survive, but you did so alone at times. Christian, surviving is succeeding. Especially out here."

I shook my head, feeling the sting of unshed tears. "That's not it."

Boyd leaned in and asked, "What's eating at you, kid?"

I looked around the table at my companions, their faces reflecting their support. My chest tightened as I struggled with my emotions. "Tomorrow, I could be on my way back to New York. But I don't have anyone there, really," I muttered.

Blue Fox placed a hand over mine and spoke gently, "You will have that job now, and with the strength of ten of the men you used to be."

I met her gaze, searching for solace. What she said was true. The wilderness had transformed me, humbled me, and made me stronger and more resilient.

Asher leaned in, smirking. "Plus, you've got some wild stories to tell when you get back. Not everyone can say they faced down the Hudson's Bay Company and lived to tell the tale. I'm sure that will make you real popular over there."

The laughter that followed lightened the mood. They were right. The journey had made me appreciate life in its rawest form and the experiences and the friendships I'd forged—they were invaluable.

Taking a deep breath, I smiled, raising my glass. "To the journey, no matter where it leads."

I'd had enough for the night, feeling the alcohol weigh down my eyelids and the fatigue of the long journey catch up to me. I pushed open the heavy wooden door to my lodgings, eager for a place to finally rest my weary bones. The room was modest—a simple cot with a few furnishings and a window that showcased the night sky.

I was about to close the door when a shadow moved just outside, and before I could react, Blue Fox slipped into the room, her presence filling the space.

I blinked, surprised. "Blue Fox?"

She looked around, her fingers brushing the rough surface of the table. "Not quite what you were expecting?"

I chuckled, still trying to understand the unexpected visit. "Not quite. Is everything all right?"

She looked up, her eyes bright, reflecting the dim light from the single lantern. "Why does something have to be wrong for me to visit?"

I swallowed, suddenly aware of the close quarters, the warmth emanating from her. "No reason, I suppose."

She stepped closer, and my breath caught. The air between us was thick with tension, unsaid words, and feelings I'd tried to ignore throughout our journey.

"You've come a long way, Christian," she began softly, her voice barely above a whisper.

I nodded, my eyes locked onto hers. "So have you."

She hesitated for a moment, then took another step, bridging the gap between us. "Am I right in thinking I got the sense you are questioning going back to New York?"

I took a deep breath, struggling to find the right words. "You are."

She smiled, that enigmatic smile that had intrigued me since our first meeting. "For me?"

"For you."

She pressed her lips against mine and wrapped her arms around my neck, pulling me close to her. I ran my hands up her hips, tugging at her dress. My linen shirt hit the floor, as did her moccasins, and we descended on the bed, lips to lips, skin to skin. It was the first night we made love.

The morning sun streamed through the gaps in the wooden structure, its light casting long, slender patterns on the floor. My eyelids flickered open, and the warm presence beside me reminded me of the night before. Blue Fox's eyes remained closed, her breathing even. For a moment, I just watched her, appreciating the peaceful expression on her face.

But the tranquility was abruptly disrupted by a firm knock on the door.

"Christian!" called out Boyd's voice, thick with an urgency that had me sitting up quickly. Blue Fox stirred beside me, blinking her eyes open.

"The governor's called for us. You best get yourselves ready."

Blue Fox and I exchanged a quick glance before getting up to dress. The sound of muffled conversation reached us from outside—Boyd was apparently filling Asher and Bear in on the governor's summons.

Just as I was tugging on my boots and Blue Fox was adjusting her shawl, the door opened slightly. Boyd peeked through the gap, his eyes taking in the scene before him. A knowing smirk crossed his lips.

"Took you both long enough," he teased with a chuckle.

Flushing slightly, I shot him a warning glare, but there was no real heat behind it. Blue Fox merely rolled her eyes, though a faint smile played on her lips.

"Let's not keep the governor waiting," she said, her tone poised as always.

Together, the three of us made our way to the governor's office, joining Asher and Bear, who were already waiting outside. The fort was buzzing with activity, traders and trappers preparing for the day's commerce. The scent of freshly baked bread wafted from the kitchen nearby, and the sounds of morning chatter and the clinking of tools filled the air.

I carefully adjusted my shirt, doing my best to appear presentable as we entered the ornate office of Sir Reginald Worthington III, as written in large letters above the front door. The room was dominated by a large mahogany desk, behind which sat the imposing figure of the governor. Heavy drapes framed the windows, casting the room in a muted light, and the walls were lined with bookshelves filled with tomes and trinkets from all corners of the British Empire.

"Ah, the American adventurers," Sir Reginald began, studying each of us intently with his piercing blue eyes. "Welcome to Fort Nez Perce."

I felt a lump in my throat. Word had traveled fast, and now we were face-to-face with a man whose opinion could determine our fates in this unfamiliar land.

"I've recently had the pleasure," he continued with a hint of sarcasm, "of reading reports detailing your… interactions with my friend Jean-Louis Foucher."

Beside me, I could feel Blue Fox stiffen, while Asher and Bear exchanged uneasy glances. Boyd shifted his weight, a slight nervousness betraying his usually calm demeanor.

"I must say," Sir Reginald went on, pausing for dramatic effect and allowing the tension in the room to mount, "it's quite a disturbing tale."

Every tick of the ornate clock on the wall seemed amplified as his silence stretched on.

But then, to our collective surprise, Sir Reginald burst into hearty laughter. "Oh, I can't hold a straight face any longer! If there's one person I've no love for, it's that conniving weasel Foucher. Good riddance!"

Our group exchanged relieved glances. Boyd even let out a short chuckle.

Sir Reginald continued, "The man's been a thorn in my side since he took charge at the Hudson's Bay post. Always looking for a way to one-up us, always pushing the boundaries. You have my thanks for sending him to his maker."

"Actually, he—" I started to say, but Blue Fox elbowed me in the ribs to shut me up. I cleared my throat. "Yes, good thing."

Sir Reginald leaned back in his chair, gesturing to a massive, intricately detailed map pinned on the wall. "Now, tell me, where have you been on this grand adventure of yours? I'm keen to plot any new territories."

Bear, always one for minimal words but precise actions, stood and approached the map, his large fingers tracing the rivers and mountains. He pointed firmly to an area, previously unmarked. "There's a lake here," he grunted, "and Paiute—they were around here."

Sir Reginald's eyebrows shot up, a glint of intrigue in his eyes. "There's a lake out there in that desert? That's uncharted territory on our maps. Fascinating!" He made a note on a paper by his side. "And this lake, does it have a name?"

Boyd chimed in, a hint of bitterness in his voice. "Considering our fortunes there, I'd call it Bad Luck Lake."

The governor chuckled, but it was evident he wasn't entirely pleased. "That's rather negative for a newly discovered body of water, isn't it?"

Memories of our ordeal flooded back—the challenges, the betrayals, MacBride's tragic end. Perhaps Boyd was on to something.

With a slight smirk, I spoke up. "Most of the HBC trappers are French-speaking, aren't they?"

Sir Reginald nodded. "Indeed they are."

"Why not call it Malheur Lake then?" I proposed. "*Malheur* is French for misfortune or bad luck."

The governor paused, considering the name. The room was thick with anticipation. Then, after a moment that felt much longer, a broad smile spread across his face. "Malheur," he repeated, savoring each syllable. "It has a ring to it. And maybe it'll keep those HBC bastards away from it. Very well, Malheur it is."

Boyd looked at me and nodded approvingly. As names went, it was elegant yet held a deep resonance for us, a testament to our journey and the hardships we'd been through. It was a name, I believed, that would endure.

"But let's get down to business," the governor said, leaning forward in his chair.

"Yes, let's," I said. "Mr. Astor sent me to strike a deal with you. He wants to utilize your shipping lines to transport our furs back to New York, in light of the fact that you are still in possession of Fort Astoria."

Sir Reginald steepled his fingers. "A curious proposition, and not the one I expected. Why would we agree to such a thing?"

I smiled, perhaps too confidently. "Exclusivity," I said. "As of right now, there are two players in these parts who can ship furs back to New York in bulk: you and the HBC. Mr. Astor plans to send many more expeditions west, and he wants to do business with you. You would, of course, take a cut from our supply."

Sir Reginald belched another hearty laugh. "John sent you all the way out here to strike this deal?"

"Of course," I said, dumbfounded.

"No, no, there must be more to it than that. He's tried a hundred times to negotiate repossession of that fort, and we simply cannot give it to him."

"He's not asking for the fort back, just your help to ship our bounty back east. And we would, of course, help you in your fight against the HBC. We've proven that to you already."

"So you killed Jean-Louis out of the kindness of your heart, did you?" Sir Reginald scoffed.

"Not at all," I said. "We merely defended ourselves, but it shows we share the same foe, and for that alone, there is an opportunity here for us to work together."

"I suppose you are right," he mused, leaning back in his chair. "What's in it for you, then?"

"I beg your pardon?"

"You. You sound educated and far too well-to-do to be running around in the forest with Indian girls."

Blue Fox growled at him. His retort took me aback. I stuttered for a moment, the right words eluding me. "Well, safe passage back to New York was one of the things," I managed to say.

"Promise you a high-paying job in an ivory tower, did he?"

The look on my face told him he was right. "Let me guess, he told you, 'You need to know what's in the sausage to sell the sausage,'" he added, reciting John Astor's quote with an over-the-top imitation of a German accent.

"That's right," I said.

"Americans," he scoffed. "Such a fool to send someone of your station into the proverbial belly of the whale. How reckless."

"I think we're getting off-topic," I said. "Are you open to negotiating a deal, or are we all wasting our time?"

"You're not wasting your time," he said slowly. "However, I did hear you say safe passage to New York *was*—past tense—one of the things that you wanted out of the deal, and seeing how close you and the Indian girl are at this present moment, I think you may have other plans. In that case, I have a counteroffer for you."

"I'll hear it."

"You see, men and women of your particular skill set are hard to come by. The wilderness is unforgiving, and the fur trade is not for the faint of heart. With Jean-Louis dead and the HBC in disarray for a short time, we at the North West Company could use a group like yours to help us regain some territory we've lost."

He paused, letting the implication of his words sink in.

"You want to poach us?" I looked at my companions, who all had wide eyes and open mouths.

"I'm prepared to offer you a lucrative contract," Sir Reginald declared, producing a neatly folded parchment from a drawer and sliding it towards us. "The terms are generous, and I believe you'll find them quite to your liking."

I reached out and grasped the parchment, carefully unfolding it and adjusting my focus as I began to read. My legal training at Columbia had provided me with a sharp eye for contracts, and as I scanned through the clauses and terms, the depth of Sir Reginald's offer began to dawn on me.

The figures and conditions were nothing short of staggering. Not only did it guarantee a base salary for our services, but it also included provisions for a share of the profits. Each line I read further confirmed what seemed too good to be true.

"This... this is unbelievable," I murmured, glancing up at the expectant faces of my companions.

"Unbelievable to you, perhaps," Sir Reginald laughed. "Astor is a miserable German miser who underpays his grunts. This is our standard contract."

"What does it say, Christian?" Blue Fox asked, her voice tinged with hope and excitement.

I cleared my throat, summarizing the contract for them. "It guarantees a base pay for each of us, which, on its own, is more than generous. But the real gold is here." I pointed to a particular clause. "We'll receive a share of the profits from our collective efforts. This... this is leagues beyond what Astor offered us."

Asher let out a low whistle. "Sounds like we hit the jackpot."

Bear grunted in agreement, a rare smile tugging at his lips.

Boyd, ever the pragmatist, asked, "But what does it mean for us, in the long run?"

I paused, gathering my thoughts. "It means, Boyd, that we don't just survive here in the West. We thrive. We have the chance to lay down roots and build a legacy. With this contract, we are not mere trappers but stakeholders in the growth and success of the North West Company in these territories."

"What do you say, then?" Sir Reginald asked. "Ready to leave Mr. Sausage behind for better things?"

The weight of our journey—the dangers we'd faced, the friends we'd lost, the trials and tribulations—seemed to merge into this moment—a moment when destiny handed us an olive branch, an opportunity to rewrite our future. But I paused. It meant not returning to New York. It meant giving up the career I had worked so hard to obtain.

"You're thinking about New York, aren't you?" Blue Fox asked, her eyes fixed on mine.

I nodded.

"Don't say you're considering turning him down," Boyd blurted out.

Sir Reginald chimed in. "Ah, yes, we could send you back if you wish. The contract would still stand for the rest of you."

Blue Fox gazed into my eyes, not with anger or resentment, but with longing and trust. After everything we had survived, after all it had taken for the two of us to consummate the love that had grown between us, why was I still hesitating? Looking around the room at the faces of the individuals who had become my family, I felt an overwhelming surge of gratitude and pride. We had faced hell together and emerged stronger, closer. And now, with a future gleaming with possibility, I couldn't let them go. I couldn't leave her behind.

"The ivory tower can wait," I said, more to myself than to anyone else. "Indefinitely."

Blue Fox jumped into my arms and kissed me. Boyd, Asher, and Bear cheered. Even Sir Reginald smiled with glee.

I put the paper on the governor's desk, reached for the plume, and signed it.

## ABOUT THE AUTHOR

C.J. Adrien is a bestselling author of Viking historical fiction novels and has a passion for Viking history. His Kindred of the Sea series was inspired by research conducted in preparation for a doctoral program in early medieval history, as well as his admiration for historical fiction writers such as Bernard Cornwell and Ken Follett. He is also a published historian on the subject of Vikings, with articles featured in historical journals such as *L'Association des Amis de Noirmoutier*, in France. His novels and expertise have earned him invitations to speak at several international events including the International Medieval Congress at the  University of Leeds, the Oregon Museum of Science and Industry (OMSI), and conferences on Viking history in France, among others. C.J. Adrien earned a bachelor's degree in history from the University of Oregon, a master's degree from Oregon State University.

C.J. was inspired to write this book in the 7th grade during a fur trade project. It's been over two decades in the making.

To learn more about the author, visit www.cjadrien.com

Made in United States
Orlando, FL
21 December 2023

41475650R00166